Beartooth Betrayal

Beartooth Betrayal

Deadly Miles Book 2

Millie Vaughn

Written by Millie Vaughn

Edited by Ameryn Tucker

Cover design by Dauntless Cover Design

Also by Millie Vaughn

Absaroka Ambush

Gina Connolly doesn't need anyone. She's built her life on control with a steady job, careful boundaries, and zero emotional risks. Depending on someone only leads to heartbreak.

Nick Davies is the last complication she wants.

He came to their small Wyoming town with no clear future and no intention of staying. The chemistry between them is instant. Inconvenient. Dangerous.

Continental Crisis

Steph Pierce has worked her whole life for one goal. Every mile she trains brings her closer to the race she has dreamed of, and nothing will stop her.

Jack Swisher thought a fresh start would be simple. A former Olympic biathlete with everything to prove, he arrives in Basin County ready to claim the race Steph has been planning and immediately makes an enemy of her.

Find these titles at MillieVaughn.com

Check out Millie's cozy post-apocalyptic fiction books, written as Millie Copper, at MillieCopper.com.

Join Millie Vaughn's Reader Club!

Receive a complimentary *Beartooth Betrayal* bonus scene. As part of my reader's club, you'll be the first to know about new releases and specials. Please sign up at:

MillieVaughn.com/BB-Bonus

Chapter 1

Brooke

Brooke Davies knew hiking alone in grizzly bear country was a terrible idea, but she needed to prove that fear hadn't won.

I should just turn around, she thought to herself. *Turn around and go back. That'd be the smart thing to do.*

She'd taken this trail before. It was a loop, about six miles total. She was maybe two miles in when she sighed and called out, "Here, bear! Here, bear!"

"Might as well let them know I'm out here," she muttered. *Pick up the pace and get this done. Everything will be fine.*

She broke into a slow, easy jog as the trail curved through lodgepole pine. This was supposed to be recovery. No training plan. No pressure. Just proof she could still do this—still trust her instincts, still move forward instead of letting nightmares and what-ifs dictate her life.

Gina was supposed to be here. Brooke saw too little of her best friend now that Gina and Nick were in a relationship. She used words like *forever* and *soulmate* as if it were simple. Maybe for them. Brooke knew better.

She pushed the thought away and lengthened her stride. This run wasn't about relationships or timelines. It was about reminding herself she wasn't broken, that she was still the same person she'd always been, no matter what had happened on that mountain.

The trail dipped slightly, and she heard the sound of running water—loud enough to sound like a small waterfall, which made no sense. There was a creek crossing, but it was still at least a mile up.

Brooke skidded to a halt, every muscle suddenly tense.

She'd heard something like that before—the sound of rushing water where there was no water. That time, it was a rattlesnake.

Her heart kicked into overdrive.

She took a careful step backward, eyes scanning the trail ahead for any sign of movement. Another step back. The sound seemed to be coming from somewhere to her left, just off the trail, but she couldn't pinpoint the exact location.

Panic fluttered in her chest. She needed to back away slowly, give the snake space, and stay on the trail where the ground was clear and visible.

Instead, she did exactly what she shouldn't have done.

She bolted off the trail to her right, crashing through underbrush and around trees, putting distance between herself and the sound. Her breath came in sharp gasps, adrenaline flooding her system.

Brooke ran until she could no longer hear the rattler, until her lungs burned and her legs shook. Then she stopped, hands on her knees, trying to catch her breath.

"Stupid," she muttered as she glanced around. "Stupid, stupid, stupid."

Why in the world had she left the trail? She knew better than that, knew she should've simply given the snake a wide berth and kept going. She was too jumpy. Still not thinking straight after the trouble from before.

And look at what that got her. There she was, standing in the dense forest with no clear sight line to where she'd come from—or where anything could be lurking. A snake seemed to be the least of her worries now.

Brooke straightened slowly.

"All right. You made a mistake, but you're okay. You're fine." She cleared her throat and talked her way through it. "Where am I? Not far off the trail. Fifty yards, maybe. I'm good."

She took a few steps as she continued her pep talk to herself. "Backtrack carefully. That's all you need to do. Watch where you're stepping in case that snake has some buddies out here, and— "

Her eyes caught on something ahead.

A mound of disturbed earth sat ahead of her, dark soil piled in a way that looked deliberately shaped. A piece of bright blue synthetic fabric stuck out of it—something that didn't belong in the forest.

Brooke moved closer, drawn by curiosity and a sick feeling that was building in her stomach.

The fabric was attached to something. A jacket, maybe, or a shirt. And next to the mound, partially covered by pine needles and forest debris, was a shoe.

A woman's shoe.

With a foot and leg still inside it.

Brooke's vision narrowed. The leg was pale and waxy, clearly not attached to a living person. And as her eyes adjusted to what she was seeing, she realized the mound wasn't just dirt. It was a cache.

A bear cache.

She'd seen photos in wildlife management presentations. Bears covered their kills, saving them for later and defending them aggressively from anything that got too close.

The ground beneath her feet seemed to tilt. She took a step back, then another, her breathing going ragged as panic set in.

Her foot caught on something, and she went down hard, landing on her hip in another pile of disturbed earth.

This one had an arm visible.

She scrambled up with a strangled sound, backing away from both caches, her mind racing through implications she didn't want to process. Two bodies. Two separate caches. Which meant the bear had been actively hunting, killing.

She needed to run. She needed to get out of here right now, because if there was a grizzly defending these kills, she was in immediate danger.

But even through her panic, she knew she'd never find this spot again. The police would need to locate the bodies. She needed to mark it somehow.

Her hands shook as she shrugged out of her daypack. Water, granola bars, jerky, a map, a multitool, an emergency blanket, and—*yes, there*—a length of paracord.

Brooke pulled out the cord and the multitool, cutting off a piece with the small blade. Her fingers felt thick and clumsy as she tied the bright orange cord around the nearest tree, knotting it multiple times to make sure it wouldn't come loose.

Is this close enough? Will this help them find it?

It would have to do. She wasn't going any closer to those bodies. She moved in the direction of where she hoped the trail was.

"Okay, okay," she said, her breath ragged and sweat trailing down her spine. As the well-worn trail came into view, she added another length of cord. Hopefully that'd be enough for whoever she called to find the bodies.

"I'm getting out of here." She shouldered her pack. The trailhead was closest if she went to the right. She'd probably have service there and could call for help.

"Take a breath, Brooke. Take several and then get going. Two miles. You can run this in fifteen minutes. No problem." She gave herself a nod and tightened the straps on her backpack.

A sound caught her attention.

Rustling. Movement. Getting closer.

Please don't let it be a bear. Please don't let it be a bear.

Her heart was pounding so hard she could feel it in her throat, in her temples, in her fingertips.

She grabbed a heavy limb from the ground and gripped it like a club. If it was a bear, maybe she could hit it hard enough to buy herself time to run.

No. Don't run. That's the worst thing you could do. Make yourself big. Threatening. Use the bear spray.

She dropped the stick and pulled the bear spray off her belt.

If the bear was within thirty feet, she'd deploy the spray. If it came around that tree line ahead, it was going to be much closer than thirty feet.

She needed to be ready.

The rustling got louder. Was there more than one? A sow with cubs would be worse. So much worse. They attacked to protect their young.

Fear threatened to overwhelm her as she gripped the bear spray. The sounds were getting louder. Closer. Too close. Then she saw it. Movement on the trail. A figure rounded the bend and stopped.

Chapter 2

Tyler

Tyler Gillis noticed the woman before she noticed them.

She was standing in the middle of the trail, bear spray at the ready. Her posture screamed terror, and his first thought was that she'd encountered a grizzly.

His second thought was that they needed to make noise immediately, so whatever spooked her knew they were there too.

"Wait," he called out, raising both hands slowly. "It's okay."

She lifted the bear spray in his direction, and Tyler got his first clear look at her. Dark hair, athletic build, late twenties or early thirties. Pretty, even with fear tightening across her expression. But what struck him most were her eyes, wild with panic but also sharp and assessing. She was terrified but not frozen.

"I'm not going to hurt you." He took a careful step forward. Behind him, he heard his friends stop moving. "You want to lower the bear spray a little?"

The woman stared at the canister in her hand like she'd forgotten she was holding it. "You're not a bear."

"I'm not a bear," Tyler agreed, keeping his voice calm and even. "*We're* not bears." He gestured back toward his hiking companions without taking his eyes off her. "Are you hurt?"

"No. I mean, yes. I mean— " She was struggling to get the words out. "I need your help. I found something. Bodies. There are bodies back there."

Tyler looked her over. She seemed sincere, and she was definitely scared.

"Take a breath."

"Seriously?" She narrowed her eyes at him, but the next line came out calmer. "I found dead bodies. Human bodies. Two of them."

Two bodies. Unlikely. But she certainly believed it. Probably an animal. Maybe a deer carcass. Yet somehow, he knew that was wishful thinking. Even though he didn't know her, his instincts told him she wouldn't be acting like this if it wasn't the real thing. "Are you out here alone?"

She took a step back and raised the canister. *Brilliant, Tyler,* he scolded himself. *You sound like a creep.*

He cleared his throat. "It's not safe to hike alone in bear country." His eyes flicked to the trees behind her, noting the flashes of orange cording. Smart. She'd known what to do even when scared. That said a lot about her and confirmed his fears. Maybe she really did find a body. "Why don't you show me what you found?"

"What do you mean *bodies*?" his friend asked.

"Dead people." Her voice shook. "Two of them. Covered with dirt and pine needles. Like . . . like something buried them. Like a bear buried them."

The pieces clicked together in Tyler's mind. Buried. Covered. "A cache?"

She nodded frantically. "Bears do that, right? They cover their kills?"

Now the danger made sense. Bodies in a bear cache meant an active grizzly nearby. One that would fiercely defend its food source.

Tyler's eyes locked with hers. She was holding it together, but barely. "Can you show us?"

"You want me to take you back there?" Her grip tightened on the bear spray. "Why?"

Fair question. Tyler glanced back at his friends. Robert had his phone out, checking for service. He shook his head. No bars in the forest.

"Because if there really are bodies in a bear cache, we need to verify it and mark the location properly before we hike out to call for help," Tyler said.

He believed her, but still wanted to see for himself, wanted to make sure it was truly human bodies before calling in Johnny Law. Dealing with the police was the last thing he wanted.

Maybe it wasn't what she thought it was. He knew, probably better than anyone, that when emotions were heightened, grasping reality wasn't always guaranteed.

The woman's shoulders dropped.

"I already marked it." She gestured toward the orange cord.

"Good thinking. That helps." Tyler took another slow step forward. "Robert and I could go. You can stay behind with Sue." He motioned to his friend's wife.

Sue gave a nod and patted the pistol in a holster across her chest.

The woman shook her head. "No, no. I'm—I'll show you."

Tyler nodded. "Okay, but listen, we need to stay on high alert. We check it so we can give accurate information to law enforcement. And then we all need to get out of this area as quickly as possible. If there's a grizzly defending those kills, we're all in danger."

The woman seemed to process that, weighing her options. Trust them or run. Tyler saw the calculation happening behind her blue eyes.

"Look, I know you don't know us," he said. "But I'd like to think you know that if we were going to hurt you, we would've already done it instead of standing here talking. Let's get this done. We all work together. We stay safe."

The logic seemed to reach her. She lowered the bear spray—not putting it away but no longer pointing it at him.

"Okay," she said. "But we need to be fast."

"Agreed. Let's keep talking. Loud voices. Make sure we don't sneak up on anything out here."

She led them through the trees, moving with the efficient stride of someone who was comfortable in the wilderness despite her obvious fear. Tyler followed, his senses on high alert.

Every sound in the forest suddenly felt threatening. Every shift in the wind made him tense.

He, Sue, and Robert kept up a steady stream of words. He wanted to include the woman, but it wasn't a true conversation, just noise to alert a bear they were there. If a bear was defending a cache, it wouldn't matter much. But if one were strolling along, it might make them keep moving away from the group.

The smell hit first. Not overwhelming, but present. Death and decay, unmistakable.

His stomach tightened.

Then he saw it. The mound of disturbed earth. The bright blue fabric. A high-heeled shoe with a pale leg still inside it.

"There," the woman whispered. "And there's another one. I fell onto it."

Tyler moved closer, careful to watch his step. The caches were exactly as she had described, mounds of dirt and forest debris covering most of the bodies. One revealed a leg, the other a hand with painted nails, some torn off. The caches looked fresh, and the covering was methodical, the way bears hid meat to save for later.

His stomach turned, but he forced himself to look, to assess. Females, obviously. The faces were covered. There was about ten feet between the caches. And bear prints were everywhere, scat along the edges of the small clearing. Staying there was dangerous. Too dangerous.

Sue stepped closer to the second cache. "I don't think it's a second body. I think . . . this is only an arm. Part of the first body."

"We need to go. Now," Tyler said quietly. "Robert, can you add another marker? Make sure officials can find it."

The woman was already moving, putting distance between herself and the bodies.

"Go with her," Tyler said to Sue. She nodded and followed.

As soon as Robert had a piece of his own paracord in place, they followed the women. He was impressed to see they'd stopped ahead and were tying an additional marker into place.

"It's about two miles back to the cars," Robert said, his voice steady but tense.

"Right," Tyler replied. He turned to the woman. "Are you parked at the main trailhead?"

"Yes."

"You driving the blue SUV?" he asked.

"Why?" She narrowed her eyes.

"Just . . . I saw it when we pulled up."

After a moment's hesitation, she nodded. "That's mine."

"We'll stick together until we get back to the cars."

They started moving back toward the main trail, with Sue leading the way. The woman followed, then Tyler. Robert was at the rear of the group, paracord and small knife still in hand to mark the trail along the way. It probably wasn't necessary on the main trail, but they didn't want there to be any issues with finding the body. Tyler gave an involuntary shudder.

Even though he was familiar with death, he'd never seen anything like this. And Sue's suggestion that it was one body in two caches added to the grossness of it.

How'd it end up in two parts?

He supposed the bear did it, but still. An even bigger question was what she was doing out here, hiking in the wilderness dressed like that. His mind ran through the likely scenarios and settled on one.

She was dumped. Killed somewhere else and dumped in the woods. Then the bear found her and did what he did. Took advantage of finding his next meal. His next several meals.

Tyler's eyes settled on the woman in front of him. From the way she held herself, it was obvious she was still tense. Of course she was. He was tense. No doubt so were Sue and Robert. Their simple hike in the woods, a way to enjoy a day off, had turned into something else entirely. And it was only going to get worse.

Now they'd be forced to call the cops. Who exactly to call, he didn't know. Probably 9-1-1, and they'd send whoever had jurisdiction. Would that be the state police?

Maybe, but most likely it'd be the Basin County Sheriff's Department. He frowned at the thought. He knew many of the deputies. And that wasn't necessarily a good thing.

If he was smart, he'd slip away before the call was made. Let Robert, Sue, and the woman handle it. He stifled a sigh. As tempting as it was, he wouldn't do that. Besides, he rode with Robert and Sue. What was he going to do, walk the fifty-odd miles back to his hometown of Irma, Wyoming?

Not only that, but he also knew he'd never leave. Not until he was certain the woman and his friends were safe.

Reaching the vehicles would eliminate the danger from the grizzly, for the most part. They'd be far enough from the cache, and that would help, though it was common for bears to saunter through parking lots and campgrounds. Especially if there was a chance food might be left out.

The hike back felt longer than it should've. Every rustle in the underbrush sparked new concern; every crack of a branch sent him scanning the tree line. Sue and Robert kept up a steady conversation, and he added a word here and there while the woman occasionally chimed in.

She kept pace easily. He couldn't help but think she was some kind of athlete. She was built like one and moved like one. A runner, maybe. He noticed her arms. She probably did some strength training too.

She'd dressed for the occasion of a long hike. A backpack with paracord, water bottle showing in an outside pocket. This wasn't her first time in the mountains, though she had made the mistake of coming out alone.

Everyone with a lick of sense knew better than to do that. At the very least, those who enjoyed hiking alone usually brought a dog with them. But this woman, out here fully alone, what was she thinking?

"What's your name?" he asked as they walked.

She glanced back at him, and for a moment, he thought she might not answer. Then she said, "Brooke."

"I'm Tyler."

"I'm Sue." Sue turned her head briefly to give Brooke a smile. "My husband is Robert."

"First time I've found something like that," Brooke said, and there was a slight tremor in her voice that she was trying to hide.

"I'd hope so," Sue said, keeping her attention forward but bobbing her head.

Tyler stayed quiet. It was a first for him, too, but not the first time death had touched his life. Not even close.

They reached the spot where the trail divided into a loop. The path widened, and Tyler felt some of the tension leave his shoulders. The path was clear and well-marked. They weren't far from the trailhead now.

"Any chance you have service?" he asked Robert.

Robert checked his phone and shook his head. "Still nothing."

"I told you we should've got one of those satellite trackers," Sue said.

"Yes, dear," Robert replied.

Tyler sighed. He wasn't certain there would be reception at the parking lot. They might need to drive up the road and make the call from the little store where they had a landline.

Brooke stumbled slightly on a root, and Tyler's hand shot out automatically to steady her elbow. She glanced back at him, and their eyes met for a moment. Blue eyes, he noticed again. Clear and intelligent, despite the fear still lingering there.

"Thanks," she said.

"No problem."

She pulled away gently and kept moving. Tyler told himself to focus on the trail, on getting everyone to safety. But part of his mind kept circling back to her. The way she'd handled herself, the strength in her despite the terror, the fact that she'd had the presence of mind to mark the location even while panicking.

The parking area came into view, and relief washed over Tyler. They'd made it. No bear encounter, nobody else to worry about. Just the quiet horror of what they'd left behind in the forest.

"Two bars," Robert said. "Maybe it'll be enough. I'm calling it in."

Brooke stopped near her blue SUV, leaning against it like her legs might give out.

Tyler moved closer, not crowding her but staying near in case she needed help. "You okay?"

She looked at him, and he saw the adrenaline crash starting. "No. But I will be."

That simple honesty struck him. No pretending, no bravado. Just the truth.

"The police will want to talk to all of us. Get our statements about what we saw."

"I know." She took a shaky breath. "I can't believe this is happening."

"Neither can I."

Robert was on the phone now, talking to what sounded like a 9-1-1 dispatcher, giving their location and explaining what they'd found. Sue stood beside him, adding occasional details.

Tyler stood beside Brooke, the perfect August day suddenly feeling off. Finding a body like that was nothing close to right. At least they were out of danger.

She pulled the water bottle from her pack and took a drink, her gaze meeting his over the rim. The look in her eyes sent a wave of something almost unfamiliar through him, a feeling he hadn't known in years and never expected to feel again.

Chapter 3

Brooke

Brooke leaned against her SUV, grateful for the solid metal at her back. The parking lot felt surreal in its normalcy. Gravel crunched under her feet, the sun warmed her face, and birds sang in the nearby trees. Everything looked as it should. No hint that the world had tilted sideways a few miles back on the trail.

Her hands finally stopped shaking. Mostly. Though she didn't dare close her eyes. If she did, she'd see them again. The women.

Or woman. The thought of one body divided between two caches made Brooke's stomach churn. She took another sip of water and tried breathing through her nose.

This was wrong. All wrong. She should've stayed home. When Gina called the night before to cancel because the hospital was shorthanded, Brooke hadn't worried. Joe and Steph would still be going.

Not even half an hour later, Joe called. Some kind of emergency had come up, and he had to leave town. He was driving to Billings to catch the first flight to LAX.

She'd called Steph, who, of course, had already heard from both of their friends. Steph said it was fine, that the two of them could still go and she'd borrow her neighbor's dog to act as their third person. Never hiking alone in bear country was a given, though Steph often ignored the rule when she was in the wilderness during the winter months and the bears were denned up. This time of year, though, they were much too active, and Brooke knew better than to be out here alone. Her friends were bound to bring this up again and again, and she couldn't really blame them for it.

Brooke always followed the rule of going out in a group. Until today. Steph called at five thirty. She'd caught her toe on the bedstead, and she was almost certain it was broken. It was already swollen and purple. "Let's try for next weekend," she'd said.

"Sure," Brooke had answered before telling Steph to take care of herself.

"See you Wednesday," Steph had added before hanging up. "Even if I can't run, I'll be there to keep you all going."

No doubt about that. Steph was the organizer of the Basin County Running Club and was an expert at motivating everyone during their weekly gatherings. Unless she was out of town, Steph didn't miss a Wednesday. She was the main reason the club kept going after what happened in May.

"You need a snack?"

Brooke looked up, startled. Tyler stood a few feet away, holding a granola bar in her direction.

"I'm good." She reached for her pack, trying to calm her nerves. "I brought things."

He smiled and nodded, and she let herself relax a little. She hadn't really looked at him on the trail. Now she noticed his height, the solid set of his shoulders, the calm green of his eyes. And his hands, streaked with grease, caught her attention.

Brooke grabbed her water bottle and took a quick sip, turning away as she realized she'd been staring.

Robert was still on the phone with dispatch, his voice carrying across the quiet lot as he answered questions and gave directions. Sue stood beside him, occasionally adding details. Their Subaru sat twenty feet away, gate open, revealing a neatly organized cargo area.

"You rode with your friends?" she asked Tyler.

"I did. Made more sense than bringing two cars up."

"Yeah, I guess it does."

His voice was easy, unhurried. The kind of voice that could talk someone through a crisis without ever raising its pitch. She'd noticed that on the trail, too, though at the time she'd been too rattled to fully register it.

He paused a beat, then said, "Why were you off the trail?"

"Pardon?"

"Where you found the, um, cache. There wasn't a trail."

"Rattlesnake. I heard one and . . . I guess I freaked." She let out an embarrassed laugh. "I know better, but I ran, and, well, that's where I stopped."

"You've had quite the day."

She met his gaze again, certain she'd see mockery or pity. Instead, she found warmth and genuine understanding looking back at her.

"Yeah." Tears stung her eyes as she took another sip of water.

Tyler gave a nod, seeming to understand both her emotions and her embarrassment. "I'm going to check and see if Sue and Robert need anything."

She watched him go, noticing he glanced back about halfway toward their Subaru. The gesture made her smile.

He was right about one thing: it had been quite a day. Her life had always been quiet, almost boring, the kind of life she liked. Work, running, friends, family. Nothing ever out of the ordinary.

Until recently, that is.

The past few months had been difficult, but she was slowly finding her footing again, little by little returning to the Brooke she used to be.

She'd lived in Irma her entire life. Thirty-two years in a town where everyone knew everyone, where the biggest crime was usually teenagers spray painting the wall of a building or the occasional rogue cattle moseying through town.

At least, that's what she used to think before she learned her friend Kelsey was being blackmailed into stealing confidential files from her employer. Brooke had been so naive.

That day had changed everything she thought she knew about not just their little town, but also about herself. Even so, owning a coffee shop meant she saw a good part of the town regularly and knew their orders, their routines, their families.

But she didn't know Tyler.

Her eyes drifted to where he stood near the other car. Instead of looking at his friends, he was scanning the tree line, like he expected something to emerge from the forest. Even from this distance, she could see the tension in his body, the way he held himself alert and ready. Like he wasn't convinced the danger was entirely behind them.

She'd been too panicked earlier to really look at him. Her brain had been locked in survival mode. Get away from the bodies, mark the location, don't die from a bear attack or become the next cache herself.

Now, standing in the relative safety of the parking lot with her heart rate finally returning to normal, she could actually see him.

He was tall, around six feet, with the kind of athletic build that came more from actual work than a gym membership, but she suspected he worked out too. His dark hair was cut short and practical, a hint of silver around the temples. Strong jaw, serious expression. He was older than her by a few years, she guessed, though it was hard to tell for certain.

He was handsome, which felt wrong to notice given what they'd just found.

But it wasn't just his looks that caught her attention. It was the way he'd handled the situation. When she'd been spiraling in panic, ready to bolt into the forest, he'd been calm and confident. He'd assessed the danger, made a plan, and executed it without drama or hesitation.

He had positioned himself between her and the caches while they marked the trail. He shot out his hand to steady her when she stumbled on the hike back. He did small, protective things without making a fuss about them.

And the way he looked at her when their eyes met, attentive and unreadable even in the middle of a crisis . . .

Heat crept up Brooke's neck. This was ridiculous. Completely inappropriate. There was a dead person—possibly two dead people—less than two miles away, and here she was cataloging some stranger's attractive qualities like she was scrolling through a dating app.

What kind of person did that?

She forced her attention back to Robert, who was still on the phone, but she kept looking back at Tyler.

Enough, Brooke, she told herself. *You are too messed up right now to even be thinking about getting involved with someone.*

She let out a sigh and turned away, her eyes moving over the forest as she took a few steady breaths. Calling herself messed up was no exaggeration. She'd been trying to keep things together, throwing herself into work, and she'd had a good race two months earlier. Not the one she'd planned, but the one she needed. Still . . . she knew herself well enough to recognize that her tendency to obsess was at an all-time high. And when that happened, she didn't make the best choices. Better to get through today and forget all about the tall, handsome Tyler Gillis.

Movement caught her eye. Robert was off the phone, and he and Sue were heading toward their Subaru. They moved to the back and started pulling out what looked like a cooler.

"They're sending someone," Robert called out. "Could be a while. Half an hour, probably longer."

Longer was more likely unless they already had someone patrolling in the mountains. She considered where they were: near the Wyoming-Montana state line but still inside Basin County, Wyoming.

Sue approached, carrying sandwiches wrapped in plastic and a handful of granola bars. Robert followed with bottles of water.

"Figured we might as well eat while we wait." Sue offered her some food. "It's going to be a long afternoon."

Brooke hesitated. Eating felt wrong. Disrespectful when someone was lying dead on the mountain. But her body was crashing from the adrenaline spike, and she knew she needed fuel. Her stomach agreed with a growl, reminding her she'd only had coffee and a bagel before leaving the house that morning.

"Thank you," she said, accepting a sandwich and water. When she unwrapped it, she discovered turkey and swiss on wheat bread. Simple but welcome.

Tyler took a sandwich as well, and Brooke noticed he looked just as conflicted about it as she did.

Stop it, Brooke. Just don't even look at him.

"I know it seems strange," Sue said gently, reading their expressions. "But we're going to be here for hours once the police arrive. We need to keep our strength up."

"She's right," Robert added. "I've been through something like this before. Years ago, when I was working construction in Colorado. Found a hiker who'd fallen off a cliff. The investigation took all day."

They settled into an awkward circle near Brooke's SUV. The food helped, grounding her in her body and in the present. She was alive. She was safe. The sandwich was good.

"You mentioned you're from Irma?" Sue asked.

Brooke nodded as she swallowed her bite. "Born and raised. I own the coffee shop on Grand Avenue. Irma Brew."

Sue's face lit up. "Oh, of course. I knew I recognized you. We've been there. You make those amazing scones. I love the variety."

"Thanks. We always have the plain but try to do a specialty scone or two each day."

"They're incredible," Sue said. "We just moved to the area a few months ago. Robert bought the auto repair shop in town."

"Morgan's place?" Brooke remembered hearing the longtime owner had finally retired.

"That's the one," Robert confirmed. "Found the listing online and made a deal quickly. He said he was ready to spend more time fishing."

Brooke glanced at Tyler. "Are you new to town too?"

Something flickered across his face, too quickly for her to read. "I work for Robert. At the shop."

It wasn't really an answer to her question. Brooke waited, expecting him to elaborate, but he took another bite of his sandwich.

"Tyler's a fantastic mechanic," Sue filled the silence. "We're lucky to have him. He was part of the team from when Morgan owned the place."

"How long have you been in Irma?" Brooke asked Tyler directly.

"Awhile," he said, his tone pleasant but vague.

Brooke felt her curiosity sharpen. She knew most people in town, at least by sight. The coffee shop saw everyone eventually—morning regulars, tourists passing through, construction crews, ranchers coming in from the outlying properties. That or at the grocery store. Everyone had to buy groceries.

But she'd never seen Tyler before.

"We try to get out hiking most weekends," Robert said, steering the conversation elsewhere. "Tyler's been showing us good trails. He knows the area well."

Tyler's jaw tightened almost imperceptibly. Brooke caught it, though, before his expression smoothed back to neutral.

Interesting.

Sue was watching her with a sly smile. The kind that said she'd seen exactly where Brooke's attention kept landing, and she found it amusing.

Brooke's face heated again. She focused on her sandwich, but she stayed aware of Tyler in a way that felt hard to ignore. The way he moved, still alert despite the casual setting. How his gaze kept sweeping the parking lot and the tree line, never quite settling.

"Do you hike alone often?" Tyler asked, and there was something in his tone that wasn't quite criticism but close.

"Not usually," Brooke admitted. "I know better. But my friends canceled at the last minute, and I needed . . ." She trailed off, not sure how to explain the desperate need she'd felt this morning to get into the mountains, to prove she could still do this, even if going out alone was a reckless decision.

"Needed what?" Tyler's eyes were on her now, focused and intent.

"To not let fear win," she said quietly.

Understanding crossed his face, like maybe he knew something about fear.

Brooke couldn't deny there was something between them. Attraction, yes, but also a flicker of recognition, as if they both understood more than either wanted to say. Like they were both carrying weight they didn't talk about, both pushing against things that wanted to hold them back.

Sue cleared her throat softly, and Brooke realized she'd been staring at Tyler.

"Well," Sue said with forced cheerfulness, "I'm glad we happened to be here today. Even if the circumstances are awful."

"Me too," Brooke said, meaning it. She didn't want to think about what would've happened if she'd been completely alone when she found those bodies. If she'd had to hike out by herself, panic building with every step. If she'd had to wait there alone for law enforcement to arrive.

Tyler made it bearable. All three of them had, but especially Tyler.

She caught his eye again and saw something warm in his expression that unsettled her in a way she wasn't ready to examine.

This was wrong. Not just wildly inappropriate when she should be focused on the victims, on who might have killed them, and on the danger that could still be lurking in these mountains, but it was risky on a personal level as well.

Her thoughts kept returning to how his voice had cut through the panic, how quickly he caught her when she stumbled, and how naturally he had taken charge without making it about himself.

Brooke took another bite of her sandwich and tried to ignore Sue's smile.

The afternoon was going to be very long.

Chapter 4

Tyler

Tyler finished his sandwich and resisted the urge to check his watch again. Thirty minutes, Robert had said. Maybe longer. Every minute that ticked by felt like time stretching too thin.

He should leave. Slip away. Today was Sunday, and it was still tourist season. The trailhead was visible from the highway, and a steady stream of cars moved along the well-traveled road. He could just walk to the pavement and stick out his thumb. Maybe someone would stop. Maybe they'd even be heading back to Irma.

Or they might take him to the seasonal store nearby. From there he could hitch again or wait for Robert and Sue. They could deal with the law and then pick him up after they were done.

The smart move was to disappear before the sheriff's department showed up. Before deputies started asking questions, taking statements, and running names through their systems. Depending on who responded, running his name might not even be necessary. Too many of them knew him by sight.

Tyler didn't trust cops, and for good reasons. The kind of reasons that left scars you couldn't see but were felt every time a badge came near. Some of those badges stung worse than others.

He shifted his weight. His muscles tightened with the familiar urge to move, to put distance between himself and what was coming. His eyes stayed on the access road, watching for the dust cloud that would signal approaching officers.

But he didn't move.

Two things kept him rooted to the parking lot, and he wasn't entirely comfortable with either of them.

First, the practical problem. They would want his statement. He had seen the bodies, helped mark the trail, and been part of the group that made the call. If he left now, they'd just track him down later.

He could make things worse by running, or at least seeming to run. Robert would cover for him and keep his name out of it, but Tyler couldn't ask that of Sue. And he certainly couldn't expect Brooke to stay silent. But Robert, he would do it. Tyler was certain of it. Robert knew about his past troubles. He knew everything.

But Brooke—she made disappearing complicated.

Tyler looked toward where she sat in the front seat of her SUV, door open and long, tan legs on the ground as she stared at the tree line. Even from here, he could see the tightness in her shoulders, the way she held herself like she was ready to bolt at the first sign of danger.

He should want nothing to do with her. Getting involved with someone in Irma, someone who'd lived there her whole life and knew everyone, was the last thing he needed. The coffee shop owner, no less. Someone who probably had her finger on the pulse of every piece of gossip and news in town.

Worse still, once she gave her name, he realized he knew her. He'd known her brother fairly well once and had even seen him in recent months.

He'd read several articles about Brooke and members of her running club being trapped during a snowstorm up at the ghost town of Bearwater. They ended up in a fight for their lives after one of the club members made a terrible choice. The article had caught his attention because it was such an odd thing for the people of Irma to be involved in.

Odd, but not unheard of. He knew from experience that bad things could happen even in Basin County.

Brooke didn't seem to remember him. He was glad about that, yet somehow disappointed.

She'd impressed him. That was the problem. Most people would've completely fallen apart after stumbling onto bear caches containing human remains. But Brooke had pulled herself together enough to mark the location, to think clearly despite her fear.

The way she moved on the trail spoke of real experience in the mountains. No surprise, considering what he'd read about her and the rest of her running club.

He'd seen them a few times, taking various routes through town on Wednesday nights. According to one of the articles about the trouble in Bearwater, they kept it short on weeknights but did longer hikes and trail runs on the weekend.

Brooke was athletic and capable, comfortable with the terrain even in a crisis. And the honesty when he'd asked if she was okay . . . no pretending, no bravado, just the simple truth.

He liked that about her.

Which was inconvenient in about seventeen different ways.

"You keep looking at her like that, she's going to notice," Robert said quietly, coming to stand beside him.

Tyler looked away. "Don't know what you're talking about."

"Sure you don't." Robert sounded amused. "Sue thinks it's sweet."

"There's nothing sweet about it. We just found a dead body."

"Two bodies, maybe. Sue likes to think she's right, but it's hard to say for sure until they get here and get a better look. I will admit, though, my wife is smart about things." An obvious look of love passed over Robert's face as he gazed at his wife.

Tyler tamped down his jealousy. He had that at one time, too, before it was ripped away from him.

"That's not the point, though," Robert continued. "The point is you can't take your eyes off her."

Tyler didn't respond. What was there to say? That he'd noticed the exact shade of blue in Brooke's eyes? That her voice had a slight rasp that did things to him? That when she'd looked at him and said she needed to not let fear win, something in his chest had tightened in recognition?

"She seems nice," Robert said. "Owns that coffee shop Sue's always dragging me to."

"I know where she works."

"You don't go there."

It wasn't a question. Robert knew Tyler's habits, knew he avoided certain places in town. Coffee shops and restaurants were on the list. Too central, too visible, too much of a gathering place for people who might ask questions.

He made an exception for a couple of the town's bars. Not because of the booze, but for darts. He liked the challenge of the game and had a few people he could trust that he played with.

"Maybe I should start going out for coffee," Tyler heard himself say, then regretted it.

Robert grinned. "Maybe you should."

Sue wandered over, carrying a bag of trail mix. "The deputies are going to want to talk to all of us, I'm sure."

Tyler stiffened. "Yeah."

"You okay with that?" Sue's question was gentle but pointed. She knew. Not everything, no one really did, but enough to understand why he might have reservations about dealing with law enforcement.

"Do I have a choice?"

She shrugged, but the look on her face was clear.

"I'm good." It was a lie, but he'd do it anyway.

His eyes found Brooke again. She was watching the road now, jaw set with determination. Handling her fear, just like she'd said. Not letting it win.

Something shifted in his chest. A feeling he hadn't experienced in years. Hadn't let himself experience, because wanting things led to losing things, and he'd lost enough for one lifetime.

But looking at her, remembering the way she'd moved through her panic with courage and intelligence, he wanted more.

He wanted to know her story, to understand the fear she was fighting, to be the person she could look at when she needed someone steady beside her.

Dangerous thoughts. The kind that led to complications.

"She's single, you know," Sue said.

"Sue," Robert warned.

"What? I'm just saying. In case he was wondering."

"I wasn't wondering."

"Uh-huh." Sue's smile was pure mischief. "That's why you've looked at her about forty times in the last five minutes."

Tyler didn't dignify that with a response.

Brooke stood and stretched, her movements fluid despite the stress. She walked a few steps toward the trailhead, then back, working out the tension. When she caught him watching, she offered a small, uncertain smile.

Tyler felt that smile land somewhere in the vicinity of his sternum.

This was a problem.

"Go talk to her," Sue suggested. "She's alone over there, probably spiraling about what she found. Distract her."

"I'm not good at small talk."

"Then don't make it small. You're both dealing with the same situation. Talk about that."

Tyler hesitated, every instinct telling him to keep his distance and hold up the walls he'd built so carefully over the past few years. Getting close to people meant vulnerability and risk. It meant danger, and not only for himself.

But Brooke looked over again, and this time her expression was uncertain, almost questioning. Maybe an invitation?

"Fine," he muttered and walked toward her before he could overthink it.

She straightened as he approached, surprise flickering across her features before settling into something more open.

"Hey," she said.

"Hey." *Brilliant conversation, Tyler. Real smooth.* "How are you holding up?"

"I don't know." Brooke wrapped her arms around herself. "I keep thinking about it. About the bodies. Who were they? What happened to them?"

"Natural response. Trauma does that."

"You think? You know stuff about trauma?"

Tyler did. More than he'd ever wanted to. "Everyone's got something."

"That's vague."

"It's intentional."

Brooke's lips quirked into what might have been a smile. "Fair enough. I'm being nosy."

"You're being curious. There's a difference."

They fell into silence, but it wasn't uncomfortable. Just two people standing in a parking lot, waiting for law enforcement to arrive and turn an already terrible day into something more complicated.

"Thank you," Brooke said after a moment. "For back there. For not letting me completely lose it."

"You didn't need me. You were handling it."

"I was panicking."

"You were scared. But you still marked the location, still got yourself to safety. You were ready to blast me with your bear spray." He smiled and she laughed, the sound of it sending a new wave of something through him.

"I was. Believe me, I was."

"That's not panicking. That's being smart under pressure."

She looked at him, really looked at him, and Tyler felt exposed in a way that should've made him uncomfortable. Instead, it felt like being seen. Like maybe she understood something about him without him having to explain it.

Behind them, Sue laughed at something Robert said. Normal sounds in an abnormal situation. Tyler became aware of how close he was standing to Brooke, close enough to smell the faint scent of her shampoo mixed with trail dust and sweat.

Close enough to notice the way her breathing had changed, steady but quick. Like maybe he wasn't the only one feeling this insane pull.

"Tyler," she started, then stopped.

"Yeah?"

"Why haven't I seen you before? In town, I mean. Sue said you've worked at the shop for a while."

There it was. The question he'd been expecting. The one he didn't want to answer but probably needed to.

"I keep to myself," he said carefully. "Work, home, play a little darts for fun. Not much else."

"That sounds lonely."

"It's safe."

The word was out before he could stop it, revealing more than he'd intended.

"Safe from what?" she asked.

Tyler opened his mouth to deflect, to change the subject, to rebuild the walls he'd just accidentally knocked down.

But then the sound of tires on gravel cut through the afternoon quiet. They both turned to see a Basin County Sheriff's Department SUV coming down the access road, dust rising in its wake.

"Guess that's our cue," Brooke said, but she didn't move away from him.

Tyler watched the vehicle approach, every instinct in him going on alert. The urge to leave rose up again, sharp and insistent.

But Brooke's hand found his arm, just briefly. A touch that said I'm glad you're here. A touch that anchored him more effectively than any rational argument could have.

"We've got this," she said quietly.

Tyler wasn't sure if she was reassuring him or herself. Either way, it helped.

The deputy pulled the vehicle to a stop, and Tyler forced himself to stay exactly where he was—for the investigation; for Robert and Sue, who'd offered him a way out and deserved his honesty; and for Brooke, who looked at him like maybe he was someone worth knowing.

Even if he wasn't entirely sure that was true.

Chapter 5

Brooke

The Basin County Sheriff's Department SUV kicked up a small cloud of dust as it rolled to a stop. Brooke wasn't looking forward to what would come next. Statements. Questions. Hours of reliving what she'd found in the woods. She squeezed her eyes shut, trying to push away the image of the waxy leg.

The driver's door opened, and a woman stepped out, hair pulled back in a low bun, sunglasses hiding her eyes until she pulled them off and hooked them on her shirt collar.

Brooke recognized her.

"Edi," she said, relief washing through her. At least it was someone she knew.

Deputy Edi Reeves had gone to Irma High School, graduating a couple of years ahead of Brooke, which meant Edi had been one of those intimidating upperclassmen when Brooke was still figuring out how lockers worked.

She came into the coffee shop sometimes and always ordered the same thing—large dark roast, black, and whatever sweet muffin they had left. She was friendly but professional, the kind of regular who knew your name but didn't overstay their welcome.

Brooke wasn't even sure if Edi remembered her from school. If she did, she never said so. She never brought up those teenage years and never attended the multi-class reunions held every summer over Irma Days.

Brooke asked her about it a couple of years ago when she saw her in the coffee shop the day before the event. Edi simply said she usually ended up on the duty roster and never felt comfortable requesting time off for something like that.

Seeing her here felt very different from seeing her in the coffee shop. Everything seemed so much more official. More real.

Brilliant, Brooke, she thought to herself. *It is real. That was a real dead body you found. A real person.* The thought stung her nose.

"Brooke." Edi's greeting was warm, but her eyes were already scanning the scene, taking in the four people gathered, the trailhead, the entire space. "You okay?"

"I've been better."

"I bet." Edi turned to Robert and Sue. "I don't think we've met officially, but you bought Morgan's auto shop, right?"

"That's us," Robert said, stepping forward to shake her hand. "Sue and Robert Toles."

Brooke noticed that Edi was not just taller than Sue but taller than Robert as well. She had always been tall, even in school, towering over the other girls and some of the boys. Being overweight didn't help, and it had earned her cruel nicknames like "Sasquatch" and "Brontosaurus."

"My condo is on the other end of your neighborhood," Edi said, her tone smooth, almost comforting. "Looks like you've been doing a lot of work on your place."

Sue smiled despite the circumstances. "Slowly but surely. We saw pictures of what it used to look like. Stunning. We hope we can bring it back to that someday."

Edi's expression softened briefly before her cop face returned. She turned toward where Tyler stood near the trailhead marker, and Brooke saw something shift in the deputy's demeanor. Not unfriendly exactly, but definitely more guarded.

"Tyler," Edi said, and there was a wealth of history in that single word.

"Edi." Tyler's response was equally loaded. His shoulders had gone rigid, his jaw tight.

There was weight in their exchange, something unspoken that made the air feel charged.

Brooke assumed Tyler was hanging back because he didn't know the deputy. That made sense—he was new to the area, or at least new enough that Brooke didn't know him. But watching them now, watching the way Edi's expression shuttered and Tyler's whole body language changed, Brooke realized she'd been wrong.

They definitely knew each other.

And whatever their history was, it wasn't comfortable.

"You're hiking again," Edi said.

"Yeah."

"Glad to see you out. I know you always loved the woods."

"Thanks."

Brooke looked from Edi to Tyler. She'd been attracted to this man. Maybe she still was, despite her reservations over the terrible timing for a new relationship.

But watching him now, tense and guarded around a local deputy, red flags were starting to wave. Brooke knew better than to ignore red flags, especially after what happened at Bearwater. What had started as a simple training run in the Absaroka Mountains with friends had turned into a life-and-death situation. All because she'd ignored warning signals that she should've recognized.

They'd been subtle, sure, but in hindsight, they were so obvious.

Kelsey had been her friend. Someone Brooke had run with so many times and trusted completely. Sweet, nervous Kelsey, who always brought extra energy bars and asked if anyone needed anything.

And she'd also been stealing files from her law firm and making illegal drops under the cover of the running club, putting all of them in danger because she'd been too scared to ask for help. Because she'd made choices that seemed reasonable to her at the time but had nearly gotten them all killed.

Brooke had completely missed it. All of it. The signs that something was wrong, the tension that must have been there, the lies Kelsey had been telling. Brooke trusted her judgment, and her judgment had been catastrophically wrong.

She couldn't make that mistake again. She *wouldn't* make that mistake again.

The problem was Brooke knew herself, knew her patterns. When she focused on something, whether it was a training plan, a race, or a person, she fixated. Obsessed. She couldn't let go even when she should.

It nearly destroyed her last year when she'd been forced to drop out while running the Moose Range Run 100. She'd spiraled, unable to see past that one failure, letting it consume her until she'd driven herself and everyone around her a little crazy.

Then, earlier this year, when training for a second try at the race, she'd put together an insanely aggressive training plan, planning every run down to the nth degree and refusing to back off when her body or her mind had had enough. She'd come close to making herself sick and then almost getting herself and others killed.

She'd promised herself she'd work on that—on giving herself grace, on not letting single data points define everything, on recognizing when her brain was sliding into unhealthy territory, and on keeping herself safe, as well as those who mattered to her.

Getting involved with someone she couldn't trust would be exactly the kind of thing she'd obsess over, the kind of thing that would consume her. And right now, watching Tyler's interaction with Edi, alarm bells were going off. The kind she wished she'd had with Kelsey. The kind she planned on paying attention to now.

Whatever was between Tyler and this deputy, it wasn't good. The strain was obvious in the careful way they spoke to each other and in the things not being said. And Tyler's whole demeanor had changed. The reliable, confident man who'd talked her down from panic on the trail was now replaced by someone guarded and closed off.

She didn't know what it meant. But she knew it meant something.

"You all were together when the bodies were found?"

Brooke shook her head.

Sue and Robert both pointed at her as Robert said, "She found them."

"I think it might be one body in two caches," Sue added.

"What makes you say that?" Edi turned to face Sue directly.

"The way the remains were positioned. The, um . . . the separation point." Sue's face went pale. "I used to be an EMT, a volunteer. I've seen trauma before. That didn't look like two separate people to me."

Edi made a note. "We'll know for sure once we get the team out there. I was hoping they'd be here by now. But that's helpful context. Thank you." She glanced at her watch and made a face. "All right, I'm going to need statements from all of you. Who wants to go first?"

"I'll go," Brooke said. Might as well get it over with and get off this mountain, away from the man who unsettled her in ways she didn't trust. Away from the man who had danger written all over him.

Edi nodded and gestured toward her vehicle. They walked over together, leaving the others by the trailhead.

"This is pretty far out for a solo hike," Edi said once they were out of earshot.

"I know. My friends canceled at the last minute. I should've canceled too."

"But you didn't."

"I needed to be out here." Brooke heard the defensiveness in her own voice and tried to soften it. "I know it was stupid. But I needed it."

Edi's expression softened. "I know what happened with Kelsey and that man. Tough business."

That man. The one who was hired to retrieve the documents from Kelsey and who intended to kill not only Kelsey but also Gina, Nick, Joe, and Brooke because they were there. He'd called them collateral damage. Like they were nothing. Like they didn't matter. "Yeah."

"And now this. It can't be easy."

"No." Brooke wrapped her arms around herself. "It really isn't."

Edi took her through the statement step-by-step. Who was supposed to be with her today, and why did they cancel? What time did Brooke arrive? What route had she taken? The sound that had spooked her, the way she'd run off trail, the moment she'd realized what she was looking at.

Tears were flowing freely, and Edi paused a moment to fish out a box of tissues, handing it to Brooke.

"Thank you. I'm . . . it's just so awful."

"Death is never easy. Take a minute, then we'll start again."

Brooke worked to collect herself while Edi made soothing sounds.

After a few minutes, Brooke said, "I'm ready. Let's just get this over with."

Brooke forced herself to keep her answers factual and to avoid embellishing. It wasn't easy, though, and she'd catch herself rambling, adding things that didn't matter. She stopped and started again, but soon discovered she was doing the same thing. It was a total word vomit. Edi seemed to understand.

"And you marked the location with paracord," Edi said, making notes.

"Orange paracord. Mine is, anyway. I tied it to a couple of trees between the cache and the main trail. You know, so we could find it again. I can't even believe I thought to do that. Everything was like . . . like I was in a dream, and I was just . . . " She pulled her lips tight. She was doing it again.

Brooke cleared her throat. "The others added their own markers too. Green. Bright green." She thought about Tyler and his green eyes. Darker than the paracord, with flecks of gold.

"Smart thinking. Especially in your state of mind."

"I'm pretty sure I wasn't really thinking. Reacting, maybe."

"Good reactions, then." Edi looked up from her notebook. "The couple—Robert and Sue—you didn't know them before today?"

"No. They found me when I was trying to get back to the trail. I was pretty shaken up."

"And Tyler was with them?"

Something in the way Edi said his name made Brooke look at her more carefully. "Yes."

"He say anything to you? About knowing the area, about what you'd found?"

"Just that we needed to stick together to make sure I got back safely." Brooke hesitated. "Why?"

"No reason. Just getting the full picture." But Edi's expression suggested there was definitely a reason.

"You know him," Brooke said.

Edi was quiet for a moment. "It's a small town. Most people know most people."

"That's not an answer."

"No, it's not." Edi closed her notebook.

The implication was clear. Whatever Edi knew about Tyler, she wasn't going to share it. Which somehow made it worse, made Brooke's imagination fill in blanks that might not even exist.

But the fact that there were blanks to fill in at all was the problem. A problem that was shouting at her, "Pay attention! Pay attention!"

They walked back to the group.

"Mrs. Toles? I'll take you next."

"Can my husband stay with me?" Sue asked, reaching for his hand.

"That's not how we usually do it."

"I understand, but . . . "

Edi checked her watch and shook her head, the hair that had slipped out of her bun at the nape of her neck brushing her cheeks. "Might as well." She glanced toward the main road before muttering. "What's taking everyone so long?"

Instead of getting into the SUV like she and Edi had, the three of them went to the front of the vehicle and spoke in low voices.

Brooke went to her car and sat in the front seat, leaving the front door open and her feet on the ground. She half expected Tyler to follow her, but he stayed near Robert and Sue's car. While she knew that was for the best, she was oddly disappointed.

"Don't go looking for trouble," she said softly. "Just let him be."

It was a good fifteen minutes before Edi finished with Robert and Sue. No one from the county or anyone else official had shown up.

Finally, it was Tyler's turn. Brooke watched as he walked over to Edi's vehicle, his movements controlled and careful. Like he was bracing himself.

As with the others, they stood near the front. She couldn't hear what they were saying, but she could see their body language. Edi's posture was professional, but there was something else there. Concern, maybe. Or suspicion. Tyler kept his arms crossed and his responses brief, based on how little his lips moved.

"Looks like they've got history," Sue said quietly, appearing beside Brooke.

"Yeah. I noticed."

"They must know each other. Tyler doesn't really talk about personal stuff. Keeps things pretty close to the vest."

"That's his right." Even as Brooke said it, she felt the doubt creeping in. Everyone had a right to privacy. But privacy and secrets weren't always the same thing.

"Absolutely," Sue agreed. "Just seems like maybe whatever history he has with the deputy is complicated."

Complicated. That was one word for it.

Tyler and Edi finished their conversation. He walked back toward the group, his expression didn't reveal anything. But when he looked toward Brooke, she saw something there. Interest, maybe.

She also saw the guardedness. The walls. The things he wasn't saying.

She looked away first.

Edi gathered them near the vehicles. "When the rest of the team arrives, we'll make sure we secure the scene. That'll take a few hours to coordinate. You're all free to go, but I'll need you to stay available. We might have follow-up questions."

"Of course," Robert said. "Whatever you need."

"And, Brooke?" Edi's expression was kind. "You might want to talk to someone. About what you saw. The county has resources for that kind of thing."

"I'm okay."

"You say that now, but finding something like this can mess with you in ways you don't expect. Just keep it in mind. That goes for the rest of you too."

Brooke nodded, though she had no intention of calling some county counselor. She was dealing with the Bearwater trauma on her own. She'd deal with this, too, and maybe someday soon she'd start sleeping properly again and stop second guessing everything in her life.

They started to disperse toward their vehicles. Tyler moved toward Brooke, and for a moment, she thought he was going to say something. Ask for her number, maybe, or suggest they meet up later to decompress. She was forming a reply in her mind—a denial, of course—ready to deliver it without hesitation.

Instead, he stopped a few feet away, hands in his pockets.

"You going to be okay?" he asked.

"Yeah. I will be."

"Good." He hesitated. "If you need anything . . . "

"I won't." The words came out sharper than she intended. "But thank you. For everything earlier. You really helped."

Something crossed his face. Disappointment, maybe. Or understanding that she was pulling away, putting distance between them.

"Anytime," he said quietly.

Traffic noise caught Brooke's attention. Two vehicles were slowing from the main road and turning off.

Tyler sighed. "I was hoping to get out of here before the rest of them arrived."

Chapter 6

Tyler

The vehicles kicked up dust as they turned onto the access road leading to the trailhead. It was a game warden truck and another sheriff's department SUV.

Tyler should've left. Should've gotten away when he had the chance, before more deputies arrived, before this whole situation became more complicated than it already was.

There was something about her that made him want to bridge the space she'd been putting between them since Edi arrived, and he hoped, against reason, that she wasn't writing him off completely.

That hope felt foolish now.

Seeing Edi had thrown him more than he'd expected. They'd known each other in high school—she was a few years behind him, part of the same small-town orbit where everyone knew everyone, whether they wanted to or not. They weren't close friends, but friendly enough. The kind of acquaintances who'd nod in the hallways, maybe exchange a few words at a football game or in the cafeteria.

Back then, she'd been quiet and kept to herself mostly. Not that she was given much of a choice. Excess weight, above-average height, and the misery of being a teenager made for a cruel combination. Add in her frizzy hair and the difficulties she had with acne, and it was an almost lethal combination as far as popularity went.

Edi's family connections should've earned her a little consideration, or at least limited some of the teasing, but kids could be cruel. Teenage girls can be downright brutal. He'd seen it happening, but he never participated and didn't encourage it. Truth be told, he went out of his way to be nice to her when he could.

That paid off after high school, when she worked at one of the county offices and helped him with business things. She'd see him walk in and make sure she took care of him, even if it meant a late lunch. Edi was always happy to help him get a title transferred over for one of his project cars.

Now she was a deputy sheriff. She'd lost some of the weight, though she was still on the heavy side. Her hair seemed to have mostly submitted to the tight knot at the back of her head, though not fully.

Most importantly, she had authority, a badge, and a gun on her hip. That shift in their dynamic had been uncomfortable in ways Tyler hadn't fully anticipated. She wasn't simply Edi anymore. She was Deputy Reeves, someone with the power to dig into his past, to ask questions he didn't want to answer, to make his life difficult if she chose to.

But what bothered him more was the way she'd looked at him. Nervous. Almost skittish. Like she wasn't sure how to act around him and wasn't sure what to say.

He didn't understand it. Before he left Basin County, Edi had sought him out. She'd told him she knew it wasn't his fault, that she believed him when others hadn't. Her support had meant something then, it was one of the few bright spots in an otherwise dark time.

So why the nervousness now? What had changed?

But that was before, when she was still just Edi. Before she managed to get hired on as a deputy. Maybe that's what changed.

Tyler shoved his hands deeper into his pockets and tried to push the question aside. It didn't matter. None of it mattered because he couldn't let it matter. He *wouldn't* let it matter.

He knew the truth in more ways than one. He'd made a mistake earlier, thinking he could get to know Brooke, thinking he could get involved with *anyone* in Basin County. He couldn't. Not Brooke. Not anyone. He'd come back here for one reason only—to face his past, stop running from what happened, and prove to himself that he could exist in this place without falling apart.

He hadn't come back to start something new. Especially not with someone like Brooke, who had her life together, owned a business, and had deep roots in the community. She had friends, family, and a real life. She deserved better than him.

What he didn't understand was how Brooke didn't recognize him. Everyone else seemed to know what happened. The whispers, the suspicions, the way people looked at him when they thought he wasn't paying attention . . . they'd done it before he left, and they've been doing it since he came back.

It wasn't a secret he could keep. Eventually, Brooke would know too. She'd hear the stories, the rumors, the truth mixed with speculation and gossip. She'd look at him the same way others did—with wariness, with doubt, with the unspoken question of whether he was dangerous.

He was poison to the people he cared about. That was the truth he'd learned the hard way. Getting close to him meant getting hurt, and he couldn't do that to Brooke.

The attraction he felt was dangerous. Not for him. He'd already paid his price, already knew what loss felt like. But for her. She'd gone through enough up at Bearwater. She didn't need his baggage added to her load.

Maybe it didn't matter anyway.

Tyler looked toward Brooke as she stared at the approaching vehicles. Since Edi had arrived, Brooke started pulling back. He'd seen it in her body language, in the way she'd stopped meeting his eyes, in the careful distance she'd put between them.

She was getting wary. Smart woman.

Did she finally realize who he was? Maybe something clicked. Maybe Edi had said something, or maybe Brooke was just good at reading people and had sensed the history between him and Edi.

Maybe she remembered how Tyler and her older brother, Phil, used to hang around together. They played football together, souped up their cars in the auto shop, spent countless hours talking about getting out of Basin County and making something of themselves.

So much for that. Phil was still in Irma after taking over his dad's print shop. Tyler had seen places and done things, but none of it had been what he wanted out of life. Coming back to Irma had made sense, at least at first. The last few months had been good. Great, even, as long as he ignored the stares and whispers. He had a job he enjoyed, and Robert and Sue treated him well.

Finding the body was rough for all of them, Brooke especially.

Brooke was definitely no longer the little kid he remembered from visits to Phil's house. She'd grown into someone impressive. Strong, capable, resilient. The kind of person who could find human remains in the woods and still have the presence of mind to mark the location. The kind of person who admitted to fear but didn't let it control her.

The kind of person he had no business getting close to.

Tyler watched as she finally looked at him, her expression troubled. Their eyes met for a moment before she looked away, and he felt the loss of that connection like a physical thing.

He'd already lost her trust, and they'd only just met.

The game warden's truck pulled into the lot first, gravel crunching under its tires. A man stepped out, surveying the scene with the practiced eye of someone who'd dealt with plenty of wilderness incidents. Tyler recognized him but couldn't put a name with the face.

The sheriff's SUV parked beside it. When the driver's door opened and the deputy stepped out, Tyler knew both the name and the face.

Deputy Adam Boverman. Of all the people who could've responded, it had to be him.

Boverman's eyes swept the parking lot, taking in the vehicles, the people, the whole setup. When his gaze landed on Tyler, something shifted in his expression. Recognition mixed with something darker. Satisfaction, maybe. Or vindication.

He walked directly toward Tyler, his stride purposeful, his hand resting casually near his belt. Not on his weapon, but close enough to send a message.

"Tyler Gillis," Boverman said, stopping a few feet away. His voice carried across the quiet lot. "Should've known you'd turn up where there's a dead body."

Tyler kept his expression neutral. "Deputy Boverman."

"Funny thing, you being here." The deputy's smile was completely fake. Not surprising. "Real funny, considering your history."

"I was hiking with friends. We helped the woman who found the remains in the woods. That's all."

"That's all?" Boverman let out a harsh laugh. "See, the problem is, people around here remember what happened last time you were involved with a dead body. Remember how that turned out?"

The words landed like a punch. Tyler heard Brooke's sharp inhale behind him, heard Robert's muttered curse.

"Deputy Boverman," Edi said, walking over quickly. "That's not— "

"Not what, Reeves? Not relevant?" His attention stayed fixed on Tyler. "He's got a history with dead bodies. Seems pretty relevant to me."

Tyler forced himself to stay still, to keep his hands visible, to not give Boverman any excuse to escalate this further. But inside, everything was crumbling.

This was why he shouldn't have come back to Irma. He should've stayed away—built a life somewhere else and lived with the ghosts that haunted him. It was also why he couldn't get involved with Brooke or anyone else.

Because in this town, he would always be a suspect. He'd always be the one they looked at first when something went wrong. The man whose past made people wonder if he was capable of murder.

Chapter 7

Brooke

The parking lot went completely silent as Adam's words hung in the air. Tyler stood perfectly still, his expression carefully blank, like he'd expected this and had already braced for the impact.

Brooke went cold. *History with dead bodies? What does that mean?*

Sue made a small sound. Shock, maybe? Robert showed no surprise at all, like perhaps this wasn't news to him.

"Deputy Boverman," Edi said sharply, moving between him and Tyler. "That's inappropriate."

Adam ignored her, his attention fixed on the small group. "People have a right to know who they're dealing with." His eyes traveled to Brooke. "So they can make efforts to keep themselves safe."

Brooke knew Adam Boverman. He had moved to town several years earlier, taking the deputy job. Brooke wasn't living in Irma when he arrived; she was away at school in Laramie.

When she came home with a degree in business and plans to buy her own restaurant, she took a job at one of the neighborhood diners while putting her plans into motion. Adam ate there regularly.

He was good-looking in that clean-cut, all-American way—sandy blond hair, pale blue eyes, and a solid build. She knew he was older than her, but wasn't sure how much. Five or six years, probably. Nice guy, or at least he always seemed nice. He popped into the coffee shop sometimes, not as regularly as Edi, but on occasion.

Until recently, he'd been in a long-distance relationship with someone he'd met online. Brooke heard through the coffee shop grapevine—because that was how information traveled in Irma—that they'd broken up a few months ago. Something about the distance being too hard, about wanting different things.

Since then, Adam had been more visible around town, stopping in at local businesses, showing up at community events, generally making himself present in ways he hadn't when he was attached.

He also had a reputation, though Brooke tried not to put too much stock in gossip. But over the years, multiple people had mentioned that Adam dated around. Nothing serious, nothing committed, just a string of relationships that never quite stuck, which was probably the reason his long-distance relationship was such a hot topic. She'd even heard people placed good-natured bets on whether he'd ever settle down.

Right now, though, watching him look at Tyler with something between satisfaction and hostility, his dating history seemed trivial. What mattered now was what he'd implied.

"What history?" The question came out before Brooke could stop it.

Adam's attention shifted back to her, his expression softening immediately. "You don't know?"

"Know what?"

He moved closer, his whole demeanor changing. Protective. Concerned. Like he was positioning himself between her and potential danger. "Tyler's wife and child died in a house fire."

The words hit Brooke like a physical blow. Wife and child. Dead. Fire. "Oh," she said, looking at Tyler. "I'm so sorry. That's . . . awful."

Tyler nodded, his face a mask that gave nothing away, though something in his green eyes had gone dark and hollow.

"It's terrible," Sue whispered. "Absolutely terrible." She gave her husband a look, and he replied with a subtle nod.

"It was ruled accidental," Adam continued, "but there were questions. Things that didn't quite add up. Tyler left town not long after, barely had them buried and memorialized before he was gone. We still had questions. We had to track him down and have the police in his new town question him."

"That's an exaggeration," Edi said firmly. "The fire marshal ruled it accidental. There was nothing suspicious about it."

"Not exactly true, now, is it?" Adam said. "There were questions. Plenty of questions. The timing, the insurance money, the way he just disappeared afterward."

"Stop." Edi's voice went hard. "You're sharing information about a closed case that has nothing to do with why we're here today. And you're doing it in front of witnesses to an active investigation, which is completely unprofessional."

Adam held up his hands. "I'm just saying people have a right to know who they're dealing with. Especially when there's another dead body involved."

"We don't even know if there's been a crime yet," Edi snapped. "Could be a hiking accident, could be natural causes, could be anything. And Tyler was with friends when they found Brooke, who had already discovered the remains. He wasn't anywhere near the scene until after it was found."

Adam went completely still. "You've already interviewed the witnesses, Deputy?"

Edi flushed. "I, uh, yes. You took so long to get here, and Brooke was upset. I wanted to get it done so she could head home."

"I see."

Brooke glanced at Edi, noting the quiet defiance in her. She hadn't done exactly what Adam expected, and part of Brooke admired that. But then her mind shifted, racing ahead to the weight of Adam's words. Tyler had lost his wife and child in a fire, the kind of loss that would destroy most people and leave scars so deep they might never heal.

But Adam's words kept echoing. *Questions remained. He left town. Insurance money.*

The implications were clear, even if Adam hadn't stated them outright. People had suspected Tyler. Maybe not officially, maybe not enough to bring charges, but enough to make him leave.

And now he was back, and there was another dead body.

The warning signs were impossible to ignore. A man with a mysterious, tragic past. Questions around death. A history of running.

This was exactly the kind of person she should avoid.

But looking at Tyler's face, at the carefully controlled pain in his eyes, she felt something else too. Sympathy. Grief for what he'd lost. Understanding of the kind of hurt that never fully healed.

She hated how conflicted she felt. Attraction warring with fear. Compassion fighting with self-preservation.

"Miss Davies?" Adam's voice pulled her attention back. He'd moved even closer, his expression concerned. "Are you doing okay?"

"I'm fine."

"You sure? Because if you need anything . . . " His smile was warm, reassuring. "Did Deputy Reeves tell you about the support systems in town? We've got some excellent resources for those who are innocent in situations. I know you've had a rough time of it lately."

There was something in his tone that rubbed Brooke the wrong way. Like he was using this situation to shine a light on himself and prove he was the good guy, the one she should trust.

"I appreciate that," she said carefully. "But I'm okay."

"Well, you know how to find me if that changes." Adam glanced back at Tyler. "And don't worry. I'll make sure you stay safe."

The implication was clear and didn't leave any doubt about who Adam planned to keep her safe from. She had half a mind to tell him what she thought about his offer and exactly what he could do with it.

She glanced at Edi, who rolled her eyes before moving over to speak with the game warden, both of them studying a map spread out on the hood of the man's truck, planning their approach to the scene.

Robert and Sue stood by their vehicle, looking uncomfortable with the whole situation and ready to leave. Brooke was too. All she really wanted was to get off the mountain, get home, and take a hot bath.

She shifted her attention toward Tyler. He remained where he was, silent and still, accepting Adam's accusations without protesting.

That bothered Brooke more than she wanted to admit. Why hadn't he defended himself? Why hadn't he explained what happened and given his side of the story?

Unless there was no good explanation. Unless the concerns were legitimate, and he knew it.

She thought about the way he'd handled himself on the trail. Calm, confident, protective. The way he looked at her, like maybe he was interested in getting to know her better. She'd felt the connection building between them.

All of it felt suspect now, tainted by what Adam had revealed.

"We need to get moving," Edi called out, gesturing toward the game warden. "Henry's going to escort me back to the scene and take pictures so we're ready when the coroner arrives. The rest of you are free to go, but stay available for follow-up questions."

"I'll go with the warden," Adam said.

"I've got it covered," Edi said firmly.

"Deputy." Adam walked toward Edi. Whatever he said was too low for Brooke to hear, but from the look on Edi's face, he'd decided she would be staying in the parking lot and Adam would be going with the warden.

Sue and Robert shuffled over to Brooke's SUV. "Would you like to ride back to town with me? Robert can drive your car."

Brooke smiled at the offer, gratitude threatening to overwhelm her. She swallowed hard before saying, "I think I'm okay."

Adam approached the group again. "As Deputy Reeves said, you may be questioned again." His attention shifted to Tyler. "Stay available."

Sue muttered that she would. Robert nodded. Brooke stayed quiet, as did Tyler.

"Miss Davies, may I speak with you?" Adam motioned her toward the front of her car. She glanced back at Tyler as she followed the deputy. His eyes followed her. She quickly looked away.

"Um, yes?" Brooke asked when they stopped.

He smiled. She was struck by how genuine it looked. She didn't plan on it, but she automatically smiled back.

"I wanted to make sure you really are okay. Do you think you can drive?"

"I'm okay. Sue offered to let me ride down with her. Robert said he'd take my car. But I'm fine. Really."

"You'd ride with Sue?" His gaze shot toward the group still standing where they'd left them. "And Tyler?"

"Um . . . I guess? They all rode up together. But, as I said, I'm fine. I'll drive myself down."

"I have a better idea. Wait until the warden and I are finished. Once I've checked the scene, the coroner should have arrived and Deputy Reeves can handle everything here. I'll drive you down."

"That's not necessary."

"I don't mind. After what you've been through today, I'd feel better knowing you got home safely."

There was nothing overtly wrong with the offer. It was kind, thoughtful even. But something about it felt off. Like Adam was trying too hard, pushing too much.

"I'm fine," Brooke said more firmly. "But thank you."

"All right. But seriously, call me if you need anything. Anything at all." He handed her a card with his contact information and gave her another smile.

Brooke tucked the card into her pocket. She wanted to get out of here, wanted to go home and process everything that had happened—the body in the woods, Tyler's past, Adam's revelations, all of it.

She felt eyes on her. When she glanced up, Tyler was watching her, his expression unreadable but his posture defeated. Like he knew exactly what she was thinking, exactly how far he'd fallen in her estimation.

Their eyes met for a moment, and Brooke saw something there that made her chest tight. Pain. Loss. Resignation.

She looked away first.

"You're sure you're okay?" Sue came over and asked.

"I'm ready to go home."

"Agreed."

Sue and Robert walked hand in hand to their car.

Brooke purposely avoided looking at Tyler as she climbed into her SUV and started the engine.

In her rearview mirror, she watched him turn away, heading for the other car. Adam stood by Henry, watching her watch Tyler, that same protective expression on his face.

Brooke pulled out of the parking lot, leaving the scene behind. But the questions followed her.

Who was Tyler Gillis? A man who'd suffered unimaginable loss and was trying to rebuild his life? Or someone with darker secrets, someone who'd been involved in deaths before and might be involved again?

She'd been wrong about Kelsey. Completely, catastrophically wrong. She'd trusted when she should've questioned, missed signs that should've been obvious. She couldn't afford to make that mistake again—couldn't let attraction or sympathy or curiosity cloud her judgment.

Tyler's wife and child had died under circumstances that made people question what really happened. He'd left town rather than face those questions.

And now he was back, and another body had appeared.

The logical part of her brain was screaming warnings, the part that had learned hard lessons at Bearwater, that had promised to be more careful, more aware, more willing to trust her instincts.

Those instincts were telling her to stay far away from Tyler Gillis.

But another part of her, smaller and quieter but persistent, kept remembering the way he'd looked at her. The gentleness in his touch when he'd steadied her on the trail. The pain in his eyes when Adam had revealed his past.

That part wondered if maybe there was more to the story. If maybe the questions people asked were just small-town gossip, tragedy twisted into suspicion because people needed someone to blame.

Brooke gripped the steering wheel tighter as she navigated the winding mountain road back toward town.

She didn't know what to believe.

But she knew one thing for certain. Whatever may have started between her and Tyler in those few hours on the mountain, it was over before it had really begun.

It had to be.

For her own safety and sanity, she needed to walk away and never look back.

Even if part of her desperately wanted to understand the truth behind those green, haunted eyes.

Chapter 8

Tyler

Despite the grisly discovery the day before, Monday morning at the auto shop began like any other. Tyler had his head under the hood of a pickup truck, running diagnostics on a stubborn engine light, when he heard the bell over the front door chime.

He didn't think much of it. Sue worked in the office most days and handled the customer interactions while Tyler, Robert, and the two part-timers focused on the actual repair work. Robert had another car on the lift and was checking the undercarriage.

Sue appeared between the cars. "Um, hey, guys, can you come up front for a minute?"

Something in her tone made Tyler straighten immediately and reach for a shop rag.

"What is it, hon?" Robert asked, not looking away from his work.

Sue looked toward the front. Tyler followed her gaze. Through the glass partition, he could see two figures.

Edi and Adam stood in the small waiting area, both in full uniform.

"The police," she whispered. "They're here."

Robert sighed. "Why?"

"Follow up. They want to talk to all three of us."

"Tell them I'm busy."

"Robert. Please."

"Fine." Robert grabbed his own shop rag as he shook his head. "Can't even let honest folks make a living."

Somehow, Tyler knew the remark was meant for him, and it brought a smile to his face.

When he returned to Irma, there was no need to tell old man Morgan about his past. Stan Morgan already knew, just like everyone else in town. To Tyler's shock, Morgan offered him a job minutes after he walked in the door.

When Robert bought the business, Tyler wasn't sure he'd be kept on. Still, he knew that if he didn't come clean from the start, it could cause trouble later. Talking about the fire and the loss of his family was hard enough. Admitting there had been accusations was harder.

Robert had only asked, "Did you do it?"

Tyler told him he hadn't.

"Good enough," Robert had said. "Let's get back to work."

And they had. No further discussion, no questions. Tyler wasn't naive enough to think Robert hadn't done an online search, and no doubt he told Sue, as a husband should when everyone had to work together. But she never said anything, and yesterday she seemed almost sad for him.

"Deputies," Robert said, his voice neutral. "What can I do for you?"

"Just following up on yesterday." Edi's tone was professional but not hostile. "We have a few more questions." She met Tyler's eyes and gave him a small smile. "Hey, Tyler. Looks like you were hard at work. You have a smudge on your chin."

He angled his sleeve to wipe at it. "Comes with the territory."

"I suppose it does," she agreed.

"Shall we get to it?" Deputy Boverman directed a look at Edi. She kept her focus on Tyler and rolled her eyes. Tyler held his smile. It was good to see Edi with more confidence as an adult than she'd had when they were younger.

"Of course." Tyler leaned against the counter, forcing himself to look relaxed even though every muscle had gone tense.

Adam's eyes were cold as they focused on Tyler. "We've been going over everyone's statements, making sure all the details line up."

"Makes sense."

"Does it?" Adam shifted his weight, hand resting casually near his belt. "Because I'm having trouble with your statement. Specifically, the part where you just happened to be hiking in the exact area where a body was found."

"We weren't." Sue shook her head. "We were on the trail. The body was off the trail." She paused for a moment and added, "Only one body, right?"

Adam ignored her, his attention fixed on Tyler. "Why were you hiking there?"

"It's a popular trail," Tyler said evenly. "Lots of people hike there."

"But not lots of people have your history."

There it was again. Boverman was on a mission.

"My history has nothing to do with what we found yesterday."

"Doesn't it?" Adam pulled out his notebook, flipping through pages with deliberate slowness. "Your wife and child died in a suspicious house fire. Questions were raised about the circumstances. And now you're present when another body shows up. That's quite a coincidence."

"I reminded you yesterday, the fire was ruled accidental," Tyler said, his voice hardening. "The investigation cleared me completely."

"Officially," Adam agreed. "But there were questions. Questions you didn't stick around and answer."

"I left because I couldn't stand being here anymore," Tyler snapped. "Because everywhere I looked reminded me of what I'd lost. Because people like you kept implying I'd murdered my own family."

"Nobody's implying anything," Adam said smoothly. "Just stating facts."

"Deputy Boverman," Edi cut in. "We're here to follow up on the discovery yesterday. Not to rehash a closed case."

"It's all connected, Reeves. You know that."

Robert stood up from where he'd been leaning against the wall. "Tyler's a good man. Been working for me since I took over in April, and I've never had a single reason to doubt his character."

"That's right," Sue added, moving to stand by her husband. "He's been nothing but professional and reliable. Whatever happened in his past, it doesn't define who he is now."

Their support caught him off guard. They barely knew him, really. A few months of working together, some weekend hikes, casual conversations over coffee. But they were standing up for him anyway.

"I appreciate the character references," Adam said. "But I need to hear from Tyler himself. Walk me through what happened that day. The day of the fire."

"Deputy," Edi said with a warning in her tone. "That is not why we are here."

"It is now. I have questions about this case that may hinge on what happened then."

Edi's mouth went into a tight line as she shook her head. When her gaze met Tyler's, she gave a slight shake of her head as if to say, *"You know how he is."*

Tyler held himself still. He'd told this story so many times it should've been easy by now. But it never got easier. Every retelling felt like ripping open the wounds that hadn't fully healed.

"Now? Here?"

Boverman smirked. "Have something to hide? Something you don't want the boss to know?"

Tyler glanced at Robert and gave a slight shake of his head. "Robert knows what happened."

"That's right, I do," Robert said.

"I know too," Sue chimed in.

The deputy ignored them and motioned for Tyler to continue.

"I was supposed to take my son hiking," he said quietly. "Garrett. He was two and a half. Loved being outside, loved the mountains. I'd planned a short trail, nothing too difficult. We'd done it before. He'd walk some, and I'd carry him in a pack some."

The memories hit him hard. Garrett's excited face when Tyler had mentioned the hike the night before. Jen had made them lunches. They'd take their time and just enjoy the day. He'd asked her to go along, but she wanted to catch up on laundry and maybe get some reading done. "I might even soak in a hot bath until the water runs cold," she'd told him with a laugh.

"That morning, Garrett woke up with a fever. Nothing serious, just a cold, but enough that taking him out wasn't a good idea." Tyler forced himself to continue. "Jen told me I should go anyway, get some air and clear my head. I'd been working a lot of overtime and was stressed about bills."

"So you went alone," Adam said.

"Yes."

"How long were you gone?"

"Four hours. Maybe a little more." Tyler's hands clenched into fists. "When I got back, the house was on fire. Fire trucks were already there, and neighbors were standing in the street. I tried to get inside, but the firefighters held me back."

His voice had gone flat, robotic. The only way to get through this was to detach, to recite facts without feeling them.

"They found Jen in the kitchen. Garrett was still in his bed. Smoke inhalation. The fire marshal determined it started in the kitchen, probably overwhelmed Jen immediately. Some kind of issue with the gas range. Completely accidental."

"But you collected insurance money," Adam pressed.

"Of course I did. That's what insurance is for. I used it to pay off our bills and cover the funeral expenses. The rest I gave to Jen's parents."

"Convenient story."

Tyler's control snapped. "My wife and son died while I was hiking because I chose myself over them. That's what I live with every single day. I chose to go to the mountains instead of staying home, and they died because of it. So don't stand there and suggest I had anything to do with that fire, because surviving when they didn't is punishment enough."

The room went silent. Sue had tears in her eyes, and Robert's expression was grim. Even Edi looked uncomfortable.

Adam's face remained impassive. "Just doing my job."

"Your *job*," Tyler said bitterly, "seems to involve harassing innocent people."

He knew that wasn't entirely fair. Adam had been new to the sheriff's department when the fire happened and was eager to prove himself. For reasons Tyler never understood, he had fixated on him as a suspect despite the evidence. He dragged the investigation out, showed up at Tyler's temporary housing with more questions, and made it clear he thought Tyler was guilty.

Edi wasn't a deputy then. She had just returned to Irma from school and was taking a semester off to help her parents after her dad's cancer diagnosis. Edi easily found a part-time job working with the county, just to keep from going crazy, she'd said.

Tyler had understood what she was going through. His mom had died in a car accident when Tyler was in middle school. His dad died while Jen was pregnant with Garrett, after battling colon cancer for more than a year. With his folks both gone, then losing Jen and Garrett, it had been easy to leave Irma.

When Tyler came back to Irma just before Christmas last year, Adam had shown up at his rental house within a week. No official business, just a "friendly" reminder that people hadn't forgotten what happened. That they were watching.

Tyler had considered leaving again, going somewhere else and starting over yet again. But he'd tried that for a dozen years, and it hadn't worked. He'd been miserable in Montana, lonely in Idaho, and restless in Utah. Indiana seemed promising, but it was just too flat. There was no place that felt like home because home was here, in Basin County, whether he liked it or not.

So, he stayed. And aside from Adam's periodic harassment, it had been okay. Better than okay, actually. His old friends seemed happy to see him.

Edi had stopped by his place a few days after Adam, not in uniform. At the time, he didn't even know she was employed by the sheriff's department. They'd chatted and caught up. When she told him she'd been on the job for four years, he'd been surprised.

She hadn't dropped by his place again, but he still saw Edi around town. He ran into her at the bank a few days ago, talking with Sheila, another woman they'd both gone to high school with. The three of them stood there catching up for twenty minutes, and for a little while things felt almost normal.

Even now, during this interrogation, Edi didn't seem to think Tyler had anything to do with the body they'd found. Her questions were procedural, professional. Adam was the only one who kept circling back to suspicion.

"Are we done here?" Tyler asked.

"For now," Adam said. "But I'll have more questions as the investigation progresses."

Sue took a step forward. "Did you find one body or two? I've been wondering since yesterday."

"Just one," Edi said.

"Deputy Reeves," Adam snapped. "We don't divulge case details to civilians."

"It's going to hit the papers soon enough. That reporter, Joe Monroe, already has the information. He approached the sheriff at the diner this morning. We've got a leak somewhere."

She emphasized the last word while looking directly at Adam. He returned her stare with a cold glare.

"Wonder who it could be," Edi added with a slight smirk.

"I'll be looking into that," Adam said. "In the meantime, all of you remember that this is an active investigation. If we have more questions, we'll be in touch."

As they left, the bell over the door chimed with false cheerfulness.

"I knew it was only one body," Sue said quietly. "Still, how terrible. I wish I'd asked if they knew who it was."

"They probably don't yet," Robert said. "These things take time. Not that they'd tell you."

"Sounds like things might be coming out in the online paper soon. Joe Monroe is a good reporter."

Tyler barely heard them. His mind was already circling back to yesterday, to the parking lot, to the moment when everything had fallen apart.

Finding the body had been terrible, traumatic in ways that'd probably stick with him for a long time. Death did that.

And he shouldn't be surprised about Adam Boverman showing up here and asking about Jen and Garrett. Tyler had a hunch it wasn't because he thought Jen's death was connected with the body in the woods. He did it to cause trouble for Tyler with Robert and Sue. He'd bet good money that was his entire intention.

Edi seemed to know it too. She seemed to understand that Adam was simply stirring the pot. He was grateful she'd come with him. He suspected that had she not been there, the accusations would've gone further than they did. He was glad Edi was the first to arrive yesterday too.

The way she'd been, especially with Brooke, was welcome and helpful. He wondered if Edi and Brooke were friends. He didn't think they were, not close anyway, but probably friendly enough.

It was interesting that he hadn't seen Brooke since he came back to Irma. Well, maybe interesting wasn't the right word. He didn't go places a woman like her would go. Seeing her after all these years was something. She looked good, even in her panic. Strong and capable. The kind of person who could handle a crisis without falling apart completely.

He was weirdly disappointed she hadn't recognized him, but he wasn't surprised. He'd been scrawny in high school, having hit his full height early but weighing maybe one-fifty soaking wet. All angles and awkward limbs.

He'd started filling out during his marriage to Jen, normal adult weight gain he kept in check by hiking and doing a little lifting, but mostly by working on cars and staying busy.

But after they died, after he'd spent months doing nothing but existing in the most minimal way possible, he'd become serious about weightlifting. Partly for something to do with his hands, partly because physical exhaustion was the only thing that let him sleep.

Twenty pounds of muscle and a scruffy beard later, he barely recognized himself in old photos. The transformation had been dramatic enough that people who'd known him casually in high school often didn't make the connection when they saw him now. Not at first at least. He always knew when the realization of exactly who he was hit. A shift in posture. A flick of the eyebrows. A glance, or a sudden cut-off in conversation.

Brooke's brother had recognized him when he'd brought in the shop's delivery van to check on a noise. Last night, Tyler had wondered if Brooke might have mentioned him when she told her brother about what happened. He liked to think Phil would put in a good word for him.

It didn't matter. Adam had shown up and destroyed any chance Tyler might've had. He'd seen it in Brooke's eyes yesterday, the way she'd pulled back and put distance between them.

But he still felt a need to make her understand, to explain what really happened. Not the version Adam presented, but the truth. Not because he thought it'd change anything between them—that ship had sailed—but because he couldn't stand the thought of her believing he was a killer.

Maybe he'd go to the coffee shop, just to set the record straight. Not because anything could happen between them. It couldn't. He'd accepted that the moment Adam started talking yesterday.

This was exactly why he couldn't get involved with anyone. Everyone in Basin County would always see him as the guy whose family died under suspicious circumstances. They'd always wonder if maybe the fire marshal had gotten it wrong, if maybe Adam's questions had merit.

More than that, Tyler had come to believe he was cursed. The people he loved died. His parents. Jen and Garrett in the fire. He was alone and always would be.

Tyler looked down at his hands, still stained with grease and oil from the morning's work, from *years* of work. The hands that had held Garrett as a newborn, that had fixed Jen's car a hundred times, that had built their life together piece by piece. The hands that had punched one of the volunteer firefighters who tried to hold Tyler back when he ran toward his burning house. It had taken three men to restrain him.

These were also the hands that people like Adam believed were capable of murder.

He'd lost Brooke yesterday. Lost any chance before it had even begun. But he could still make sure she knew the truth.

Tomorrow, he decided. Tomorrow he'd go to the coffee shop and explain everything. Set the record straight, even if it didn't change her opinion of him.

At least then he could walk away knowing he'd tried.

Chapter 9

Brooke

Brooke stared out over the coffee shop. The lunch rush seemed to be over, leaving a brief lull. It wouldn't last long, only until the afternoon crowd started trickling in.

"I'm going to tidy things up in the back," she told Becky, her full-time weekday employee.

Becky tilted her head. "You sure? I'm happy to clean up."

That was their usual division of labor. Becky handled things in the back while Brooke took care of the front, straightening tables and making everything look as good as it could.

"I could use a change. You mind?" Brooke gestured to the tables. Things looked okay, but not the way she liked them.

Becky furrowed her brow. "Is everything okay? You seem distracted today."

Distracted. That was one word for it. Brooke hadn't told Becky about yesterday. She wanted to, but somehow the words wouldn't come.

She'd expected one of the customers to say something, but so far, no one had mentioned how she'd found a body in the Beartooth Mountains. "Lots on my mind," she said, which was the absolute truth. "I thought the change in duties might do me good."

"Sure, no problem. Let me know if you decide to switch. I'm off at two thirty."

The implication was clear. Brooke may be the owner, but doing dishes was not her forte. Becky was right to be concerned. It was highly possible that Brooke would still be working in the kitchen by the time her shift ended. "It's fine. I'll get it done. Who's on this afternoon?"

Becky named the two high school girls on for the evening, both confident, if not go-getters. Brooke liked giving the youth a chance to work, but it wasn't always easy. So many times, they'd rather be on their phones than doing the side work necessary in food service. She tried to remind them that if they had time to lean, they had time to clean, but it did little good.

As she started rinsing dishes, her mind drifted to yesterday. Finding the body had been awful. Traumatic, even. She slept little last night, caught between replaying the scene in her mind and waking from strange dreams. Not exactly scary dreams, but definitely odd. Tyler was in them, and so was Deputy Boverman.

She hadn't even made it all the way home, only as far as a stable internet connection, before pulling over and searching for Tyler's name. As she read the first article, she vaguely remembered hearing about the tragedy.

She'd been away at college when the fire happened. Phil had mentioned it during one of her calls home. A house fire. A young wife and a toddler dead. Tyler Gillis—Phil's friend from high school—came home to find his life destroyed.

At the time, Brooke had struggled to place Tyler. Phil kept insisting she knew him, that he was in Phil's graduating class and had even come over to the house, but she couldn't picture his face. She was much younger, focused on her own friends and activities. The older kids had been background noise, faces she passed without really seeing.

Yesterday, after reading the article and seeing an old photograph of Tyler with his wife and child, she realized he did look familiar from that time in her life, and she could even remember Tyler at her house a time or two, exactly as Phil said.

The pictures in the article were very different from how he looked now. It was no surprise she hadn't recognized him on the trail. He'd aged well. In fact, if she was being honest, he looked better now than he did when he was younger.

His eyes were different. The green was the same, of course, but while they had danced with laughter in the family photo, yesterday they were solemn, almost haunted.

Once she realized Tyler was her brother's friend, she'd been tempted to drive straight to her father's house, where Phil still lived in a basement apartment. But if she did, she'd have to tell them about finding the remains, or if Sue was right, one body in two separate piles. The thought alone turned her stomach.

Instead, she spent several minutes searching archived files. A local tragedy. Questions raised. The investigation closed.

Tyler's wife, Jen, had a bump on her head, but it was consistent with a fall after being overcome by smoke. The fire started in the kitchen, and she might have tried to put it out before being overcome by the smoke and fumes.

The official cause of death for both Jen and their little boy was smoke inhalation, but the pictures of the house and the damage still made Brooke's heart ache. She was grateful the smoke had been the culprit and not the flames.

No charges had ever been filed. The fire was blamed on a faulty gas line on the stove. But reading between the lines, Brooke could still see the suspicion that had lingered. The insurance payout was mentioned multiple times, and Tyler had left town shortly afterward. The timeline invited questions without providing answers.

After she got home last night, she called Phil, wanting to hear his perspective.

"Tyler Gillis?" Phil had said immediately. "Why are you asking about him?"

"Just curious. I was reading about the fire."

"After all these years?"

"Please, Phil. What can you tell me?"

"That was a rough time." Phil's voice had gone somber. "Tyler was a good guy. Still is. I never believed he had anything to do with it."

"Really?"

"Brooke, I knew Tyler. We were friends all through school. Even later, when he was married, I went to his place a few times. He worked at the gypsum factory back then, but always had a love for cars. I worked with him on a couple of his project cars. He used to buy old cars cheap and fix them up to turn a profit. It helped pay the bills so his wife could stay home with their baby. That man loved his family more than anything." Phil had been adamant. "No way he set that fire. It had to be an accident, just like they said."

"But people suspected him."

"Some people suspect everyone. Doesn't make them right." Her brother had paused. "Why the sudden interest?"

Brooke had deflected, saying she'd just been curious about old news. Phil hadn't pushed, though she suspected he didn't believe her.

He wasn't going to be happy when he found out about yesterday. And no doubt the news would get out, even if it hadn't already. It was impossible to keep a secret in Basin County.

As far as Tyler was concerned, she trusted her brother's instincts. Phil could be too blunt sometimes, saying things that made people uncomfortable, but his read on people was usually accurate. If he said Tyler was innocent, that carried weight.

But so did her own experience with Kelsey.

Brooke finished loading the dishwasher, added soap, and hit start, her movements automatic while her mind continued turning.

She thought about calling her dad, too, but decided not to. She couldn't quite explain why, but she wanted to keep yesterday private. Not secret exactly, just not discussed. Not analyzed and dissected and turned into family conversation over dinner.

Her dad would understand. They were very much alike. Both needed time to sort things out before talking about them. Her mom, though, had been different. Like Phil, she sometimes spoke before giving herself time to process. Phil definitely got his bluntness from her.

Their mom had died three years earlier. She went to bed one night and never woke up. Her dad and Phil had both been out of town at a convention. Brooke had found her when she stopped by to pick her up for church. Finding her mother like that had nearly broken her.

Even then, she'd needed several minutes to pull herself together before she started making the phone calls. That was just how she was built.

Keep quiet. Process. Then talk. The trouble was the talking didn't simply stop. Her mind would go into overdrive, and she would end up replaying things over and over to the point of obsession. She was trying hard to tamp down that tendency now, and failing miserably.

Gina had found out about the body in the woods. It wasn't surprising. She worked at the hospital, was a volunteer with Basin County Search and Rescue, and seemed to hear everything eventually. She'd called the night before while Brooke was once again searching for information about Tyler, this time on her laptop.

"Are you okay? I heard about what happened."

"Is it all over the town?"

"All over? Not yet. The news of a body being found is out, but not who found it. I only know because I ran into Edi Reeves. She knows we're friends."

"I'm fine," Brooke had assured her. "Shaken up, but fine."

"I'm at work right now, but I can come by later if you need to talk."

"Really, I'm okay. Just trying to stay busy."

They'd talked for a few more minutes before Gina had to go handle something at the hospital. Not fifteen minutes later, the doorbell had chimed, and her cousin Nick was there.

He looked worried, his usual smile replaced by concern. "Gina called me. Said you found a body?"

"News travels fast." It made sense that Gina called Nick. They'd been dating since Bearwater. Something good had come out of that nightmare after all. Both had been burned before, so they were taking things slowly.

"Gina worries." Nick had settled onto one of the stools at the breakfast bar. "You want to talk about it?" Brooke had given him the abbreviated version. Nick had been staying with her until a few weeks ago, when he finally found his own place, a studio apartment over someone's garage. It was small, but it was his, and Brooke was happy for him, even if she missed having him around.

"You're sure you're okay?" Nick had asked when she finished her story.

"I will be. It's just a lot to process."

"Yeah, I bet." He'd studied her face. "Is there something else? You seem more rattled than just finding a body would explain."

She'd laughed, but the sound came out hollow. "Really? You think finding a body wouldn't mess me up?"

"Sorry. That was a poor choice of words and not what I meant. But really, is there something else?"

Brooke had hesitated, then told him about Tyler. About the history, the suspicions, and the way Adam had revealed everything in the parking lot. Nick wasn't from Irma and didn't know the story. He nodded when it was appropriate, asked a few clarifying questions, and waited until she was done to say more.

"Sounds complicated."

"That's one word for it."

"What does your gut tell you?"

That was the question, wasn't it? She hadn't had an answer for Nick last night, and she didn't have one for herself today.

Brooke moved to the sink and wiped down the stainless steel while she tried to organize her thoughts into something coherent.

She was attracted to Tyler. That much was undeniable. The way he'd handled the situation on the trail, his calm competence, the protective instinct that had kicked in without him making a big deal about it. She'd felt something building between them, brief but real.

Her brother believed in him. Phil had known Tyler personally, spent time with him and his family, and was certain Tyler was innocent. That had to mean something.

But so did her history with Kelsey. She had trusted the wrong person before. How could she be sure she wasn't doing it again?

Then there was Adam Boverman. He'd been kind yesterday, protective in a way that felt safe and straightforward. No mysterious past, no questions about his character. Just a local deputy doing his job, making it clear he was interested in her.

That should be appealing. That should be exactly what she wanted after everything with Kelsey—someone uncomplicated, someone whose life was an open book.

But something about Adam's interest felt off. Too eager, too calculated. Like he was positioning instead of genuinely connecting.

Plus, he had a reputation as a player. She couldn't get into a relationship with someone like that. Brooke was no prude, but she also didn't do short-term situations. And she most certainly avoided one-night stands, which is what Adam was known for.

Even worse, she couldn't get Tyler out of her head. His pain was real, raw in a way that cut through all the suspicion and doubt. When Adam revealed his past, Tyler hadn't defended himself or made excuses. He had just stood there and taken it, like he was used to being accused.

That acceptance bothered her. If he were truly innocent, wouldn't he fight harder?

Unless he was simply too tired to fight, too worn down by years of suspicion to keep defending himself.

Brooke dried her hands and leaned against the counter.

She wasn't going to pull away completely. Not yet. She'd give Tyler the benefit of the doubt, at least for now. She'd trust Phil's instincts and admit that tragedy didn't equal guilt.

But she'd keep her guard up. She needed to know more. She needed answers to the questions that kept circling in her mind. To get those answers, she needed to talk to Tyler and hear his side of the story directly, not filtered through Adam's accusations or old news articles. She needed to look him in the eye and see what was really there.

Brooke made a decision. She'd finish cleaning the kitchen, make sure the high school girls were all set for their shifts, and drive over to the auto shop to give Tyler a chance to explain. If her gut still told her to be wary after that, fine. But she owed it to herself to at least listen.

The kitchen was almost finished now, the mess not nearly what it often was on a busy Monday. Brooke checked her watch. Another half hour until the next shift came in, and then she'd need twenty minutes to get them situated. She could get through that and stay busy enough to stop obsessing over Tyler Gillis.

She was wiping the counters when Becky stuck her head in the kitchen door.

"Hey, Brooke?"

"Yes?"

Becky's expression was amused, her eyebrows waggling in that way that meant something interesting was happening. "Someone's asking for you."

Brooke's heart jumped. "Who?"

"A cutie." Becky grinned. "Tall, nice smile. Looks like he works out."

Tyler? Had he come to talk to her before she could go to him?

Brooke quickly dried her hands on a towel, then smoothed down her hair. She was in her work clothes—jeans and an Irma Brew T-shirt topped with an apron that served as their uniform. She slipped out of the water-spotted apron, hanging it on a hook.

She pushed through the kitchen door and scanned the shop for Tyler.

Disappointment hit hard.

Adam stood at the counter, still in uniform, wearing that easy smile on his face. Not Tyler. Not even close.

"Hey, Brooke. I hope I'm not interrupting anything."

Brooke forced a smile, trying to hide her disappointment. "No, not at all. What can I do for you?"

"Actually, I was hoping we could talk."

Chapter 10

Tyler

Wednesday morning found Tyler under the hood of a Chevy Silverado, but his mind was nowhere near the transmission problem he was supposed to be diagnosing. Three days had passed since the mountain, and he still couldn't stop thinking about Brooke. He'd planned to talk to her before now, but kept chickening out.

What could he say to her? If he was smart, he'd do the right thing and forget all about her. Stay away from her. He knew they couldn't get involved. That wasn't an option. She deserved better than someone with his history, his baggage, his curse of losing everyone he cared about.

But logic didn't seem to matter when it came to Brooke. He needed to talk to her, to make sure she understood he hadn't killed his wife and his son, no matter what Deputy Dawg thought.

"You planning to fix that transmission or just stare at it?" Robert's voice cut through his thoughts.

Tyler straightened and wiped his hands on a shop rag. "Sorry. Distracted."

"I've noticed." Robert leaned against the workbench and gave Tyler a look that said he understood more than Tyler wanted him to. "You want to talk about it?"

"Just tired."

"Uh-huh." Robert didn't push, but his expression suggested he knew exactly what—or who—was really on Tyler's mind.

Tyler tried to refocus on the transmission, but it was useless. His thoughts kept circling back to Brooke. The way she'd looked at him on the trail before everything went wrong. The brief connection he'd felt building between them. Then the way it all came crashing down.

He needed to see her, just once, to make sure she was okay after finding the body and to explain his side of the story without Adam's accusations coloring everything.

Or maybe he just needed an excuse to be near her again.

"I'm going to grab some coffee," Tyler announced, already pulling off his work gloves.

Robert raised an eyebrow. "We've got coffee here."

"Better coffee. From that place on Grand Avenue."

"Irma Brew?"

"Yeah."

Robert's knowing smile widened. "The place Brooke Davies owns?"

Tyler didn't respond, just headed for the door before Robert could say anything else.

The drive to downtown Irma took less than five minutes. Tyler parked his truck down the street from the coffee shop, suddenly nervous in a way he hadn't been since he was a teenager asking a girl to prom.

This was a bad idea. He should turn around, go back to work, and forget about the woman who had gotten under his skin in the span of a few traumatic hours.

He looked at his reflection in the rearview mirror, then reached under the seat and pulled out the container of wet wipes he kept handy. He spent several minutes scrubbing grease from his chin and hands.

"Here goes nothing," he muttered, shaking his head as he headed inside.

The bell over the door chimed as he entered Irma Brew. The shop was moderately busy, with a few people working on laptops, some retirees chatting over coffee, and a young mom with a stroller talking with another woman. The space was warm and welcoming, with exposed brick walls, mismatched furniture that somehow worked, and the rich smell of fresh-brewed coffee.

And there was Brooke.

She stood behind the counter, laughing at something a customer had said. Her dark hair was pulled back in a ponytail, and she wore jeans with an Irma Brew T-shirt. No makeup that Tyler could see, just natural beauty and genuine warmth as she handed over a latte with a smile.

This was her world, her element. And she was magnificent in it.

She looked up and saw him. Something flickered across her face—surprise, maybe wariness, but also something else. Something that looked like relief.

"Tyler." His name on her lips did things to him that he wasn't prepared for. "Hi."

"Hi, I was hoping we could talk."

Brooke glanced around the shop, assessing the crowd. "Give me a minute. Becky?" She called to the woman working the espresso machine. "Can you cover the counter?"

"Sure thing."

Brooke came around from behind the counter and gestured toward a quiet corner table. Tyler followed, acutely aware of the eyes tracking their movements. Small towns meant everyone saw everything.

They sat across from each other, and for a moment, neither spoke.

"How are you?" Tyler finally asked. "After everything?"

"I'm okay. Still processing, I guess." Brooke's eyes searched his face. "What about you?"

"Same."

"I read about what happened," she said quietly. "The fire. Your wife and son."

Tyler forced himself to hold her gaze. "What did you read?"

"Everything I could find. The articles, the investigation, the questions people raised." She paused. "My brother Phil knew you. He said you were innocent."

"Your brother's a good man. Always was."

"He said you loved your family. That there was no way you'd hurt them."

"He's right." Tyler kept his voice level despite the emotion churning underneath. "I loved them more than anything. Losing them destroyed me. The fact that people thought I might have . . ." He couldn't finish the sentence.

"I don't think you did it," Brooke said, and the simple certainty in her voice made something crack open in Tyler's chest. "I wanted you to know that. Despite everything that Deputy Boverman said, despite his suggestions, I believe you."

Tyler stared at her, hardly daring to hope he'd heard correctly. "You do?"

"My brother's instincts are usually good. And something about the way you looked when the deputy was talking . . . that wasn't guilt I saw. It was grief."

They sat in silence for a moment, the weight of her trust settling between them. He wanted to cheer, to cry out in relief, to tell everyone in the building he might just have a chance with the beautiful Brooke Davies. "Thank you. You have no idea what that means."

Brooke's smile was small but genuine. "I think I do. I was going to come talk to you the other day, but I got sidetracked. I'm glad you came to me."

The conversation shifted then, becoming easier. They talked about the shop, about Tyler's work at the garage, about nothing and everything. She told him about opening Irma Brew five years ago, about the challenges of small business ownership, how she'd borrowed from far too many people to make her dream a reality, and about the regulars who had become like family.

Tyler found himself relaxing in a way he hadn't in years. Brooke was easy to talk to, quick to laugh, and genuinely interested in what he had to say. What he'd felt on the mountain was still there, stronger now without the trauma overshadowing it.

"So, you really don't remember me from high school?" Tyler asked.

Brooke's expression turned sheepish. "When we were on the mountain, I didn't recognize you at all. Phil said I should remember you. You used to come over to our place. Then I saw the older pictures . . ." She stopped talking, looking like she thought she may have said something wrong.

"The pictures from the articles about the fire?" he asked with measured calm, though the question carried its own sting.

She nodded. "Seeing those, I did recognize you then and remembered you a little."

He smiled. "I admit, I was pretty forgettable back then. Scrawny kid. I tried all the sports but wasn't really good at any of them."

"You're not forgettable now."

Brooke's cheeks flushed slightly, like she hadn't meant to say it out loud.

Tyler leaned forward slightly. "Brooke— "

"I should probably get back to work," she said, but she didn't move. He needed to head back too. He'd been gone far too long for a coffee break. This would have to count as his lunch break.

"I was hoping . . . " Tyler took a breath, gathering his courage. "Do you want to have dinner sometime? Just the two of us?"

Brooke's eyes widened slightly. "Are you asking me on a date?"

"Yeah. I am." Even he was surprised by how easily the words came out.

She smiled, and it transformed her entire face. "I'd like that."

Relief rushed through him. "Really?"

"Really. I'd like to get to know you better."

He was about to respond when the bell over the door chimed. Tyler glanced up, and his happiness crumbled.

Edi and Adam walked into the coffee shop, both in uniform, both wearing expressions that said they were there for a reason, and it wasn't coffee.

The conversation in the shop died down as people noticed the deputies. Edi's face was grim, apologetic. Adam's held barely concealed satisfaction.

They walked directly to Tyler's table.

"Tyler Gillis," Edi said, her voice formal but her eyes sad. "I need you to stand up, please."

Panic hit hard. "What's going on?"

"We need you to come with us," Adam said. "We have some questions about the body found on Sunday."

"We already went through all that," Tyler said, but he was standing now, his body responding to the authority in their voices even as his mind raced.

"The victim has been identified," Edi said quietly. "It's Sheila Jones. You probably knew her as Sheila Mayers."

Sheila Mayers from high school, the bank teller he and Edi had been talking to just days ago. The woman who'd laughed with them and suggested they all get together to hear a local band.

"No." Tyler shook his head. "That can't be right."

"You knew her," Adam said.

"Of course I knew her. We went to school together."

"You dated her," Adam continued. "She broke up with you."

"That was years ago," Tyler said, his voice rising. "What does that have to do with anything?"

"It has everything to do with it." Adam pulled out his handcuffs. "You were on the mountain where her body was found. You have a history with the victim. And you've been seen at her workplace, keeping in contact."

"We were just talking! Edi was there too."

"Tyler Gillis, you're under arrest for the murder of Sheila Jones."

The words seemed to echo in the sudden quiet of the coffee shop. Tyler was vaguely aware of gasps, phones being pulled out, and the entire shop watching as Adam moved behind him.

"You have the right to remain silent," Adam began, snapping the handcuffs around Tyler's wrists.

Tyler looked at Brooke. She stood up from the table, her hand over her mouth, her face pale with shock. Their eyes locked, and Tyler saw everything he'd hoped for crumbling in real time.

The trust she'd just given him. The date she'd just agreed to. The connection they'd been building.

All of it was destroyed in the space of thirty seconds.

"Anything you say can and will be used against you in a court of law," Adam continued, gripping Tyler's arm.

"I didn't do this," Tyler said, still looking at Brooke. "I didn't kill Sheila. You have to believe me."

But Brooke's expression had shifted. Her walls were going up, and doubt was creeping in.

"You have the right to an attorney," Adam droned on.

"Brooke," Tyler tried again, but Adam was already pulling him toward the door.

Tyler caught one last glimpse of Brooke through the window. She stood frozen at their table, surrounded by staring customers, her hand still covering her mouth.

He'd lost her. Just when he'd thought maybe, impossibly, he might have a chance, he'd lost her.

Because in Basin County, Tyler Gillis would always be the man they suspected first.

The handcuffs bit into his wrists as Adam guided him into the patrol vehicle. Through the window, Tyler could still see inside the coffee shop, could see Brooke processing what had just happened and believing he was guilty.

Adam made sure Tyler was in the back seat before Edi went around to the driver's side. A second patrol car was in front of the SUV.

Edi met his gaze in the mirror as she buckled her seat belt. "Sorry about this. We went to your work first. Robert said you went out for coffee. I wanted to wait . . . "

Tyler nodded. Adam knew arresting him in front of Brooke would make an impact and ruin any chances Tyler might have with her once this whole mess was straightened out.

The patrol car pulled away from the curb, and Tyler closed his eyes.

Sheila was dead. Someone had killed her and left her body in the mountains.

And everyone, including Brooke, would think that someone was him.

Chapter 11

Brooke

The bell over the door chimed as the deputies led Tyler out, and for a moment, the entire coffee shop remained frozen. Then everyone started talking at once.

"Did you see that?"

"He was arrested for murder."

"Who was he?"

"Tyler Gillis. He used to live here but moved away."

"I always knew something was off about him."

"Wasn't his wife and kid— "

Brooke stood rooted to the spot, her hand still covering her mouth as her mind struggled to understand what just happened. One minute, she'd been agreeing to go on a date with Tyler. The next, he was being led out in handcuffs, accused of murder.

Sheila Jones. The name echoed in her head. She knew Sheila. Everyone in Irma knew Sheila. Sweet, chatty Sheila, who worked at Basin Federal and always had a smile for anyone who came through the door.

Dead. Found in a bear cache in the mountains.

And Tyler was accused of killing her. Her stomach turned, and her knees became wobbly.

"Brooke?" Becky appeared at her elbow, concern evident on her face. "Are you okay?"

"I don't know." Brooke's voice sounded strange to her own ears, distant and disconnected.

Becky took her arm and led her to the chair she'd been sitting in only minutes earlier—when she'd been smiling and happy and excited about going on a date with Tyler.

Around them, the coffee shop had erupted into conversation and speculation. Some customers were gathering their things, clearly uncomfortable with the drama. Others had pulled out their phones, probably texting the news or even posting on social media. A few remained seated, leaning toward their companions with excited whispers, treating the whole thing like entertainment.

Outside, people were gathered on the sidewalk. Customers from other businesses had come out to watch the patrol cars pull away. Not just customers, but shop owners and their employees too. Brooke dropped her gaze.

This would be all over Irma within the hour. Maybe less.

Her coffee shop—her pride, her life's work—had just become the scene of a very public arrest.

The bell chimed again, and Deputy Boverman walked back in. He surveyed the shop with a professional eye, taking in the gawkers and gossipers.

"All right, folks," he said, his voice carrying authority. "Show's over. Either order something or head on your way."

A few people looked affronted, but Adam's firm expression got them moving.

"You need anything?" Becky whispered.

Brooke waved her away.

Within minutes, half the customers had left, mumbling among themselves as they exited. The remaining patrons at least pretended to return to their coffee and laptops, though Brooke could see them sneaking glances in her direction.

Adam approached her table. "Mind if I sit?"

Brooke gestured to the chair Tyler had just vacated.

"I know that was difficult to witness," Adam said, his tone gentle. "But I wanted to make sure you understood what was happening. What we found."

"You said Sheila Jones. She was the one on the mountain?"

"You knew her, right?"

"I do my banking at Basin Federal." Tears stung Brooke's eyes. She hadn't seen the face of the body. She was glad of that now. If she'd seen Sheila dead . . . her stomach tightened again. For a moment, she thought she might be sick. "You're sure?"

"We're sure. She was reported missing on Monday morning. We thought it might be her, but we needed to make a positive identification. That took time."

What did that mean? Everyone knew Sheila. They could've asked just about anyone to identify her. Unless . . .

Brooke wrapped her arms around herself, suddenly cold despite the heat of the shop. "And you think Tyler killed her?"

"We have strong evidence pointing in that direction." Adam leaned forward, his expression serious. "Did you know Sheila and Tyler dated?"

"Since he's been back?"

He shook his head. "In high school."

Brooke snorted out a laugh. "You can't be serious. Everyone dated everyone in high school. That's what happens when your graduating class is barely a hundred people. We all knew each other."

"But she broke up with him. That kind of rejection can stick with a person."

"It was high school."

"Feelings can simmer for a long time, especially when someone's already demonstrated they have trouble with loss." Adam's implication was clear. "Based on the condition of the body and the bear cache, the coroner believes she'd been there for over a day when you found her. She was last seen leaving work Friday night around six o'clock."

"Poor Sheila."

"Tyler was seen at the bank where Sheila worked around that same time," Adam continued. "We can make a solid case."

He sounded confident. Convinced, even. But Tyler . . . no, she couldn't believe it.

"I'm glad we got him before he could hurt you." Adam reached across the table like he might take her hand, but Brooke pulled back before he could. He set his hand on the table. "When I saw him in here, talking to you, sitting so close . . . I won't lie, Brooke. It scared me."

"He wasn't going to hurt me."

"How can you be sure? A man with his history, his pattern of loss and violence— "

"There was no violence with his family," Brooke interrupted. "The fire was ruled accidental."

"Officially," Adam said. "But I was part of that investigation, and I had questions. Questions that were never fully answered. And now we have another woman dead, another person connected to Tyler's past."

Brooke's head spun. Evidence pointed one way. Her instincts pointed another. Phil's certainty that Tyler was innocent warred with the case Adam was presenting.

After being so catastrophically wrong about Kelsey, could she trust her judgment about people at all? She was starting to wonder.

"You're safe now," Adam said. "That's what matters. Tyler Gillis can't hurt anyone else."

But what if Tyler was innocent? What if the real killer was still out there while an innocent man sat in jail?

"I knew something was off about him the first time he was under investigation," Adam continued. "The way he acted, the things he said . . . my gut told me he was guilty, even if we couldn't prove it. Now we have a chance to get justice for Sheila. Maybe even for his wife and child."

Brooke thought about Tyler's face when Adam had said Sheila's name—the genuine shock and grief, the way he'd looked at Brooke as they led him away, pleading for her to believe him.

That hadn't looked like guilt. It had looked like devastation.

"Listen," Adam said, his tone shifting to something softer, more personal. "I know this is a lot to process. Finding a body, then discovering someone you were talking to might be the killer, that's traumatic. Please be sure to take care of yourself, okay?"

She nodded, grateful he was being so good about this. Adam had asked her out on Monday, showing up at the coffee shop not long after the lunch rush. She'd told him she was too shaken up about finding the body and needed time before thinking about dating. He'd said he understood and would ask again when she'd had time to settle.

Even then, Brooke already knew the truth. She didn't want to date Adam. The attraction wasn't there, and the interest wasn't genuine. He was nice enough. Handsome too. But he wasn't the man for her. She knew that without a doubt.

What she'd wanted, what she'd been planning since Monday but kept chickening out of, was to talk to Tyler, get to know him better, and give that connection a chance to grow.

And now Tyler was going to jail, accused of murder.

"Remember, I have a list of resources if you need them," Adam said, standing. "You've been through a lot. You still have my card, right? Just let me know."

"Thank you."

He left with a final concerned look, and Brooke sagged in her chair as soon as the door closed behind him.

"Brooke." Becky appeared again, her phone in hand. "You need to see this."

"What?"

"Social media is blowing up." Becky turned the phone so Brooke could see the screen.

Posts were flooding in from multiple platforms—photos of the patrol cars outside her coffee shop, speculation about what had happened, and the name Tyler Gillis appearing over and over with varying degrees of accuracy about his history.

And there, in multiple posts, people were calling Irma Brew "murder central." Joking about coffee served with a side of crime, wondering if they should avoid the place until things settled down. There was even someone who said they had inside information that the unnamed hiker who had found the body on Sunday was none other than Brooke Davies, the owner of Irma Brew.

Brooke's stomach dropped. "This is going to hurt business."

"Maybe," Becky said carefully. "Or maybe people will be curious. They might want to see where the arrest happened. People are weird that way."

"That's not the kind of attention I want."

"I know. But we'll get through it. The shop's been here for years. People know us, know we're not involved in whatever happened."

But Brooke was involved, wasn't she? She'd found the body. She talked to Tyler on the mountain. She'd just agreed to go on a date with him minutes before his arrest.

The gossip mill wouldn't care about nuance. They'd just see connections and make assumptions.

"Why don't you take the rest of the day off?" Becky said. "Go home and decompress. I can handle the shop."

"Are you sure?"

"Positive. Take care of yourself. But, Brooke . . . "

"Yes?"

"This one." Becky pointed at the comment saying Brooke had been the one to find Sheila's body. "Why would they say that?"

Brooke's shoulders drooped. Becky was staring at her, waiting, and Brooke knew she couldn't dodge it anymore.

"It's true. I found her while I was out on my Sunday run."

"Oh, I'm so sorry. That must have been awful."

Brooke nodded.

"You didn't say anything."

"It was . . . there was an investigation." The truth, but Brooke knew she could've still told Becky—had she wanted to, but she hadn't. It seemed so much easier to pretend it hadn't happened. She hadn't even told her dad or brother, and even though there was an article in the online newspaper, her name had been kept out of it thanks to her friend Joe Monroe, another member of her running club and a fellow survivor of Bearwater.

"Still." Becky shook her head. "You should've taken some time off."

"I'm fine. Really. But I think I'll go now if you're okay here."

"Absolutely. I'll see if I can get someone to come in early. We'll be fine."

Brooke nodded, grabbing her jacket and bag. She needed to get out of there, away from the stares, whispers, and phones recording everything.

She glanced at the table where she'd sat with Tyler. Where he'd asked her out. Where she'd said yes, feeling hopeful for the first time in months. Feeling like maybe she could trust herself to have a chance at a relationship without messing things up. Without her usual tendency to fixate and then second-guess every choice.

Instead everything had fallen apart, and this time it wasn't even her fault.

She looked out the front window. People were gathered on the sidewalk, talking in clusters.

Brooke headed for the kitchen to go out the back and into the alley where she parked.

Her phone buzzed as she reached her car. It was a text from Phil: *Heard Tyler got arrested in your coffee shop. You okay?*

News really did travel fast in a small town.

She didn't respond. She didn't know what to say. How could she be okay when she was this confused, this conflicted about everything?

The case Adam laid out sounded possible: a history with the victim, being at the bank Friday night, his presence on the mountain, a pattern of suspicious circumstances.

But Phil believed in Tyler, and when Tyler looked at her as they led him away, Brooke hadn't seen a killer. She'd seen a man who'd already lost everything once and was watching it happen again.

Her phone buzzed again, another message from Phil: *Rumor is, you're the one who found the body??????*

"Sorry, bro," she muttered. "I'm not up to talking right now."

She drove home on autopilot, her mind churning through possibilities. What if Tyler was innocent? What if he was guilty? Could she even trust herself to know?

Brooke pulled into her driveway and sat in the car, staring at her house without really seeing it.

She was worried about her business—the social media posts, the gossip, the way "murder central" would stick in people's minds whenever they thought about Irma Brew.

She was worried about Tyler and whether he was guilty or innocent. Worried about him sitting in a jail cell, facing murder charges, his life destroyed again.

And she was confused. About everything. About what to believe, who to trust, and how to move forward when every instinct she had seemed suspect.

The only thing she knew for certain was that nothing would be simple from here on out.

Not her business, not her peace of mind, and definitely not her feelings about Tyler.

Even if she wanted to walk away, she couldn't. She was already too involved, too invested in what happened next.

For better or worse, her life had become entangled with Tyler's the moment she stumbled across that bear cache.

And now she had to figure out what that meant, and whether she was brave enough—or foolish enough—to believe in him despite everything pointing the other way.

Chapter 12

Tyler

The interrogation room at the Basin County Sheriff's Department was exactly what Tyler expected. Beige walls, fluorescent lights, a metal table bolted to the floor, uncomfortable chairs. He'd been in this exact same room before, twelve years earlier, when they'd questioned him about the fire.

History was repeating itself.

Deputy Boverman sat across from him, a folder opened on the table between them. Edi stood near the door, arms crossed, her expression unreadable. A camera was visible in the corner, its red light blinking steadily. He looked at the mirror. Was someone watching on the other side? Maybe, though he hadn't seen anyone after they finished booking him and led him in.

"Let's go through this again," Adam said in a deceptively casual tone. "You knew Sheila Jones."

"We went to high school together." Tyler struggled to keep his tone even. How many times was Adam going to ask the same question?

"You dated."

"Briefly. I'd just graduated, and she was heading into her junior year." Tyler kept his voice level, forcing himself not to react to Adam's baiting tone. "We went out for a few months."

"So you were, what, eighteen? She was sixteen? What are you, a pedophile?"

Tyler shook his head. "I was only seventeen when I graduated, one of the youngest in my class. Turned eighteen on September 4th. Sheila was held back a year, so she was the same age as me."

Adam glanced toward Edi, who gave a nod. "Sounds right."

Tyler tried not to take pleasure in Adam looking a little foolish, but he failed. He was reminded of a lawyer show he'd watched once that said, "Never ask a question unless you already know the answer." Too bad Adam had missed that one.

"But Sheila broke up with you, right?"

"Yes."

"That must have hurt."

Tyler met Adam's eyes. "It was years ago. I got over it."

"Did you?" Adam leaned forward. "Because it seems like quite a coincidence that you come back to town and your ex-girlfriend suddenly ends up dead."

"Suddenly? I've been living here since December."

Adam narrowed his eyes. "Still seems like quite a coincidence to me."

"I had no interest in Sheila then or now. We dated. It ended. I met my wife the next year. Married her. Built a life with Jen. Sheila and I were kids when we dated. It meant nothing in the long run."

"You were seen at the bank where she worked," Adam said, flipping through papers in his folder. "Multiple times in recent weeks."

"I do my banking there. Most people in Irma do."

"You were seen talking to her. Laughing with her."

"Edi was there too. We ran into each other at the bank last week and caught up. It was a friendly conversation, nothing more."

Edi shifted but didn't speak.

"And Friday night?" Adam pressed. "Security footage shows you at the ATM around six o'clock, the same time Sheila was leaving work."

"I stopped to get cash on my way to the pub. I play darts there on Friday nights and needed money for drinks and the game buy-in."

"Convenient."

"It's the truth."

Adam gave a cold smile. "So, you just happened to be at the bank at the exact time your ex-girlfriend was leaving, and you had nothing to do with her death?"

"I had nothing to do with her death," Tyler said firmly. "I was with friends when the body was found. You already know that. Robert and Sue were with me the entire time."

"The body had been there for over twenty-four hours before it was discovered, which means Sheila was killed either Friday night or early Saturday. Where were you Friday night?"

"As I said, playing darts at the pub. There were at least a dozen people there who could verify that."

Adam made a note. "And what time did you leave?"

"Around ten. Went straight home."

"Alone?"

"Yes. Alone." Of course, alone. Always alone.

"So, no one can verify your whereabouts after ten o'clock."

This was exactly the problem. He had an alibi for most of the evening, but after he left the pub, no one could account for his time.

"What about Saturday?" Edi asked, her voice quiet but clear.

Tyler looked at her, grateful for the intervention. "I was at the shop. We open one Saturday a month for people who work during the week."

"What time?" Edi asked.

"Seven thirty to three thirty. Robert was there the whole time. One of our part-timers was there too. We had customers in and out all day."

"Can anyone verify you didn't leave during that time?" Adam jumped back in.

"I already told you. We were there all day."

"You and Robert?"

"And Andre, he works part-time. He was there too."

"Robert's your boss," Adam said skeptically. "Your friend. The man who's been vouching for you. You expect us to believe he's an objective witness?"

"He's an honest man. He has no reason to lie for me."

"Doesn't he? You work for him. He needs mechanics. Seems like he'd have plenty of reason to protect his employee. In fact, you're his only full-time employee, right?"

Tyler shrugged. He wanted to argue, but he could see it from Adam's perspective. Robert's testimony would be seen as biased, tainted by their developing friendship and professional relationship.

"Look," Tyler said, forcing himself to stay calm. "I understand how this looks. But I didn't kill Sheila. I had no reason to. We were casual friends. I ran into her occasionally around town. That's it."

"Friends," Adam repeated. "Is that what you call it when you show up at her workplace?"

"I went to the bank. Where I do my banking. Where half the town does their banking."

"Rumor is Sheila wasn't invited to your wedding."

"My wedding? To Jen? Why would I have invited her?"

"If you were such great friends, why wouldn't you?"

Tyler leaned forward. "You heard she wasn't invited? Did you hear who was invited?"

"We're talking about why Sheila wasn't there."

"Jen and I eloped. We went to Reno, just the two of us. Not even our families were there."

Adam leaned back in his chair, studying Tyler with open suspicion. "Here's what I think happened. You started seeing Sheila again, and those old feelings came back. Maybe she rejected you again. Maybe she said something that triggered memories of your wife leaving you— "

"My wife didn't leave me," Tyler snapped. "She died."

"Under suspicious circumstances."

"Under accidental circumstances."

"Officially," Adam said. "But we both know there were questions. Just like there are questions now."

Edi pushed off from the wall. "Deputy, can I speak with you outside?"

Adam's jaw tightened, but he stood. "Five minutes."

They left the room, and Tyler buried his face in his hands. This was bad. Worse than he'd thought. Adam was building a narrative that tied everything together—the fire, Sheila's death, Tyler's return to town. It didn't matter that the connections were circumstantial. It was a story people would believe because it fit their existing suspicions about him.

If he were smart, he'd tell Adam he was done talking and wanted a lawyer. Maybe he should've done that from the start. But why would he? He was innocent and had nothing to hide.

Adam could think whatever he wanted. Tyler knew the truth. He'd done nothing wrong involving Sheila or his family. He lifted his head and stared into the camera, daring it to find fault in him. A noise from outside drew his attention.

Through the small window in the door, Tyler watched Adam and Edi. Edi's body language was tense, her gestures sharp. Adam's face was flushed with anger.

Tyler's mind drifted to Brooke. She probably thought he was guilty now. How could she not? The evidence seemed plausible, and the timing looked suspicious. She'd be smart to write him off.

But part of him—the part that had felt something real when they talked in her shop, when she'd agreed to go out with him—wished things could be different. He wished he could start fresh and build something with someone who saw him as more than just the cursed man from Basin County.

The door opened, and Adam returned alone. "Deputy Reeves had to take a call. We'll continue."

They went through it again. And again. Adam asked the same questions in different ways, trying to catch Tyler in a contradiction. Tyler gave the same answers, knowing how weak they sounded.

An hour passed. Then two. Tyler's exhaustion was showing. His answers got shorter, and his patience thinner.

Finally, a knock on the door interrupted them. A man in an ill-fitting suit stepped in carrying a worn briefcase.

"I'm here for Tyler Gillis," he said, setting his briefcase on the table. "My client has nothing further to say."

Tyler studied the man. Young, maybe late twenties. Nervous energy radiating off him. Not exactly inspiring confidence.

"Fine." Adam stood. "We're done here anyway. For now."

The lawyer—he introduced himself quickly, but Tyler didn't catch the name—sat down as Adam left. "Let me see what we're dealing with."

"Who called you?"

"Pardon?"

"How'd you know to come here and represent me?"

"Oh, a call came in that you needed representation. My boss sent me."

"I don't understand. I didn't call, nor did I put down a retainer."

He shrugged. "I was told to come here, so I came. Now, what's the problem?" The lawyer flipped through some paperwork, and Tyler felt the reality of his situation settling over him.

He was in serious trouble. Real, life-destroying trouble. The kind that didn't go away just because you were innocent.

The evidence was circumstantial, but it was there. The motive was thin, but Adam was making it sound convincing. The community already suspected him because of the fire. Now they had a new reason to believe the worst.

He could go to prison for something he didn't do. Just like with the fire, he was being accused of a crime he didn't commit. Only this time, it seemed they might have something on him. They had to have something, right? Otherwise, they couldn't have arrested him. Something manufactured, but it might be enough to convince a jury.

But alongside the fear and despair, anger was building. Hot and bright and clarifying.

Someone had killed Sheila. Someone had taken a woman Tyler had known since childhood and ended her life. Left her body in the mountains to be scavenged by bears.

And that same someone—intentionally or not—was framing him for it.

The timing was almost too perfect. Tyler came back to town, reconnected with old friends, started building a life again, and then Sheila died in a way that pointed directly at him.

Tyler needed to figure out who and why. But from a jail cell, with a nervous young lawyer and the entire sheriff's department convinced of his guilt, what could he possibly do?

"So," the lawyer said, looking up from the papers, his face pale, "you've been accused of murder?"

"Uh, yeah? What did you think you were coming here for?"

The man shook his head. "I didn't know. As I said, this is uncommon. I've only been on the job a few weeks, and my boss told me to get down here. It's usually traffic stuff. DUI sometimes. A fight in a bar. But murder . . . this is Irma."

Tyler shrugged. "I didn't do it."

"Oh, yeah, of course not. Is this the first time you've been accused of murder?"

Tyler laughed at the absurdity of the question.

"Is that a yes? If so, that's good. Juries like first-time offenders."

"I'm not an offender at all."

"Right, right. I get it. I just meant . . . " The lawyer trailed off, shuffling papers nervously.

This was not going well.

Hours later, Tyler sat alone in a holding cell. The attorney had left after explaining the bail hearing process and the timeline for arraignment.

Now there was nothing to do but wait.

Tyler lay on the narrow cot, staring at the ceiling. In the span of a few days, he'd gone from hoping for a fresh start to being accused of murder, from asking Brooke on a date to watching any chance with her disappear, from rebuilding a life to possibly spending it behind bars. Or worse. Wyoming had the death penalty.

Somewhere out there, the real killer was free, maybe laughing at how perfectly this had worked out.

And Tyler was stuck in jail, powerless to do anything but hope the justice system he'd already learned to distrust would somehow work in his favor this time.

Tyler closed his eyes and thought about Brooke's smile when she said yes to dinner and about how different things might have been if it hadn't been Sheila who'd died. If he hadn't been in the wrong place at the wrong time yet again.

And he thought about who might have killed Sheila and how he was going to prove his innocence when everyone had already decided he was guilty.

Chapter 13

Brooke

The Wednesday evening group run met at the golf course. The group followed a variety of routes around town. One amazing thing about Irma was the number of biking and walking paths the town had added a few years earlier as part of a development plan to attract more tourism. While most of the paths were paved, some were packed dirt.

The club's system was to check the weather report after each run to see what was predicted for the coming week. Rain had been expected for today, which made the paved trail surrounding the greens the perfect choice.

Instead of rain, they were met with oppressive heat. Brooke would've preferred one of the trails outside of town, where the trees offered shade or the path followed the river. But they were here.

She knew the run's location was not what truly bothered her. What lingered was Tyler's arrest earlier that day. She had nearly skipped the run altogether, but she hoped the miles might help. Even as she stretched, she doubted they would.

Tonight, there were maybe fifteen people milling around, stretching and chatting while they waited for the stragglers. Brooke recognized all of them—this was her community, her people, the ones who understood that sometimes you just needed to run until your mind went quiet.

Yet she recognized their discomfort. They deliberately avoided mentioning what they all knew had happened earlier at her coffee shop. Some avoided her altogether; others looked away when she glanced their way. The tension settled hard in her gut.

"Hey." Gina appeared beside her, touching her arm. "How are you holding up?"

"I'm okay," she lied, staring at her shoes.

"Really?" Gina's skeptical tone said she didn't believe it for a second.

"Really," Brooke insisted, meeting her gaze with a smile, trying to convince herself as much as Gina. "This will help keep me from thinking too much."

Nick joined them and slipped an arm around Gina's waist. "Thinking about anything in particular?"

Before Brooke could answer, Joe jogged up. "Sorry I'm late. I had a call with an editor that ran long."

"I heard you were back in town," Brooke said, genuinely happy to see him. "How was your trip?"

Something shifted in Joe's expression. It was brief, but Brooke caught it.

"It was good."

"Everything okay?"

"Yeah. Sure. Fine. Glad to be back. Sorry to hear about what happened to you. I feel terrible that I canceled at the last minute like that. If I had known . . . "

"I know." Brooke nodded. "When did you get back? You had the article out on Monday."

"Yeah, I was back Sunday on the late afternoon flight. I heard about it while I was at Denver Airport waiting for my connecting flight. I didn't know it was you then."

"You heard about it while you were in Denver?" Brooke shook her head. Joe was new in town, having only moved there earlier in the year, but he still seemed to know everything that happened before anyone else.

"Only the basics. At that time, I didn't have all the details."

"Thanks for keeping my name out of it as long as you did." She gave him what she hoped passed for a grateful smile.

Joe's expression turned sympathetic. "I heard about what happened today. At your coffee shop. Are you okay?"

"Everyone keeps asking me that."

"Because everyone's worried," Gina said gently.

"I'm fine. I just want to run and not think about dead bodies or murder arrests or any of it for an hour."

"Fair enough," Nick said. "Looks like they're about ready." He gestured toward the rest of the group.

Steph motioned them over. "You all ready?" she asked as they approached.

"Are you running?" She was wearing sandals instead of runners, her right pinky toe taped to the toe beside it.

"Not today. It hurts to even walk. I'm not at all happy about it."

Brooke understood. "Have you started training?"

"Am I ever not training?" Steph laughed. "But yeah. Loosely. The real training happens when the weather shifts."

Like Brooke, Steph loved trail running. But, unlike Brooke, she'd successfully completed several one hundred milers, including the elusive Moose Range Run 100 that Brooke couldn't seem to conquer.

A few years earlier, Steph had started winter racing, taking on shorter distances in snow and cold before tackling an ultramarathon that crossed the Continental Divide. Brooke admired Steph's spirit and dedication, but thought her goal was way too ambitious. Even the training, alone in the snow and cold, could be deadly.

"Okay, gang," Steph said. "I'll be waiting here to cheer you on when you finish the loop."

They were about to head out when a red sports car pulled into the parking lot. Adam climbed out, dressed in running gear.

"Who invited him?" Gina murmured.

"I didn't know he ran with the group," Nick said quietly.

"He doesn't," Brooke replied, watching as Adam grabbed a water bottle from his vehicle. "Or at least he never has before."

Adam jogged over. "Hope you don't mind me joining. I need to keep in shape for work, and running alone gets boring."

"The more the merrier," Joe said, though his tone suggested he wasn't entirely convinced.

They set off on the loop, the group naturally spread out based on pace, with faster runners pulling ahead and slower ones dropping back.

Brooke found herself in the middle of the pack with Gina, Nick, Joe, and Adam. Exactly where she didn't want to be, given Adam's presence.

"So," Adam said, matching her stride, "how are you doing? Really?"

"I'm fine."

"You've been through a lot. Finding the body, then discovering Tyler was involved."

"Allegedly involved," Brooke corrected, her breath coming faster as they hit a slight incline.

"Sure, sure. Allegedly." Adam's tone suggested he didn't believe in Tyler's innocence for a second. "I just want you to know we're building a strong case. We'll get the evidence to convict him, not only for Sheila's death but for his wife and son too."

Brooke stumbled, caught off guard by the vehemence in Adam's voice, but she caught herself before she went down. "You really believe that?"

"I know it. Tyler Gillis is a dangerous man, Brooke. I don't want you anywhere near him."

"He's in jail."

"For now. But he sees the judge in the morning and might get bail. If he does, I need you to promise me you'll stay away from him."

Something about the way Adam said it—the assumption that she'd agree, the proprietary tone—rubbed Brooke the wrong way. "I appreciate your concern, but I can make my own decisions about who I spend time with."

"Even when that person is a murderer?"

"Innocent until proven guilty," Joe said. "That's how it's supposed to work, right, Deputy?"

"Of course," Adam said smoothly. "But the evidence is convincing. It's only a matter of time before we can prove what he did."

They ran in silence for a few minutes, the only sounds their steady breathing and the rhythm of feet hitting pavement. Brooke's thoughts were moving faster than her legs.

"Tyler's story would make a great series," Joe said suddenly. "The angle, the narrative arc—wrongly accused man returns to town, or actually guilty and finally caught. Either way, it's compelling."

Brooke shot him a look. Joe's journalist's brain never really turned off, but she'd hoped for a little more sensitivity given the circumstances.

"Once I've nailed him, I'll get you an exclusive," Adam said. "Full access to the investigation files, interviews with everyone involved. Could be a career-maker for you."

The words hit Brooke wrong. Not the offer itself, but the way Adam said it. Like convicting Tyler was already a done deal. Like the truth didn't matter as much as closing the case.

"What if he's innocent?" Brooke asked.

Adam's laugh was humorless. "He's not."

"But what if he is?"

"He's not," Adam repeated, more firmly this time. "Brooke, I understand you want to believe the best in people. That's only natural. It's one of the things I admire about you. But Tyler Gillis has a history. He left here under mysterious circumstances. Sheila, his old girlfriend, is dead. I've been in touch with the places he's lived in over the past twelve years. They're looking into unsolved murders and disappearances. I wouldn't be surprised if we found out Tyler was involved in those too."

Adam moved closer to Brooke, his voice dropping so only she could hear. "He's dangerous, I'm convinced of this. Please, promise me you'll stay away from him."

Brooke wanted to argue, but something in Adam's expression stopped her. He genuinely believed what he was saying.

Was that dedication to justice, or something else?

"I'll be careful," she said finally, which wasn't exactly a promise but seemed to satisfy him.

The rest of the run was quieter. Adam stayed close to Brooke, occasionally making conversation but mostly just . . . there.

Gina caught Brooke's eye more than once, her expression concerned. Nick looked thoughtful. Joe was unreadable, his journalist mask firmly in place.

Back at the parking lot, people dispersed to their vehicles. Adam lingered, clearly hoping to talk more, but Gina intervened smoothly.

"Brooke, Nick, and I were going to grab a soda. Want to come?"

"Sure."

"Joe? You in?" Nick asked.

"Yeah, sounds good."

Adam looked disappointed but didn't push. "I'll see you around, Brooke. Call me if you need anything."

They watched him drive away before turning toward Nick's truck. Steph was there, standing near her car.

"Want to join us?" Joe asked. "We're going for sodas at Annie's."

"Not tonight, but thanks. I'm going home and icing my foot."

They piled into Nick's SUV.

"So, that was intense," Joe said, sitting next to Brooke in the backseat.

"He's really got it bad for you," Gina added.

"And he really thinks Tyler's guilty," Nick observed.

Brooke shook her head but stayed quiet. What made Adam so sure Tyler was guilty? Did he know more than he was saying? Of course, he probably did. He certainly wouldn't tell her about all the evidence he had in an active investigation.

They drove to the small diner on the edge of town and slid into a booth in the back. They ordered sodas and a couple of appetizers to share.

"Talk to us," Gina said once they were alone. "What are you thinking?"

Brooke traced patterns in the condensation on her water glass. "Adam's a good guy, right? A good deputy?"

"Seems like it," Nick said carefully.

"He truly believes Tyler's guilty. He's not lying to me or trying to manipulate me. He really thinks he's protecting me from a dangerous man."

"But?" Gina prompted.

"But that comment to Joe bothered me. 'Once I've nailed him.' Like it's already decided. Like the investigation is just a formality."

"He's confident," Joe said. "Law enforcement types often are."

"Or he's more interested in being right than finding the truth," Brooke countered.

"That's a serious accusation," Nick pointed out.

"I know." Brooke took a sip of her water. "And maybe I'm wrong. Maybe Adam is exactly what he seems—a good cop trying to protect the community. But something about tonight felt off."

"What are you going to do?" Gina asked quietly.

Brooke's thoughts drifted to her brother. Phil had always been blunt, sometimes to the point of rudeness, honest even when it hurt, and utterly incapable of lying convincingly.

Phil wouldn't defend someone without reason. He'd known Tyler. There had to be a reason he'd been so certain of his innocence. After Tyler's arrest earlier today, Phil had texted her several times and even left a voicemail. In each one of them, he'd basically said the same thing: They've got the wrong guy.

"I'm going to talk to Phil," Brooke said. "I want to know why he was sure Tyler was innocent back then and what he thinks now."

"Are you sure that's a good idea?" Gina's concern was evident. "Getting involved in this?"

"I'm already involved. I found the body. Adam arrested Tyler in *my* coffee shop. The whole town is talking about me and speculating about my connection to all this, even calling my coffee shop murder central. I can't ignore that."

"That doesn't mean you have to investigate," Gina argued.

Nick cleared his throat. "Actually, maybe she does."

Gina turned to him, surprised. "You think she should get involved?"

"I think she needs answers. And I think waiting for the sheriff's department to find the truth might not be the best plan, especially if Adam's already decided Tyler's guilty." Nick looked at Brooke. "I get it, wanting to know for yourself instead of taking someone else's word."

"Even if it's risky?" Gina pressed.

"If she's careful," Nick said. "And if she's not doing it alone."

Joe had been quiet, but now he leaned forward. "Look, I'll be honest. The journalist in me is fascinated by this story. But the friend part of me is worried about you, Brooke. You've been through a lot lately."

"I know what you're going to say— "

"Do you?" Joe interrupted gently. "Because I remember earlier this year how you were when you were training for the Moose Range Run 100. You were a nervous wreck. Your judgment was off. You made poor decisions."

"Like not turning around when the storm started," Gina added quietly. "That hike outside Bearwater. You insisted we keep going when we should've turned back."

Brooke flinched. The memory of that day, of Kelsey and the hired killer and how close they'd all come to dying, was still sharp. Maybe if she hadn't been so stubborn and turned around when the weather first started, they would've been able to get off the mountain before the road flooded, trapping them there in a storm. Trapping them with a killer. "I know. I screwed up."

"But after everything that happened, you seemed better," Nick said. "You switched to the shorter distance and finished strong. You've been taking it easy, being more careful."

"Until Sunday," Gina said. "When you went hiking alone in the mountains. That was poor judgment, Brooke. You know better."

"I do," Brooke admitted. "Going alone was stupid. I should've made a few more calls and found someone to go with me, or just skipped it. But that doesn't mean meeting Tyler was a bad thing. And it doesn't mean he's guilty."

"Are you sure about that?" Joe asked.

"No," Brooke said honestly. "I'm not sure about anything. But I don't think he killed Sheila. And I don't think he killed his family. And what's that whole story Adam had about looking for unsolved murders and disappearances where Tyler lived? That seems odd, like he's grasping at straws."

"It's a reasonable thing to check." Joe shrugged. "I'd do it, too, if I were investigating the case."

"Bottom line is, I need to know if I'm right or if I'm making another mistake in judgment."

The table went quiet as the waitress brought their sodas. "Food'll be right out," she said before leaving them alone.

They all took a moment to drink and think.

Finally, Gina spoke, "If you're sure about this—really sure—I'll support you. But you have to be careful. No going off alone. No taking unnecessary risks. And if at any point you think Tyler might actually be dangerous, you walk away. You tell Adam or Edi or someone everything you know about Tyler. Deal?"

"Deal," Brooke agreed.

"I can help," Joe offered. "Research, background checks, that kind of thing. I know how to dig into records without raising red flags."

"And I can ask around," Nick added. "Construction sites are gossip central. If there's talk about Tyler or Sheila or anything related, I'll hear it."

Brooke felt something ease inside her. These were her people. Her tribe. The ones who'd been with her through the worst day of her life and were still standing by her now.

"Thank you," she said, her voice thick with emotion.

"Just be careful," Gina repeated. "Adam's not wrong about one thing—if Tyler is guilty, he's dangerous. And even if he's not, the real killer is still out there."

The food arrived, and they purposely shifted to a new subject before wrapping things up.

Nick gave everyone a ride back to their vehicles. When they reached the parking lot, Gina turned to Brooke. "Remember, be smart."

"I will," she promised.

"I'm going to do some checking around," Joe said. "I'll call you if I find anything substantial. I think I'll go to the arraignment too. You planning to be there?"

"I hadn't thought about it," Brooke admitted. She shook her head. "No, I won't be there."

She knew that was the right decision, though part of her felt like she should go, to show her support for Tyler if nothing else.

But the idea of seeing him there bothered her. She assumed he'd be in jail clothes. What did they even wear at the Basin County Detention Center? Orange jumpsuits with some kind of slide sandal? She didn't know, but that's the kind of outfit they wore on television, and she didn't want to see Tyler dressed like that.

As Brooke climbed into her SUV, she thought about Adam's certainty, his determination to "nail" Tyler. About her brother's conviction that Tyler was innocent. About Tyler's eyes when they'd led him away in handcuffs.

Someone was wrong. Either Adam, who genuinely believed he was protecting her. Or her brother, who'd never been wrong about people before, to her knowledge. Or Brooke herself, whose judgment had failed her catastrophically in the recent past.

She needed to find out which. She needed to understand the truth, whatever it was.

Even if that truth turned out to be something she didn't want to face.

Tomorrow, she'd talk to Phil and find out what he knew, try to understand why he'd believed in Tyler all those years ago.

And then she'd decide for herself whether Tyler was a man wrongly accused or a killer who'd fooled them all.

But tonight, driving home through the quiet streets of Irma, Brooke couldn't shake the feeling that Adam's interest in her was about more than just protection. And that his determination to convict Tyler was personal in a way it shouldn't have been.

That maybe the real danger wasn't Tyler at all.

Maybe it was trusting the wrong person to keep her safe.

Chapter 14

Tyler

Five days. It had been five days since they'd arrested him in Brooke's coffee shop. Five days since his world had imploded in front of part of the town and the rest of Irma learned about it on social media.

The arraignment never happened. Before Tyler even stood before the judge, the prosecutor had pulled his lawyer aside and admitted they'd been hasty. The evidence was circumstantial at best, and without something more concrete, they couldn't justify keeping Tyler in custody.

Tyler had walked out of the detention center, gone straight home to shower away the smell of jail, and called Robert about work.

"Your job's here when you're ready," Robert had said without hesitation. "Innocent until proven guilty, remember?"

True to his word, things had been fine at the shop. Robert treated him the same as always. Sue had been wonderful, bringing in pastries and making sure Tyler was welcome.

But the rest of the world wasn't so understanding.

Especially Adam Boverman, who was everywhere. Tyler would leave work and see his patrol vehicle parked across the street. He'd stop at the grocery store and find him two aisles over. Would drive home and catch the tail end of a red sports car—Adam's personal vehicle—turning the corner.

Stalking. That's what it was. Legal stalking, done under the guise of keeping an eye on a suspect. Adam wanted him to slip up, to do something that could justify another arrest.

Tyler tightened a hose clamp and straightened, wiping his hands on his shop rag. Through the shop window, he could see a handful of customers in the waiting area. Some were regulars who'd been faithful since Morgan owned the shop. Others were new faces, people who didn't know him or his history but couldn't help wanting to catch a glimpse of the accused killer.

Not everyone was fascinated by Tyler and his situation. The reactions had been mixed. Some customers had canceled appointments, citing vague reasons that didn't hide their discomfort. Others had gone out of their way to be supportive, making a point of saying they believed in his innocence.

Robert emerged from the office, a work order in hand. "Got a brake job coming in at two. You good to handle it?"

"Yeah, no problem."

Robert studied him for a moment. "You doing okay?"

"I'm fine."

"You say that a lot."

"Because it's true."

"Tyler." Robert's voice was gentle. "I know this is hard, being accused of something you didn't do and having people look at you differently. But you're not alone in this."

The words hit harder than Tyler expected. He'd spent so long thinking of himself as cursed, as poison to everyone around him, that support felt foreign. Uncomfortable, even. And difficult to accept.

"Business might take a hit," Tyler said. "People might associate the shop with me."

"Let them." Robert's tone was firm. "This is my shop, and I employ who I want. If customers have a problem with that, they can take their business elsewhere."

"You could lose money."

"Money comes and goes. Good people are harder to find." Robert clapped him on the shoulder. "Besides, Sue would have my head if I let you go. She knows you're innocent, and when that woman makes up her mind about something, there's no changing it."

Tyler's throat tightened. "Tell her thank you. For everything."

"Tell her yourself. She's bringing lunch around noon."

Robert headed back to the car he was working on, leaving Tyler alone with his thoughts and the Ford's engine.

Work was supposed to be a distraction, a way to keep his hands busy and his mind focused on something other than the case against him, the suspicion in people's eyes, and the way his life had fallen apart again.

But he couldn't stop thinking about Brooke and the moment they'd had in her coffee shop before the arrest. The way she'd smiled when he asked her out. The yes that had made him feel, for the first time in years, like maybe he could have a future. Maybe be able to build a new life and have a second chance at a family.

Then Adam had walked in and destroyed it all.

Tyler wanted to see her again. He needed to apologize for dragging her into this mess. She'd found a body and met him on the same day—how could that not cast suspicion on their connection?

But more than that, he wanted to know if that moment had been real. If the connection he'd felt was something she'd felt, too, or if it had been one-sided hope from a lonely man who should've known better.

Maybe he'd been wrong about being poison, wrong about not deserving happiness, wrong about needing to stay away from people he cared about.

Maybe everyone didn't die or leave. Maybe sometimes they stayed.

The thought was dangerous. Hope was dangerous. But Tyler couldn't quite shake it.

He couldn't even count the number of times he'd thought about calling her or going to her coffee shop. But he'd stopped himself.

He'd seen the social media posts and the things people were calling the coffee shop. Murder central. Mostly it was made in jest, but Tyler knew there was some truth to it. Not to mention the accusations being thrown at Brooke. Someone had leaked that she was the one to find Sheila's body, which made things worse. The news that he was there with Robert and Sue did nothing to improve the situation and only added to the rumors.

Tyler had driven past her shop every day on his way to and from work. Surprisingly, she seemed busier than usual. That was saying something.

Morbid. That's what people were. Just like the ones coming here now, hoping to see him, to say the killer had worked on their car. He'd noticed it after Jen and Garrett died. People drove past his job back then, or by his friend's house where he slept on the couch. They were curious, yes, but it was a morbid curiosity.

The morning passed in a blur of oil changes and diagnostic work. Customers came and went, some making eye contact and offering greetings, others avoiding his gaze entirely. Tyler tried not to care.

Sue arrived at noon with sandwiches and homemade cookies, settling into the break room with Robert and Tyler like this was any other day.

"How are you holding up?" she asked, passing out food.

"Been better," Tyler admitted. "Been worse too."

"The whole thing is ridiculous," Sue said firmly. "Anyone with sense knows you didn't kill Sheila."

"I wish the sheriff's department had sense then."

"They will. Eventually." Sue's confidence was reassuring. "The truth has a way of coming out."

Tyler wanted to believe that, but experience had taught him that truth and justice didn't always align. Sometimes innocent people get convicted while the guilty walk free.

"I can't just sit around waiting, hoping they'll figure it out."

"What do you mean?" Robert asked.

"I mean someone killed Sheila. Someone left her body in the Beartooth Mountains. And whether it was intentional or not, that same person has made me look guilty." Tyler set down his sandwich. "I need to prove my innocence. Actively. Not just hope the investigation clears me."

"How?" Sue asked.

"I don't know yet. But I can't keep pretending everything's normal while my life hangs in the balance."

Robert exchanged a glance with Sue. "What do you need from us?" Sue asked.

The question caught Tyler off guard. "You'll help me?"

"Of course we'll help you," Sue said, like it was obvious. "You're innocent. You need support. That's what friends do."

Friends. The word felt strange. Tyler had gotten so used to being alone, to keeping people at arm's length, that friendship seemed like something from another life.

"I don't even know where to start," Tyler admitted.

"Start with what you know," Sue suggested. "Who had a reason to hurt Sheila? Who might want to frame you?"

"I don't know. I've been gone since shortly after Jen and Garrett died. I don't know who Sheila was close to, who she had conflicts with, anything."

"Then we find out," Sue said. "Talk to people who knew her. People who knew you back then."

Tyler thought about his old friends. Phil, Brooke's brother, who'd believed in his innocence during the fire investigation. And others from high school might remember both him and Sheila.

And Edi. She'd been there when they found the body. She'd questioned him at the shop. But before all of that, she'd sought him out after the fire to say she believed him.

Maybe she still did.

"Yeah, maybe," Tyler said.

"Sheila's funeral is tomorrow," Sue said. "I thought I'd go." She looked at Robert, raising an eyebrow.

"I'll join you," he quickly offered.

Sue smiled. "I thought you might."

"Are you sure that's a good idea?" Tyler asked, shaking his head.

"Why not? We knew her from the bank." Sue broke a cookie in half and offered the second piece to her husband.

"Yep. It's the right thing to do." Robert met Tyler's eyes. "You'll stay here and hold down the fort. Wouldn't do for you to go to the funeral. Not with that deputy lurking around."

"You've noticed?"

"Hard not to. Remember, you've got us," Robert assured him.

"And maybe others," Sue added. "People who know you, who can vouch for your character. We've had more than one customer mention you were being framed."

Tyler nodded slowly, the outline of a plan forming. He'd reach out to old friends, talk to people who'd known Sheila, and try to piece together who might have wanted her dead and why they'd want him to take the fall.

"One other thing," Tyler said, working up the courage to ask a question that had been on his mind for days. "Did you have an attorney sent to the jail?"

Sue shook her head while Robert said, "I wish I had. But by the time I heard about what was happening, you already had representation."

Tyler scrunched his face. "Who told you I had a lawyer?"

"Social media." Sue shrugged. "That's pretty much where we learn everything in this little town. That Irma Chit Chat page has all the prattle."

"Most of it's fake," Robert added, "but once in a while, they hit the nail on the head."

"Did you happen to read who sent the attorney to the jail?"

"Nope. Sorry. Did you ask him?"

"He didn't know, and I called their office and was told it was confidential and their services were pro bono."

"That seems . . . odd," Sue said. "A blessing for sure, but still odd."

"Yeah, I thought so too."

"Well, maybe we can solve that mystery along with everything else," Robert said. "Now, I suppose we ought to get back at it. Andre should be here in about fifteen minutes. Sue and I will be taking off when he arrives. You'll close down the shop."

"Yep," Tyler agreed. "Our usual Monday schedule."

Tyler was looking forward to the day ending. He wanted to see Brooke. *Needed* to see her, to explain to her what had happened with the arrest. Not that he understood it all himself, but he'd put it off long enough, and she deserved an explanation for what had happened at her coffee shop.

The thought of facing her made his chest tight. She probably thought he was guilty. No doubt she wanted nothing to do with him.

But he owed her the truth, unfiltered by Adam's accusations. And maybe—impossibly, irrationally—she'd give him a chance to explain.

Maybe she'd even believe him. But first, he had something else he needed to take care of. He had someone else to see.

The afternoon dragged. Andre came in right on time, smiling at Tyler like any other day. Robert and Sue left after asking Andre if he could cover for them the next day while they went to Sheila's funeral. He agreed to do it before starting on a brake job. Tyler helped a customer with a flat tire and ran diagnostics on a check engine light. Normal work. Normal Monday.

Except nothing was normal anymore.

When five o'clock finally came, Tyler cleaned up and headed for his truck. He scanned the street for Adam's patrol vehicle or his personal car but didn't see either. Small mercy.

He climbed into his truck and started it up, checking his watch. If he timed things right, he might get another person on his side.

Chapter 15

Brooke

The print shop sat on a side street off Grand Avenue, tucked between an antique store and a law office—the same law office Kelsey used to work at. That's how they met. Brooke was picking up some printing she'd had her brother do for the coffee shop when Kelsey was at her car, fumbling with too many things in her arms and trying to get her door open. They were instant friends.

Now she didn't even know where Kelsey was. After the terrible incident at Bearwater, Kelsey had been taken into police custody—which, according to Joe, turned into federal custody—until one day she was just gone. Joe was convinced she had been put into witness protection, and they'd never see her again.

She wasn't sure how she felt about that. Not entirely, anyway. She couldn't deny she missed their friendship, but she was still angry about the entire situation.

Stop it, Brooke, she chided herself. *Kelsey is no longer a concern. She did what she did, and now she's paying for it.*

She didn't know if Kelsey was actually "paying" for it. The way Joe put it, things might be pretty good for her. A new life where no one knew her. Certainly, she wasn't a lawyer now, but Brooke knew there were plenty of days Kelsey hated her job. Of course, so did most people, but they didn't resort to theft.

It was rare for Brooke to have a bad day at work. Sure, there were customers she could do without, especially during tourist season, and a few regulars who could be a little much, but for the most part, she loved what she did. That made it even more difficult to understand and accept Kelsey's poor choices.

She sat in her car for a moment, gathering her thoughts. Coming here felt like the right move—Phil was always honest with her, even when that honesty hurt. If anyone could help her understand Tyler's past and whether she was being foolish to even consider believing in his innocence, it was her brother.

Phil was always practical. More than practical. It used to drive Brooke crazy the way he was. Her dad would be annoyed by it, too, but he admitted it made Phil good at the business end of things. After their dad retired, Phil had taken over, modernizing some equipment but keeping the small-town feel that made the business successful.

Just get it done. She opened the car door and strode up the sidewalk. She pushed through the front door, the familiar chime announcing her arrival. The smell of ink and paper filled the air, comforting in its consistency.

"Be right with you," Phil called from somewhere in the back.

"It's just me," Brooke called back.

"Brooke?" Phil appeared from the production area, then his expression shifted. "Oh. Uh, hey. I didn't expect to see you here. I have a visitor."

Tyler stepped around the corner.

Brooke froze. Of all the places she might have expected to run into Tyler, her brother's print shop wasn't on the list.

"Hi," Tyler said, his voice carefully neutral.

"Hi." Brooke's heart was pounding, and her stomach was making that annoying little flip. She looked at Phil. "I didn't mean to interrupt."

"You're not interrupting," Phil said quickly. "Actually, this might work out. Tyler came to talk to me about . . . well, about everything. Any chance that's why you're here too?"

Brooke nodded slowly, not taking her eyes off Tyler. He looked tired but composed, dressed in work clothes with grease on the collar. Real. Solid. Not the dangerous criminal Deputy Boverman kept insisting he was.

"Sorry," she said. "I'll come back later."

"No need, Brooke," Phil said. "I've got another chair back here. You know that."

"Okay. I guess."

"Good. Turn the sign to closed. It's near enough time anyway."

Brooke did as he asked, then made her way to the small room and settled into a chair, acutely aware of Tyler sitting a few feet away. The chemistry she'd experienced between them was still there, humming beneath the surface.

Dangerous and undeniable.

"So," Phil said, leaning against his desk. "While it's been a minute since I've seen my baby sister, we've been texting back and forth." He looked at Tyler. "She asked me why I believed you were innocent before. When Jen died."

"It's a fair question." Even though Tyler's words were calm, Brooke didn't miss the tension radiating off him.

"And Tyler came here to tell me he's innocent now. Seems like a good time for everyone to get on the same page."

"You still believe I'm innocent?" Tyler asked. "Even with everything that's happened?"

"Of course I do," Phil said without hesitation. "For the same reasons I believed it then."

"Which were?" Brooke prompted.

Phil looked at her before shifting to Tyler. "What grade were you in when you moved here, Tyler?"

Tyler shrugged. "Second grade, I guess."

"Yeah. That sounds right. And we've been friends ever since."

"Mostly," Tyler agreed. "I do seem to remember that first day when you came at me acting all tough."

Phil chuckled. "And you smiled and said, 'Hey, I'm Tyler. What's your name?' Your friendliness took the tough right out of me."

Brooke smiled at the thought of Tyler and Phil as children. She could almost imagine it. The differences in their personalities were evident in that exchange as young children.

Phil turned back to Brooke. "You remember Tyler coming over to our place?"

She shook her head. "Maybe. I know you had plenty of friends."

"Right. Tyler was one of them. We played football in junior high and high school, though I was better at that than Tyler. He only played because his dad insisted on it. Tyler preferred track."

"You're a runner?" Brooke asked.

Tyler raised his hand. "In school. Not as much now."

"Tyler's a natural athlete," Phil said. "Always was. Even when he was too lanky, he had skill. But football wasn't his thing. He was too nice on the field, and coach hated it. He wanted us tough. That's the point I'm making. How could Tyler be a killer when he didn't even like roughing people up on the turf?" Phil shook his head.

"I know his character. Besides, he loved Jen and Garrett with his entire being. And Tyler starting the fire never made sense. Why would he kill his family when he was working overtime to provide for them?"

"They said that was one of the reasons," Tyler corrected. "I was tired of working all the time."

"You still work all the time, right?"

Tyler shrugged. "Not like then. I was working at the factory then and reworking cars on the side. That's one of the reasons Jen and I chose that old house. It had an extra-large lot with a separate double-car garage at the back of it. The extra income helped make ends meet."

"Yup. That's right. You did good work. Buy a car cheap and fix it up. You don't do that now?"

"No place at my rental. Besides, I'm working with cars every day now instead of doing factory work."

"Coming home was a risk." Phil scratched his chin, leaving an ink mark on it.

"And now there's Sheila," Brooke said quietly.

"Yeah, now there's Sheila," Phil said. "But the whole idea makes no sense. They dated years ago. So what? Lots of people dated Sheila. I even went out with her a couple of times in high school."

"You did?" Brooke didn't know that.

"For like two weeks. She broke up with me to go out with someone else. Didn't bother me." Phil looked at Tyler. "When did you two date? After you graduated?"

"Yeah. We went out for a couple of months. She ended it before school started again. I moved on."

"Exactly. Ancient history. No reason to kill someone over something that happened back in high school."

"Unless he's been nursing a grudge all this time," Brooke said, repeating things she'd heard others say.

"Does Tyler seem like the type to nurse grudges?"

Brooke studied Tyler's face. He looked tired and stressed, but not angry. Not vindictive. Just . . . weary.

"No," she admitted. "He doesn't."

"Besides," Phil continued, "Sheila was one of the popular girls. But she was also a mean girl. She and her friends would go out of their way to make life difficult for whoever they decided was their current target."

"I forgot about that," Tyler said quietly. "Sheila was the leader of that group."

"That's for sure," Phil said. "No one was safe. They played jokes on people. Remember that one kid? What was his name? Walt? Warren?"

"The brainiac?" Tyler nodded. "They were terrible to him."

"Yeah. You hear about him? He's like a gajillionaire now. Got into digital currency before it was a thing. Sheila was trying to track him down a few years back. Said she wanted to make amends. Wanted to figure a way into his wallet was more like it."

Phil laughed, and Tyler joined in, though his was more subdued than her brother's.

"So, Sheila wasn't nice in high school?"

"She was awful." He lifted his chin at Tyler. "Remember how she was with Edi? She's the one who came up with those names. Yeti?"

"Sasquatch," Brooke corrected softly. "I always thought that was terrible."

Tyler frowned. "They were awful to her, but Edi never seemed to care. She let it slide right off."

"Like water off a duck's back," Phil agreed.

"Besides," Tyler added, "Edi had something Sheila and her gang didn't."

They looked at each other and said simultaneously, "Money."

Phil laughed. "Right. But I do think it bothered Edi more than you realized. She had money, and her family had power, but she wasn't always as strong as she is now. She put up a front when she was around you."

Tyler shook his head. "I don't think so."

"Sure, she did," Phil insisted. "She had a thing for you and didn't want you to see her as weak."

"Wait," Brooke said, trying to follow. "Edi had feelings for Tyler?"

"No," Tyler replied. "We were only ever friends."

"A friend she had feelings for," Phil corrected. "Trust me, everyone knew. Except you, apparently."

Tyler looked genuinely surprised. "I had no idea."

"Because you were oblivious." Phil turned to Brooke. "Anyway, the point is, Sheila didn't really outgrow her mean girl tendencies. I mean, sure, she was nice to people at the bank because she had to be, but get a few beers in her, and she'd say some pretty rotten things. More than one person took their business elsewhere because of Sheila's mouth. I heard she'd even been written up over it."

"I never heard about this." Brooke shook her head, trying to recall anything that sounded like what Phil was talking about.

"Sure, why do you think she was still a teller after all these years? Because she was too much of a blabbermouth and drunk to move up. If I were the cops, I'd be looking at some of the folks she'd been badmouthing. Not Tyler, who moved on from their brief relationship years ago."

The conversation shifted, and Tyler began explaining his side of the story directly to Brooke.

When he was finished, he swallowed hard. "The fire marshal said it started in the kitchen. A problem with the gas stove that ignited and exploded. Completely accidental."

"But people suspected you anyway," Brooke said softly.

"Some people. Deputy Boverman especially. He was new to the force and eager to prove himself. He decided I was guilty and kept pushing, even after the investigation cleared me." Tyler met her eyes. "I left town because I couldn't stand the suspicion. Couldn't stand all the memories and being in a town where everyone looked at me and wondered."

"Why come back?" Brooke asked.

"Because nowhere else felt like home. I moved around for years trying to find somewhere I fit. But I kept thinking about Basin County. About the mountains I grew up hiking. About people like Phil who believed in me." Tyler's gaze held hers. "I thought maybe enough time had passed. Maybe I could start over."

"And then Sheila died," Phil said quietly.

"And then Sheila died." Tyler's frustration was evident. "I'm being framed. I don't know by who or why, but someone wants me to take the fall for this."

Brooke processed everything she'd heard. Phil's unwavering faith in Tyler. Tyler's explanation of the fire, which matched what she'd read in the articles but carried the weight of lived experience. The timeline of his relationship with Sheila—so long ago it seemed absurd to hold a grudge.

The evidence against Tyler didn't add up. None of it was proof of murder.

The people who didn't like Sheila made much more sense as being the culprits.

Someone could be setting him up. But who? And why?

"I believe you," Brooke said. And that scared her more than if she didn't.

Tyler's expression shifted. "You do?"

"I think so. Yes." She looked at her brother. "Phil's judgment matters to me. And your explanation makes sense."

"Thank you." Tyler's voice was rough with emotion. "You have no idea what that means."

They talked for another hour, going over details and discussing possibilities. Phil threw out names of people who might have had issues with Sheila: two ex-husbands, people at the bank, people from the bars in town. Tyler admitted he'd been gone too long to know who she'd had conflicts with recently.

Eventually, Phil needed to wrap up a print job that was due the next morning. Brooke and Tyler walked out together, the early evening sun warm on their faces.

At her SUV, they paused. The awkwardness was back, that awareness of each other that made conversation difficult.

"Thank you for listening," Tyler said. "For believing me."

"I'm not sure I have a choice," Brooke admitted. "Everything about this feels wrong. The timing, the evidence, the way Deputy Boverman is so determined to convict you."

"He's been following me," Tyler said. "Ever since that night I spent in jail. Watching me. Trying to get me on something. Even a traffic stop is my guess."

"That's not right."

"It's legal enough." Tyler shoved his hands in his pockets. "I appreciate you giving me a chance to explain. You didn't have to."

Brooke knew she should say goodbye and drive away, keep her distance until this was all sorted out. But instead, she said, "Stop by the coffee shop tomorrow. At closing time."

Tyler's eyes widened slightly. "Are you sure?"

No. She wasn't sure at all. But the invitation was out there now, and she couldn't take it back. She *wouldn't* take it back.

"I'm sure," she said, hoping her voice sounded more confident than she felt. "I usually take the closing shift on Tuesday. Can you be there at six?"

"Okay." Tyler's smile transformed his face. "I'll be there."

They stood for another moment, neither quite ready to leave. Then Brooke opened her car door.

"Tomorrow," she said.

"Tomorrow," Tyler agreed.

She drove away, watching him in her rearview mirror as he headed to his truck. Her heart was pounding, her mind racing with questions about what she'd just done.

She believed Tyler was innocent. Phil believed it too. But belief and proof were different things. And getting involved with him—even just to talk, even just to help—was risky in ways she couldn't fully calculate.

Brooke couldn't shake the feeling that she'd just made a decision that would change everything.

For better or worse, she was choosing to trust Tyler.

Chapter 16

Tyler

Tyler arrived at Irma Brew ten minutes before closing time, parking down the street so his truck wouldn't make it obvious which shop he was going into. The last thing either of them needed was more fuel for the town gossip mill.

He stayed in his truck for a few minutes, waiting and replaying the day. Sue and Robert had gone to Sheila's funeral, as they said they would. They came in afterward and told him all about it.

"Adam Boverman was there," Robert had said with a tilt to his eyebrows. "In uniform."

"That was just weird," Sue said. "It made people uncomfortable. I was actually surprised more people didn't go. There were a few people from the bank and others I recognized from around town, but really not that many. Her ex-husband was there. The most recent one—at least that's what people said. Randy or something."

"Rusty," Robert corrected. "We've done work for him before. You know him?"

Tyler had shaken his head, unable to put the name with the face.

"Has that old Trans Am."

"Oh, yeah. Him. Works at that new factory on the edge of town."

"Yup, he's the one," Sue said. "If you ask me, they should be looking at him for her murder. You know who else was there? The game warden. The one that came up to the trailhead that day. What was his name?"

"Henry," Robert said, his tone clipped.

Sue gave him a questioning look, to which he shrugged. "What? His name is Henry."

"Anyway," Sue said. "Someone told me they dated."

"Sheila and the game warden?"

"Yup." Robert's nod said more than the single word.

Tyler wondered if Adam Boverman was harassing Henry the same way he was harassing him. After all, he, too, had been on the mountain that same day, a man who had dated Sheila and answered the call of a dead body. That sounded suspicious to him, but somehow he knew Boverman would explain it away. As far as he was concerned, Tyler was his man.

He checked his watch. Two minutes to six. He took a breath and headed for the door.

Through the front window, he could see Brooke moving around inside, clearing tables and wiping down surfaces. The shop was empty of customers, but she had yet to turn off the open sign.

The bell chimed as he entered. Brooke looked up from where she was arranging chairs, and her expression softened when she saw him. Not fear. Not wariness. Something warmer that made his chest tight.

"Hi," she said, moving to the open sign and switching it off.

"Hi." Tyler felt suddenly awkward, standing near the doorway of her business like a teenager picking someone up for a first date. "I can come back if you need more time to close up."

"No, you're fine. I let my staff go home early. I'm almost finished, but . . . " She gestured at the chairs she'd been stacking. "Want to help? It'll go faster with two people."

The request caught him off guard. He'd expected to sit and talk, not to help close her shop. But there was something appealing about the idea of working alongside her in her space.

"Sure."

They fell into an easy rhythm. Tyler stacked chairs while Brooke wiped down tables. She showed him where supplies were kept when he offered to sweep. The movements were practiced and comfortable, like they'd done it dozens of times instead of this being their first.

"You're good at this," Brooke observed, watching him maneuver the broom.

"Worked in the student union during college."

"I didn't know you went to college."

"Community. Did one year, taking business classes. I married Jen and started working at the gypsum factory. Didn't take long to realize I liked working on cars a lot better than dealing with numbers." Tyler paused. "Seems like a different lifetime now."

Brooke nodded, understanding in her eyes. "A lot can change over the years."

They finished the main dining area and moved to the kitchen. Brooke offered to make them cappuccinos.

"Not necessary. I usually just drink the stuff from a canister."

"How about an Americano?"

"Sure, I guess." He wasn't sure what that was, but he was willing to try something different.

She went back to the counter area. As the machine fired up, Tyler rinsed the few dishes left in the sink and loaded the dishwasher.

"You don't have to do that," she said, coming back with a mug in each hand.

"I don't mind. Tell me where the soap is, and I'll start it."

With the dishwasher providing a quiet background hum, they took chairs at a small table tucked in the corner of the kitchen. This wasn't the public dining area but her private workspace, where she probably sat to do paperwork and plan menus. The lighting was dim, just the overhead fixtures turned low for closing. It felt intimate in a way that made Tyler's pulse quicken.

They sat across from each other, coffee mugs between them.

"Can I ask you something?" Brooke said after a moment.

"Anything."

"What was it like? After they died. How did you . . . how did you keep going?"

The question caught Tyler off guard. Not because it was inappropriate, but because no one had asked him that in years. People avoided the topic, uncomfortable with his grief.

"Honestly?" Tyler stared into his coffee. "I'm not sure I did keep going. Not really. I existed. Went through the motions. But actually living? That took a long time to figure out again."

"What changed?" She leaned forward, and Tyler caught a whiff of her perfume, or maybe it was her shampoo. Whatever it was, he liked it.

"Nothing dramatic. Just . . . eventually the pain wasn't quite so sharp. I could think about them without feeling like I was drowning. Could remember the good times instead of just the end."

He looked up at her. "Being away was good. Necessary. And then it wasn't. For the last three or four years, all I could think about was being here. In Irma. Around the mountains. Being home. But now . . . " He shook his head as his shoulders sagged.

Brooke was quiet for a moment. "I'm terrified of losing people," she said softly. "My mom died three years ago. Just went to sleep one night and didn't wake up. I found her when I went to pick her up for church."

"I'm sorry."

"It broke something in me. Made me realize how fragile everything is. How quickly someone can just . . . be gone." She wrapped her hands around her mug. "That's part of why I struggle with trust. With letting people in. Because what if they leave? What if I lose them?"

"Trust isn't easy," he admitted.

"You're telling me. You know about my friend Kelsey? About what she did?"

"I read the paper and heard people talk about it. It must have been pretty terrible."

"That day was terrible, but losing Kelsey as a friend . . . I trusted her, and look how that turned out."

They were quiet for several minutes, each sipping their coffee. Finally, Brooke said, "If I can't even pick my friends properly, how am I ever going to pick out a boyfriend? A husband? I'm totally afraid I'm going to mess that up and then be alone for the rest of my life."

Tyler understood that fear intimately. "I get it. It's hard to date. Much easier to stay single, isn't it?"

"That and Basin County isn't exactly overflowing with options." She gave him a small smile, then quickly glanced at her mug. "Until recently."

Tyler's own smile grew. Was she saying what he thought she was saying? He was going to ask, but she changed the subject.

"I'm sorry I don't remember Phil bringing you over to the house."

"I don't think I was very memorable then." He laughed. "Tall and skinny. Awkward."

"Nothing wrong with being tall."

Her smile came again, and with it, warmth spread through his chest. He could like Brooke. He could like her a lot. He already did.

They talked about Phil for a while, about his steadfast loyalty and blunt honesty. "That's not always easy," she said with a laugh. "Having a brother who rarely sugar-coats things is challenging."

Then the conversation shifted to the case against Tyler, to Sheila and what she'd been like in high school.

"Phil said she was a mean girl," Brooke said. "That she never really outgrew it."

"Yeah. I was thinking about that last night. He's right. They'd pick a target and make that person's life miserable for weeks or months." Tyler took a sip of coffee. "I'd sort of forgotten how bad it was until Phil mentioned it. No one was safe from Sheila and her gang."

Brooke nodded. "I was looking at one of those websites last night that people set up for their class reunions. Some of her friends from high school still live in Irma. I know them. They come into the coffee shop."

"Yeah. I've seen a few people from high school in passing. There's a girl who works at the craft store across from the auto shop."

"Monique. Her aunt owns the place. I saw pictures of her and Sheila."

"Monique." He nodded. "Pretty sure that's her. Sheila had mentioned some of us getting together for drinks and live music."

"I don't go to bars much," Brooke said. "So, I miss out on some of the juicier gossip. But Phil sure seemed to know things about Sheila and how she wasn't always as sweet as she seemed at work."

"Nobody's perfect. But that doesn't mean she deserved to die."

"No," Brooke agreed softly. "She didn't."

The conversation deepened from there. Tyler found himself opening up about things he hadn't talked about in years. The grief over losing Jen and Garrett. The guilt that still plagued him, wondering if he could have prevented the fire somehow. He still didn't understand what had caused the gas line to fail. To cause the entire system to ignite and the house to explode.

And he shared with her the loneliness of the past twelve years, moving from place to place without ever feeling like he belonged. About how he would imagine what Garrett would be like now. Nearly sixteen. He liked to think they'd be working on a car together. Something they bought and could fix up for him.

"I kept thinking maybe the next town would be different," he said. "Maybe I'd finally feel at home somewhere. Maybe I'd finally stop dwelling on what my life should be like. But nowhere felt right. Nowhere felt like Basin County."

"So, you came back."

"So, I came back. And walked straight into another nightmare."

Brooke reached across the table, her hand covering his. The touch was meant to be comforting, a simple human connection. But the moment her skin met his, heat spread up his arm.

Tyler looked up and found her eyes already on him. The awareness that had been building between them since they'd met intensified, becoming almost tangible in the quiet kitchen.

"I believe you're innocent," Brooke said quietly. "I don't think you killed Sheila. And I don't think you killed your family."

"Thank you." His voice came out rougher than intended. "That means more than you know."

Her hand was still on his. Neither of them moved to break the contact. Tyler could feel his heartbeat in his throat, could see the way Brooke's breathing had changed.

He should pull away—remember that Boverman was still watching him, still waiting for a reason to make another move—but he couldn't make himself step back.

"Tyler," Brooke said, and there was something in the way she said his name that made his chest ache.

"I should go." But he didn't move. "You don't need more complications in your life."

"Maybe I do." Her eyes held his.

"Brooke— "

She stood and went around to his side of the table. Tyler stood too.

They were close. Close enough that he knew the lovely scent from earlier was her shampoo, an intoxicating mix of coconut and vanilla.

Tyler fought the urge to kiss her. Knew he shouldn't. Getting involved with Brooke, with everything going on, was selfish and wrong.

But the pull was magnetic. Undeniable. He wanted to touch her so badly it hurt.

"Sorry," he said, even as his hand came up to cup her cheek. "You deserve better than this mess."

"What if I don't want better?" Brooke's voice was barely above a whisper as she turned her cheek into his hand. "What if I want you?"

Tyler started to pull back, to do the right thing and walk away. But Brooke moved in, closing the distance between them.

The kiss was brief. Gentle. Her lips were soft against his, her hand coming up to rest against his chest. It lasted maybe three seconds, but it felt like the world had shifted.

When they pulled apart, both breathing harder, Tyler knew he was in trouble. Because that kiss—brief and gentle as it was—had been amazing. Unforgettable. The kind of kiss you don't come back from.

"I really should go," he said again, but this time there was less conviction in his voice.

"Probably." But Brooke didn't move away.

They stood there for another moment, the tension between them thick enough to cut. Finally, reluctantly, Tyler stepped back.

"When can I see you again?" The question was out before he could stop it.

"Soon." Brooke's smile was small but genuine. "We'll figure something out."

He thought about saying how much he liked the sound of that, how much he liked that she was ready to work things out. Instead, he nodded, wearing what was no doubt a goofy smile.

"Let me make sure everything's locked up, then we'll head out the back, okay?" Brooke said, grabbing her jacket and purse.

"Can I help?"

"No, I've got it." She waved him off and disappeared through the kitchen door into the main part of the coffee shop.

Tyler rinsed the mugs and placed them in the sink before waiting by the door. A couple of minutes later, she returned and ushered him out into the alley.

The evening air was cool, the heat of the late August day burning off. Tyler walked Brooke to her SUV, parked behind the shop.

"Thank you," he said. "For believing me. For listening. For . . ." He trailed off, not sure how to finish.

"For kissing you?" Brooke supplied, a hint of humor in her voice.

"Yeah. That too."

She unlocked her door but didn't get in immediately. "Be careful, Tyler. Don't give Boverman a reason to arrest you again."

"I'll be careful."

"Promise me."

"I promise."

She stood on her toes and pressed a quick kiss to his cheek, then climbed into her SUV before he could react. Tyler watched as she started the engine, backed out of the alley, and drove away.

He stood there for a long moment after her taillights disappeared, his hand touching the spot where she'd kissed his cheek.

Something was building between them. Something real and powerful and terrifying in its intensity. He'd come to Basin County hoping to start over, to build a new life in the place that had always felt like home.

He hadn't expected to find Brooke.

Hadn't expected to feel this way about someone when his life was such a disaster.

But here he was, standing in an alley behind her coffee shop, still feeling the ghost of her kiss on his lips and knowing that everything had changed.

Tyler walked to his truck, scanning the street for any sign of Adam's patrol vehicle or sports car. Nothing. Another small mercy.

As he drove home, Tyler thought about Brooke's smile, her laugh, the way she'd looked at him in the dim kitchen light. He thought about the kiss that had lasted only seconds but felt like it had rewired something fundamental inside him.

He was in trouble. Deep, serious, wonderful trouble.

And for the first time in years, that didn't feel like a curse.

It felt like hope.

Chapter 17

Brooke

Brooke wiped down the espresso machine, her mind anywhere but on the gleaming chrome surface in front of her.

She couldn't stop thinking about last night—Tyler in the dim kitchen, the heat of his chest under her hand, the way he'd kissed her back.

That kiss had kept her awake for half the night. She replayed it over and over until she finally gave up on sleep around four in the morning.

What must he think of her? She'd basically thrown herself at him. Sure, he hadn't pulled away, had even seemed to welcome it, but still. How embarrassing to be so forward when the man was dealing with so much.

"You okay?" Becky asked, appearing beside her with a tray of dirty mugs.

"Of course. Why?"

"You've been cleaning that same spot for like five minutes."

Brooke stepped back from the machine, realizing she'd been staring at it without seeing it. "Guess I'm distracted."

"Thinking about Tyler Gillis?"

"What? No. Why would you— "

Becky's knowing smile stopped her. "Small town, remember? People saw his truck parked down the street last night around closing time. They're talking."

Of course they were. Brooke suppressed a groan. "We were just talking."

"Uh-huh." Becky didn't sound convinced. "For what it's worth, I think he's innocent. Deputy Know-It-All's got it wrong."

"You think so?"

"Sure. Tyler's been nothing but polite. And I've seen enough true crime shows to know that circumstantial evidence doesn't mean anything. Besides," Becky lowered her voice, "Boverman has a thing for you. Have you noticed the way he looks at you? Intense."

Brooke wanted to argue, to defend Adam as just doing his job, but she couldn't. Because Becky was right. Adam's attention had shifted from professional concern to something more personal.

Truth was, a few weeks ago, she may have welcomed his attention. He was easy to look at and pleasant enough. He was the type of guy she might have liked to get to know better.

Now, though, she hated how he was about Tyler, how he was so convinced Tyler was guilty. And she didn't welcome Adam's attention because she couldn't think of him in that way, couldn't think of a fling with the deputy when Tyler was the man she wanted to spend time with.

The bell over the door chimed, and Brooke looked up to see the man himself walking in.

"Speak of the devil," Becky muttered, then plastered on a customer service smile. "Morning, Deputy. Want a cup of coffee?"

"Please." Adam's attention was already on Brooke. "Got a minute?"

Not really, Brooke wanted to say. But small-town politeness won out. "Sure."

He nodded toward a table. "Look good?"

Brooke nodded. "I'll grab you a cup of coffee and be right there."

He reached for his wallet.

"It's on me." She smiled. Even though she truly wasn't interested in Adam, buying him a cup of coffee and hearing him out was the right thing to do. Plus, maybe he'd let something slip about the investigation that could help her figure out who really killed Sheila, because she knew it wasn't Tyler.

Mug in hand, she joined him at the table, acutely aware of Becky watching from behind the counter and several other customers trying not to obviously eavesdrop.

"Here you go." She set his mug in front of him.

"Nothing for you?"

"I'm running on too much caffeine as it is. Hazard of the job."

"I bet." He gave her a smile. "I wanted to check on you and make sure you're okay after everything."

"Sure, everything's great."

"Is it?" He leaned forward, his voice dropping. "Because I heard Tyler Gillis was here last night. After closing."

There it was. The real reason for this visit. She leaned back in her chair. "And?"

"And I'm worried about you, Brooke. This man is dangerous. He's already cost two women their lives— "

"Allegedly," Brooke interrupted. "The fire was an accident, and he was released because of a lack of evidence concerning Sheila, right?"

Adam's expression shifted, surprise flickering across his features. "You're defending him now?"

"I'm saying innocent until proven guilty. That's how the system works. I'm sure you know that." She forced herself to drop her shoulders and smile. "Right, Deputy?"

"The system isn't perfect. Sometimes dangerous people slip through because we can't prove what we know in our gut." He reached across the table, his hand covering hers before she could pull back. "I'm trying to protect you."

"I'm fine. I don't need protection from Tyler." She tried to keep her voice light.

"Yes, you do." Adam's voice had gone harder. "I'd like to get to know you better, Brooke. I think you know that, right? And part of caring about someone is keeping them safe, even when they don't know they need it."

Brooke carefully extracted her hand. "I'd better get back to work. The lunch crowd will be here soon."

"Just promise me you'll be careful. That you won't see him alone again."

The request sounded reasonable on the surface. But something about it—the way he was looking at her and the proprietary tone his voice took on once again—made her uncomfortable.

"I'll be careful," she said, which wasn't exactly a promise.

He tipped back his coffee. "You make the best coffee. I don't know why when I make it at home, it never turns out nearly as good." He smiled. "And don't even get me started on the coffee at the station."

Brooke forced a polite laugh. "I can only imagine."

Adam took a step toward her. "I know I sound obsessed as far as Tyler is concerned. And maybe I am. There was just always something about the fire that bothered me. I can't explain it. I know the official report came back as an accident, but . . . " He shrugged. "And now, with Sheila . . . "

"But you don't know for certain that Tyler had anything to do with either."

"You're right. I don't. But my gut tells me they both circle back to him. He's at the heart of it. I'd hate to be right about this and have you in danger."

Even though she wasn't interested in Adam, she could hear the sincerity in his tone. As weirdly possessive as he'd seemed, she now wondered if he was more scared than anything. Scared that he might be right about Tyler and another person may die.

"Tyler isn't dangerous."

"How do you know?" He dropped his voice to a whisper. "Because he told you he's innocent? Because you want to believe him? Brooke, you were wrong about Kelsey. What if you're wrong about him too?"

The words hit hard because they echoed her own fears. But hearing them from Adam, delivered with that mixture of concern and condescension, made her defensive instead of doubtful.

"I need to get back to work," she said firmly.

"Brooke— "

"Have a nice day." She walked away before he could say anything else, not stopping until she reached the kitchen. She stood there, staring at the room. Her attention shifted to the table where she and Tyler had sat last night.

She'd had her doubts before, but after talking with Phil and getting to know Tyler better, she was positive he was innocent. And she was going to help prove it. She grabbed her phone and found the number for the auto shop, her heart pounding as she dialed.

"Morgan's Auto Repair," a woman's voice answered.

"Hi, Sue? This is Brooke. Brooke Davies?"

"Oh, Brooke! Hi! How are you doing? I know things haven't been easy."

That was certainly an understatement, but what could she say? "I'm fine, thanks. I was wondering if I could leave a message for Tyler? Ask him to call me?"

"Don't be silly. He's right here. I'll grab him. He's due for a break anyway."

Before Brooke could respond, Sue was already calling his name.

"Brooke?" Tyler said, slightly breathless.

Her stomach did that annoying flip again. "Hi. Sorry to bother you at work."

"You're not bothering me. Is everything okay?"

"Yeah, I just— " She took a breath. "I wanted to see if you wanted to have dinner. An early dinner. I'm off at three, and I have running club at six, so maybe four? Would that work? At my place?"

The words tumbled out in a rush, and as soon as they stopped, Brooke wanted to take them back. Dinner at her place? What was she thinking? Why not suggest a restaurant, somewhere public?

"I'd like that," Tyler said. "I'm off at three-thirty today, so four is perfect."

"Great. Okay. Um, I'll uh, give you my address."

"How about I give you my number so you can text it to me?"

"Yeah, yeah. That's a good idea."

He gave her his number before saying, "Brooke?"

"Mm-hmm?"

"I'm glad you called."

Her chest felt tight in the best way. "Me too."

They hung up, and Brooke stared at her phone. Dinner at her place. She'd actually invited him to her house.

This was either brave or incredibly stupid, and she wasn't sure which. Not because she thought he was guilty, she didn't. But rather because inviting a man to her house was . . . was what? Something her mom had told her she should never do? Especially not on a first date. They should go out to a public place. Oh, well. Too late now.

The rest of her shift crawled by. Brooke kept checking the clock, counting down the hours until three. They were slow, so as soon as the next crew arrived, she scooted out about fifteen minutes early, stopping at the grocery store on the way home.

Lemon chicken pasta—light and quick, and just fancy enough to impress Tyler. She grabbed the ingredients, plus a loaf of sourdough bread, and hurried home to start cooking.

By 3:45, her house smelled amazing and she was second-guessing everything—the menu, the bread, and the fact that she'd invited him over instead of suggesting somewhere more public.

The doorbell rang at exactly four o'clock.

Brooke took a breath and rushed toward the door. She checked herself in the entryway mirror, tucking a strand of hair behind her ear. "Here goes nothing," she whispered.

Tyler stood on her porch, in jeans and a salmon-colored button-up shirt, his hair damp like he'd taken time to wash up before coming over. He held a small bouquet of flowers.

"Hi," he said, offering them to her.

"Hi." She took them, and something warm spread through her chest. "These are beautiful."

"They have them at the gas station. You know, the one on the corner down the road. Thought you might like them."

She found a vase for the flowers while he looked around her living room.

"Nice place," Tyler said.

"Thanks. It's on the small side but has two bedrooms upstairs and an office on this floor." She blinked a few times. Why in the world had she mentioned the bedrooms? "Um, and, you know, the main space downstairs." She gestured toward the kitchen. "Dinner's almost ready. I hope you like lemon chicken."

They moved to the kitchen, falling into an easy rhythm as Brooke plated the food and Tyler filled water glasses. The domesticity of it felt natural, comfortable, like they'd done this many times before.

At her small dining table by the sliding patio door, they settled in, the view of the yard lending a pleasant ambiance. She should've suggested eating outside, but it was too late now. For a few minutes, they ate and made small talk about their days, the tension still there, bubbling beneath the surface.

Finally, Brooke set down her fork. "Deputy Boverman came by the coffee shop this morning."

Tyler's expression tightened. "What did he want?"

"To warn me about you. Again. He heard you were there last night."

"Of course he did."

"I defended you. He noticed. I think it made him uncomfortable, and he admitted maybe he was wrong." That wasn't exactly what he said, but it wasn't an outright lie either.

"I don't want to cause problems for you."

"You're not causing problems. He is." She reached across the table, her hand covering his. "Tyler, I believe you're innocent. I'm happy to tell everyone. Not because I'm naive or because I want to believe it. Because I've looked at the evidence, listened to Phil, and talked to you. I believe you."

Tyler turned his hand over and laced his fingers with hers.

"Tell me about her," Brooke said softly. "About your wife. Not about the fire. About before. About when things were good."

Something shifted in Tyler's expression. Not pain exactly, but a bittersweet warmth. "Jen was amazing. Smart, funny, completely unimpressed by my attempts to be cool." He smiled at the memory. "We met at a car show. She was there with her dad, and I was working a booth, helping out a friend. She asked more intelligent questions about engines than half the guys there."

"Sounds like she was perfect for you."

"She was. We got married young—not even twenty yet. Everyone said we were crazy, but it just felt right." His thumb traced circles on the back of Brooke's hand. "Garrett was born a little over a year later. He looked just like her. Same smile, same laugh. He loved trucks and dinosaurs and being outside."

"You had a good life," Brooke said.

"I did. For almost four years, I had everything I'd ever wanted." Tyler's voice was thick with emotion. "Then it was gone. And for a long time, I thought that was it. That I'd used up my chance at happiness."

"And now?"

"Now I'm sitting in your kitchen, holding your hand, and wondering if maybe I was wrong." He met her eyes.

"But I'm terrified, Brooke. What if getting close to me puts you in danger? What if Adam's right? Not about me being guilty." He shook his head. "But maybe I'm cursed. Maybe I'll put you in danger simply because I'm me."

"You're not cursed," Brooke said firmly. "Bad things happened. Terrible things. But that doesn't make you cursed."

"You sure?"

"I'm willing to take my chances." She squeezed his hand. "What if you could be happy again? What if you could have something good?"

The question hung between them. Tyler stood slowly, and Brooke stood with him. They were close now, the tension from last night back in full force.

"I'm scared," Brooke admitted. "I don't know if I'm any good at relationships. I get so wrapped up in things that I can become a little . . . obsessive."

"I'm not sure I mind you being obsessed with me." Tyler's hand cupped her face. "It seems like we might be a good pair, don't you think?"

Brooke's breath caught. This was right. Tyler was right. Whatever was building between them was real and worth the risk.

She closed the distance. Her hands gripped his shirt as she pulled him down to meet her. The kiss was everything—passionate, desperate, and perfect. All the tension that had been building between them since that first moment on the mountain released in a rush.

Tyler's arms wrapped around her, pulling her close as the kiss deepened. This wasn't the brief, tentative kiss from last night. This was them choosing each other despite the risks, despite the fear, despite everything that said they shouldn't.

When they finally broke apart, both breathing hard, Brooke rested her forehead against his chest.

"What have we done?" she whispered.

"Something either really smart or really stupid." Tyler's voice was rough. "But I don't regret it."

"Me neither." She looked up at him.

They stood there for a long moment, holding each other.

Finally, Brooke pulled back slightly. "I have running club in forty-five minutes. Come with me?"

"To running club?"

"Why not? Show everyone you're not hiding. That you have nothing to be ashamed of." She gave a mischievous smile. "Plus, it'll drive Adam crazy."

Tyler laughed. "When you put it that way, it's tempting. But I don't have running clothes on." He motioned to his jeans.

"Go change. We're meeting at Meadowlark Lane this week. You know the trail there?"

"I know it, but I'm going to pass. There're a few things I need to do at home. You all run every week?"

"Every Wednesday, rain or shine. Next week, maybe?" While she wanted him to join them, she knew it might not be the best idea. Adam showed up last week. He might show up again, and then what? It could be super uncomfortable . . . or worse.

"Next week, sure. Let me help you tidy the kitchen."

They cleaned up the dinner dishes together, the comfortable domesticity from earlier back in full force. When they were done, she walked him to the door.

She wanted to kiss him again, have a repeat of earlier. But she worried that if she did, she might beg him not to leave, and then she'd miss her run. Instead, she gave him a hug.

"You have my number now," she reminded him. "Maybe call me tomorrow?"

He nodded before stepping outside.

She stayed in the doorway, giving him a wave when he reached his truck. He returned the gesture before climbing in and starting it up. As he pulled away from the curb, she started to close the door. That's when she saw the little red sports car pull away from the curb down the block.

Chapter 18

Tyler

Tyler arrived at the shop fifteen minutes early, which wasn't unusual. What was unusual was the fact that he'd been awake for hours, lying in bed staring at the ceiling, replaying last night.

Brooke's kitchen. Her smile. The way she'd pulled him close and kissed him like she meant it.

He pocketed his keys and headed inside, whistling some tune he didn't even recognize.

"Hey," a guy said, getting out of the truck parked next to him. "Shop open yet?"

Tyler checked his watch. "You're a few minutes early, but the lights are on." He smiled at the man and realized he looked familiar, though he couldn't place him.

"Mind if I follow you in?"

"Might as well, but you may need to wait a minute or two if Sue doesn't have the computer up yet."

"No problem."

As expected, the front door was unlocked. Robert was behind the counter and gave Tyler a nod and a smile when he saw him. His eyes traveled to the man with him, and his smile faltered.

"Something I can help you with?" Robert's tone was stiff and more businesslike than usual.

"Yeah, uh . . . " the man hesitated.

"Henry, isn't it?" Robert asked.

Tyler looked to the man, putting the face and name together. Henry, the game warden. The one who had worked with Edi and Adam on the day they found Sheila and who, according to Sue and Robert, was also at Sheila's funeral and used to date her.

What is he doing here?

"Yep. Henry Ayers. I want to order a case of oil." He fished in his pocket and pulled out a piece of paper, handing it to Robert.

Robert shrugged. "I can order it for you, but it's just a common grade. You can buy it off the shelf at the box store down the road. Cheaper there too."

"Okay, then." Henry took his note back before stepping toward the door. His gaze traveled to Tyler. "Take care of yourself, Tyler."

Henry gave a short nod and pushed the door open.

"That was weird," Robert said, shaking his head, as they watched the man walk toward his truck.

"Did he just threaten me?" Tyler muttered.

"Might have," Robert agreed with a nod.

Tyler shook his head and got to work on the job waiting in bay two. The morning passed quickly, the familiar rhythm of work settling his mind. The thing with Henry was weird, but his time with Brooke last night still occupied his thoughts. Every twenty minutes or so, he'd find himself reaching for his phone.

He'd pull it out, stare at the blank screen, and type a message.

Had a great time last night.
Delete.
Thanks for dinner. I can't stop thinking about
Delete.
Hey, just wanted to say

Delete.

What was wrong with him? He'd faced down murder accusations, survived losing everything, and rebuilt his entire life. But texting a woman he'd kissed made him feel like a nervous teenager.

Play it cool. Don't come on too strong. Give her space.

He shoved the phone back in his pocket and focused on the brake pads.

"You've checked that phone about forty times," Robert said, appearing beside the car. "Why don't you just call her?"

"I'm working."

"You're obsessing." Robert's grin was infuriating. "Just text her. What's the worst that could happen?"

Tyler didn't answer. Because the worst that could happen was that she'd realize getting involved with him was a mistake. That the reality of dating someone accused of murder was too much. That last night had been a moment of weakness she regretted in the light of day.

"What have you got to lose?" Robert said, walking away. "Think about it."

Tyler did think about it—for an entire hour, while he finished what he was working on and then moved on to the next car. His phone stayed in his pocket, a constant weight against his leg.

Finally, at noon, he wiped his hands on a shop rag. "I'm going to grab lunch. Want me to pick up something?"

"Subs from Riverside?" Sue suggested. "Haven't had those in a while."

"Sounds good. Robert?"

"I'm in. Thanks, Tyler."

After taking their sandwich orders, Tyler headed to his truck.

He climbed in and reached for the keys. That's when he saw it.

A piece of paper, folded once, was tucked under the windshield wiper on the driver's side.

He got out and pulled the paper free.

Generic printer paper. Plain black text.

You should've stayed away. You have blood on your hands. Who's next?

Tyler read it twice. Three times. The words didn't change.

You have blood on your hands.

Jen. Garrett. The fire. Sheila? Someone was throwing that in his face. Someone who thought he was guilty, who wanted him to know they were watching.

He scanned the parking lot. There were a few cars belonging to customers, but the street beyond was mostly empty except for a handful of vehicles. No one was watching. Not that he could see, at least.

Who's next?

Brooke.

His chest constricted. He looked around the parking lot again, more carefully this time. Someone had been there. Someone had put this on his truck while he was working fifteen feet away.

Henry the game warden. He'd threatened him earlier, subtle but there, even Robert had noticed it. Now this?

Tyler's hands shook as he pulled out his phone. He didn't care about playing it cool anymore. Didn't care about seeming desperate or overeager. He needed to know Brooke was okay.

Hey. Just wanted to say dinner last night was great. Thanks for having me over.

He hit send before he could second-guess the message. It was weak and generic, not what he wanted to say. But it was something, a way to check on her without alarming her.

He stared at the screen, willing her to respond. Thirty seconds. A minute. Two minutes.

Nothing.

She's at work, he reminded himself. *Probably busy with the lunch crowd. She'll respond when she can.*

But the panic didn't ease.

Tyler folded the note carefully and shoved it in his pocket, then climbed back in the truck. He needed to get lunch. Robert and Sue were expecting it. And sitting there obsessing over a threatening note wasn't going to help anything.

I'll swing by the coffee shop. See if I can see her through the window. Maybe check the alley for her car.

Driving past the alley, her SUV was right where it should be. That eased the pounding in his heart a little. He took a left to drive in front of the building. He couldn't see inside the window, but the door opened as someone went in. They did look busy. Maybe he should stop and pick up bagel or croissant sandwiches instead. He'd heard they were good from Irma Brew.

Get a grip, Tyler, he told himself as he kept going up Grand Avenue. He drove toward Riverside Subs on autopilot, his mind racing. The note was typed. Generic. It might have been from Henry, but it could've come from anyone. But someone had put it on his truck in the middle of the day, in a public parking lot, without being seen.

Or maybe they had been seen. Maybe someone noticed but didn't think anything of it. A piece of paper on a windshield could be a flyer, an advertisement, anything.

Tyler stopped at a red light and checked his phone again.

Still nothing from Brooke.

His chest felt tight. He forced himself to breathe. She was fine. She was at work. It's busy, he'd seen that with his own eyes. She'd text back when she had a chance.

Movement caught his eye. It was a sheriff's SUV. Deputy Adam Boverman sat in the driver's seat, watching Tyler.

Their eyes met. Adam didn't look away, didn't pretend he wasn't watching. Just sat there, obvious and unapologetic.

Tyler's grip tightened on the steering wheel. Had Adam put the note on his truck? Was this some kind of intimidation tactic, trying to scare him into leaving town or confessing to something he didn't do?

But even as the thought formed, Tyler dismissed it. Adam was a lot of things—obsessive, convinced of Tyler's guilt, inappropriate in his pursuit of Brooke—but he wasn't subtle. If Adam wanted to threaten Tyler, he'd do it face to face, with his badge visible and his authority clear.

This note was different. Sneakier. Someone who wanted to stay hidden.

Could be Henry, but if so, why stop by the shop this morning with some lame story of ordering oil?

The light turned green, and Tyler drove on, leaving Adam in his rearview mirror.

Maybe Adam had seen something. Maybe he'd been watching the shop, watching Tyler, and had noticed someone messing with his truck.

Tyler almost turned around, almost pulled over to ask. But what was the point? Adam would either deny seeing anything or use it as another reason Tyler was guilty.

People are threatening you because they know what you did.

Not worth it.

Tyler pulled into Riverside Subs, placed the order, and checked his phone while he waited.

Still nothing.

The panic was building now, irrational but impossible to shake. The note said *who's next,* and all he could think about was Brooke, about someone watching them last night, seeing them together, and deciding she was a target.

His phone buzzed.

Tyler nearly dropped it as he pulled it out of his pocket.

Thanks for coming over. I had a really good time. :)

Intense relief flooded through him. She was okay. She was at work, slammed with customers, but she'd taken the time to respond.

She was okay.

Tyler paid for the sandwiches and drove back to the shop, the note in his pocket feeling heavier with every mile. He needed to figure out what to do about it.

He needed to decide whether to tell Brooke.

Back at the shop, he found Robert and Sue in the break room, plates and napkins already set out.

"Perfect timing," Sue said. "I'm starving."

Tyler set the bag on the table but didn't sit down. Instead, he pulled the note from his pocket and handed it to Robert.

"Found this on my truck when I went to get lunch."

Robert read it, his expression darkening. He passed it to Sue without a word.

"Oh no, Tyler," Sue said. "This is a threat."

"Seems to be. I was thinking the game warden might have left it this morning."

"The game warden?" Sue asked, shaking her head.

Robert explained the weird visit before saying, "You need to report this. Henry or whoever left it didn't mean it as a joke."

"Report it to who? Deputy Boverman?" Tyler shook his head. "He'd probably use it as evidence I'm guilty, say I wrote it myself to throw suspicion elsewhere."

"Not to Boverman," Sue said. "To Edi. You two are friends, aren't you? She'll take this seriously."

Tyler wasn't sure she would, but Sue was right that Edi was the better option.

"I'll call her," Sue offered, already reaching for her purse. "I still have her card from when we found— " She stopped, not finishing the sentence: from when they found Sheila's body.

"I'll do it," Tyler said. "This is my problem."

He made the call. Edi answered on the third ring, sounding harried. "Deputy Reeves."

"Edi, it's Tyler. Tyler Gillis."

A pause. "Hey. Everything okay?"

"Not really. Someone left a threatening note on my truck. I think you should see it."

Another pause. "Where are you?"

"Work. The shop."

"I'm in the middle of something, but I'll be there when I can."

Edi showed up around two o'clock, her expression serious as Tyler and Robert entered the office. Sue opened a file folder.

"I put it in here."

Edi read the note, her face giving nothing away. "When did you find this?"

"A couple of hours ago. When I went to lunch. It was under my windshield wiper."

"Anyone see who put it there?"

"Not that I know of. I was working inside. Didn't notice it until I went out."

Sue told her about the visit from the game warden while Edi turned the note over, examining both sides of the paper. "Could've come from anywhere. But Henry?" She made a face and shook her head. "I can't imagine him leaving something like this."

"Well, someone did," Sue said. "Whether it was him or whoever. It's a threat. What are you going to do about it?" Her voice was sharp.

"I'll file a report, make sure it's on record." Edi looked at Tyler. "But honestly? This is probably just a prank. Your name's all over social media right now. People are talking about you in the grocery store, at church, everywhere. Someone probably thought it'd be funny to scare you."

"Funny?" Sue's voice rose. "You think it's funny? 'Who's next?' That's not funny, Deputy. That's dangerous."

"I understand your concern— "

"Do you? Because if something happens to Tyler, or to someone he cares about, and you dismissed this as a prank, how are you going to feel?"

Edi's jaw tightened. "Mrs. Toles, I'm taking this seriously. I'll make sure it's documented. I'll ask about increasing patrols in this area. But the reality is, we get stuff like this sometimes. Especially in high-profile cases. Nine times out of ten, it's nothing."

"And what about the one time it's not nothing?" Sue pressed.

"Then we'll deal with it." Edi pulled a baggie out of a pocket and put the note inside. "In the meantime, I'd suggest you all use precautions. Lock your vehicles. Be aware of your surroundings. Don't go anywhere alone if you can help it."

"That's it?" Sue asked. "Lock your doors and hope for the best?"

"That's all I can do right now. I'm sorry, but without more to go on . . . " Edi trailed off. "Look, Tyler, I know this is scary. But try not to let it get in your head."

Tyler shook his head. Easy for her to say.

Edi left, taking the note with her. The three of them stood in the office.

"She's wrong," Sue said finally. "This isn't a prank. Someone's threatening you."

"Maybe." Tyler wasn't sure what he believed anymore.

"Brooke needs to know," Sue said. "If someone's watching you, if they know about her— "

"We don't know that they do," Robert interrupted. "The note doesn't mention her specifically. Could just be general intimidation."

"Who's next?" Sue repeated. "That's specific enough."

They both looked at Tyler, waiting for him to decide.

He thought about Brooke's smile last night. The way she'd kissed him. The hope he'd felt this morning, fragile and new and terrifying in how much he wanted it.

He thought about Jen and Garrett. About the fire. About how everyone he loved seemed to end up hurt.

What if Edi was wrong? What if this wasn't a prank? What if getting close to Brooke was the worst thing he could do for her?

"I don't know," Tyler said quietly. "I don't know what to do. Maybe I should just, you know, not see her again."

"You can't push her away," Sue said firmly. "Tyler, that woman chose you while knowing you came with baggage. You don't get to make that decision for her."

"But what if knowing me puts her in danger?" Tyler's voice was rough. "What if the person who wrote this goes after her because of me?"

"Or what if they don't? What if you push away the best thing that's happened to you in years because you're too scared to take a chance?"

"Distance might be safer, though," Robert said quietly. "Not forever. Just until this is sorted out. Until we know who killed Sheila and why they're coming after you."

Tyler looked between them. Sue, passionate and certain. Robert, practical and cautious.

Both of them were right. And both of them were wrong.

"I need to think," Tyler said finally.

They let him go, let him retreat to the bay where a simple job waited. Tyler threw himself into work, trying to quiet the war in his head.

He wanted Brooke. Wanted what they'd started building. Wanted to believe he could have something good without destroying it.

But the note in Edi's evidence bag suggested something else.

You have blood on your hands. Who's next?

What if it was Brooke? What if his curse, his poison, his whatever-it-was that killed everyone he loved, reached out and took her too?

Could he live with that? Could he look at himself in the mirror if something happened to her because he'd been too selfish to stay away?

His phone buzzed. It was another text from Brooke.

The running club is planning a trail run this weekend if you want to come. No pressure though. :)

Tyler stared at the message. He could go. Could see her, be near her, and pretend everything was fine.

Or he could stay away, keep his distance and protect her the only way he knew how.

He didn't know which choice was right, or even if there was a right choice.

Chapter 19

Brooke

Brooke laced up her trail runners and checked her watch. She had twelve miles mapped out, a nice, long Saturday run on one of her favorite loops. The weather was perfect—cool enough that she wouldn't overheat, but sunny enough to lift her mood even higher than it already was.

Which was saying something, because lately her mood had been pretty good.

She grabbed her water bottle and headed out, smiling as she thought about the past two weeks. Tyler had told her about the note someone left on his truck—creepy and unsettling, sure—but like Edi said, it was probably just some bored person trying to stir up drama.

Tyler thought it might be the game warden who had shown up the day they found Sheila. He had dated Sheila and even went to her funeral. Plus, he had gone to the shop earlier in the day when the note was left, wanting to order something that Tyler said he could buy anywhere.

Brooke agreed it was weird that he'd shown up at the shop, especially since he had a history with Sheila, but that didn't mean much. Lots of people in town had a history with Sheila.

They had both agreed to be careful, to pay attention, but not to let fear run their lives.

And they hadn't. Tyler had shown up for the trail run that Saturday, keeping pace with the group like he'd been running with them for years. Natural athlete, that man.

He'd been to each Wednesday night run since then, and they'd gone out running on their own a handful of times, even celebrating his birthday together earlier in the month. Dinners, running together, talking, building something that felt real and solid and good.

The trail wound through familiar terrain, pine trees thick on either side, the path well-worn and easy to follow. Brooke settled into her rhythm, breathing steadily, mind drifting.

She'd asked Tyler if he wanted to come today, but the shop was open. They stayed open one Saturday a month, and this was the day. He'd sounded genuinely disappointed when he said he couldn't make it, which made her smile even as she'd told him it was fine, that she'd see him later.

Things were good. Really good. Even Adam had backed off—no more following Tyler around, no more random appearances at the coffee shop or the running club. She liked to think he realized Tyler was innocent. At the very least, he received the message she wasn't interested, so that was a plus.

She felt a little bad that she was spending so much time with Tyler. Gina understood, of course, since she was deep in her own relationship with Nick. But Brooke got the sense that Steph was feeling left out, so they had gone out together for dinner and the community theater's newest production last night.

It was fun. At dinner, they caught up on all sorts of gossip, especially about how Steph was upset over a guy who had recently moved to nearby Elkridge and started a running club there. Brooke thought it sounded like a great thing. Another running club might mean they could do things together.

But Steph said he'd called her, suggesting his new running club and Basin County Running Club plan a weekend run together to get to know each other. He was totally stuck-up and arrogant, and Steph wanted nothing to do with him or his club. He was some sort of failed Olympian and had people in his pocket. He not only started a running club, but he was also planning to start hosting races.

Brooke understood why Steph was upset. She had long dreamed of hosting road and trail races that would draw people not only from the state and region, but eventually as a world-class event. She had come close a few times, but something always got in the way. While she'd been instrumental in organizing dozens of fundraiser runs, turning it into a business was a completely different challenge.

More than once, Brooke and Steph had discussed ways to do a major event on the cheap. Plenty of famous races started with bare-bones funding, but Steph always came up with an excuse as to why they couldn't do it.

And now this guy showed up, planning the very thing Steph had dreamed of, and she couldn't help but take it personally. Brooke decided that reminding Steph she'd had plenty of opportunities for a big race in the past was a bad idea and simply let her talk. Knowing Steph, eventually she'd come to realize the truth.

The play was amazing. It was opening night, and their friend Jocelyn, cofounder of the community theater and a member of their running club, had put on an amazing production. Brooke admired Jocelyn's creativity.

After the play, Steph and Brooke joined the cast for the afterparty, making for a late night. She'd been a little slow to start this morning, but the run was finally starting to feel like it should.

Brooke rounded a bend, her feet automatically finding purchase on the rocky section. She knew this trail well, having run it dozens of times over the years.

She lost her footing as something slammed into her from the side. The world tilted—trees, sky, ground—and then she was down, rocks digging into her shoulder, her breath gone. She groaned. *What just happened?*

A hand clamped around her arm and yanked her across the hard ground. The person was big and strong, dressed in dark clothes with a ski mask covering their face, sunglasses in place.

Brooke screamed and twisted, fighting to break free.

A kick hit her hard in the ribs, stealing her breath. The grip tightened, dragging her deeper into the trees. Away from the trail. Away from anyone who might hear.

No, no, no!

She twisted and kicked out. Her shoe connected with something solid. Her attacker groaned, and their hold loosened just enough. She scrambled free and got to her feet, hands still on the ground.

She pushed off, ready to sprint. She made it two steps before a hand caught her jacket and jerked her backward. She stumbled but caught herself and spun around swinging. Her fist grazed the mask.

The attacker grabbed her wrist and twisted it behind her back. Pain shot up her arm.

She kicked, connecting with a shin. The person didn't even flinch. Didn't make a sound. Not a word, not a grunt, nothing but breathing. She raised her knee and connected again. The attacker made a fist and punched Brooke in the jaw.

Brooke's hands went to her face. The attacker shoved her backward, hard. Her foot caught on a root, and she went down, hitting the ground with a sickening thud. Stars burst across her vision as pain exploded through her skull.

Get up. Have to get up. But her body refused to listen.

The figure loomed above her, vast and imposing. A boot rose into the air, and Brooke hurled herself aside just as it slammed into the ground where she'd been moments before.

"Hey! What's going on?"

"Someone call 9-1-1."

Voices. People on the trail.

The attacker's head snapped toward the sound, then back to her, and then they bolted, crashing through the trees and disappearing.

Brooke lay there, breathing hard, her head screaming with pain. Warm wetness dampened her scalp. Blood.

"Hurry, she needs help."

Hikers. Thank goodness. Brooke tried to sit up but only made it halfway before everything tilted sideways.

"Don't move," a woman's voice said, close now. "You're bleeding. We're calling for help."

"Thank you," Brooke managed. Her voice sounded strange.

"Just stay still, okay? Help's coming."

Brooke closed her eyes. Her head hurt. Everything hurt. But she was alive. She'd fought back, and she was alive.

She closed her eyes and let herself relax.

★★★★★

180

The emergency room was too bright, too loud, too much. Brooke sat on the exam table, trying not to move her head as Gina worked on cleaning the laceration.

"This is going to need stitches," Gina said, her professional mask firmly in place. But Brooke could hear the worry underneath. "Probably four or five."

"Okay."

"Brooke." Gina's hands stilled. "What happened out there?"

"I told you. I've told everyone. They came out of nowhere. I don't know who. They wore a ski mask."

Gina's expression darkened. "Did they— "

"No. They didn't. They just grabbed me and tried to pull me off the trail. I fought back, and then some hikers came, and whoever it was ran away."

"Thank goodness for those hikers." Gina resumed cleaning, her touch gentle despite the circumstances. "I called Steph to come sit with you. I've got another couple of hours on my shift, but I don't want you alone."

"Gina, I'm fine— "

"You have a concussion. Someone needs to monitor you. It's either Steph, or Phil, or your dad."

Brooke closed her eyes. Phil would lose his mind. Her dad would, too, and that was a whole other level of drama Brooke didn't have the energy for right now.

"Steph," she said quietly.

"Smart choice. She'll be here soon."

While Gina worked, Brooke replayed what had happened. The attack had been so sudden, so violent. Random? Had to be. Wrong place, wrong time, some crazy person on the trail. It didn't make sense otherwise.

But the silence bothered her. The attacker hadn't said a word. Not a threat, not a demand, nothing. Just grabbed her and tried to—what? Drag her away? Hurt her?

"Hey, hey," Gina said, handing Brooke a tissue. "You did great. You got away, and you'll be fine."

"I will," Brooke whispered. "It's just so weird."

They tried to kill me. Brooke pushed the thought away. As Gina said, she was fine. Bruised, battered, and bleeding, but fine.

Gina finished the stitches and moved on to other patients. Brooke lay on the uncomfortable exam table, ready to be discharged. Gina said the doctor wanted to see her again before she was released and to just hang tight.

Steph arrived and sat in the chair beside the exam bed, her usually cheerful face tight with concern.

Deputy Boverman showed up half an hour later. When he entered, Steph stood and went to Brooke's side.

"Ouch," Adam said, making a face. "You're okay?"

She nodded, regretting the movement.

"Don't do that," Steph said, touching her arm.

"No kidding."

Steph turned to Adam. "Brooke gave her statement to the city police. They responded."

"Yeah, the park is inside Irma city limits. I'm following up to determine if it's connected to any of our county cases."

"Such as?" Brooke asked, narrowing her eyes.

"Can you walk me through what happened?"

"I'm sure you can get a copy of the report." Steph smiled, but there was a bite to her tone.

"It's fine," Brooke said. "I'll tell him." She kept her tone even as she described the attack—the figure in dark

182

clothes, the ski mask and dark glasses, the fighting, the hikers, everything.

"Can you describe the attacker's build?" he asked.

"Tall. Maybe six feet? Big, strong."

"Did he say anything? Make any sounds?"

"Nothing. Complete silence the entire time."

"Where was Tyler Gillis today?"

"Really?" Steph shook her head.

Brooke blinked. "What? Why?"

"Tyler Gillis. Where was he?"

"At work. Why would you— "

"Someone attacks you on a trail, and you don't think it's relevant that you've been dating a man accused of murder?"

"That's seriously inappropriate." Steph's voice held a note of warning.

Adam ignored her, his eyes fixed on Brooke. "You've been spending time together."

"That's not— " Brooke stopped herself. *Stay calm. Stay polite. Don't engage.* "Tyler didn't attack me. He was at work."

"You sure about that? Because from where I'm standing, this looks like a pattern. Tyler's connected to two dead women, one of them his own wife, and now someone attacks you right after you start dating him."

"So we're back to this again?" Brooke asked.

Steph took a step forward. "Deputy Boverman, I think you need to leave. Brooke's been through enough without you making accusations."

"I'm not making accusations. I'm doing my job." Adam's jaw was tight as he kept his focus on Brooke. "Someone attacked you. Don't you want to know who?

Don't you want to consider the possibility that the man you're defending isn't who you think he is?"

Brooke looked at him, at the intensity in his eyes, the certainty. She was foolish to think he'd moved on from accusing Tyler. He sincerely believed he was dangerous, that he was somehow behind what happened today.

"Tyler didn't do this." She pressed her fingers to her temples.

"How do you know?"

"Because I know him."

"You thought you knew Kelsey too."

The room went silent. Even Steph looked shocked at the low blow.

Brooke felt something cold settle in her chest. "That's not fair."

"Fair?" Adam's voice rose. "What's not fair is that I'm trying to protect you and you won't listen. What's not fair is watching you make the same mistakes over and over— "

Steph stepped between Brooke and Adam. "This is inappropriate."

"Doing my job is not inappropriate."

"Let's see what the sheriff thinks about the manner in which you are doing your job."

Adam stared at Brooke for another long moment, then turned and left.

Steph reached for Brooke's hand. "That was intense."

"Threatening to call the sheriff, Steph. Really?" Brooke let out a breath.

"Well . . . " Steph shrugged. "Obviously, it worked. Boverman left." She paused and met Brooke's gaze. "He really does think Tyler is guilty. Thinks he killed Sheila and his family."

"He's not."

"You're sure?"

"I know him, plus Phil believes him. And you know how Phil is."

"Phil's been wrong before." Steph waggled her eyebrows.

"Don't tell him that." Brooke smiled. Steph and Phil had casually dated several years earlier. He'd broken up with her, saying he didn't think they wanted the same things. Truth was, he couldn't keep up with her, and he was embarrassed to admit it. "Will you grab me my phone?"

"For?"

"I'm calling Tyler."

Steph hesitated before shuffling through the plastic bag holding Brooke's personal belongings. There wasn't much, only what she had on her when the paramedics arrived. Her car was still in the parking lot. She'd need to get that later.

"Thanks." Brooke swiped the phone until she found his number. It rang four times, then went to voicemail.

"Hey, it's me. Can you call me when you get this? It's important."

She hung up and tried the shop. The line rang, then an automated message: "Thank you for calling Morgan's Auto Repair. We're currently closed. Our hours are— "

Closed? But Tyler said they were open today. He said that's why he couldn't come on the run.

Brooke checked the time. 1:15. Maybe they'd closed early?

She called his cell again. Voicemail.

"Tyler, it's me again. I really need to talk to you. Please call me back."

Gina came back in, her shift finally over. "Ready to go? You're staying with me tonight."

"I should go home."

"Too bad. You're concussed and shouldn't be alone." Gina's tone left no room for argument. "Come on. Nick is making dinner. Want to join us, Steph?"

"What time?"

"Six?"

Steph checked her watch. "I don't think so. I've got a run to get in."

Gina shook her head. "Not today. Not after . . . " She gestured toward Brooke. "They're still out there."

"Joe's going with me."

Gina sighed. "Fine."

Brooke let herself be led out, Steph walking on her other side.

After she got settled into Gina's car, Brooke tried Tyler's number one more time. Voicemail. Again.

Where was he?

Chapter 20

Tyler

Tyler wiped his hands on a shop rag and surveyed the parts spread across the workbench. Three hours of solid work, and he was finally making progress. The familiar rhythm of diagnosis and repair had kept his mind occupied, kept him from checking his phone every five minutes like some lovesick teenager.

Not that he wasn't lovesick. He definitely was. But he'd left his phone in the office on purpose, forcing himself to focus on work instead of wondering if Brooke had texted.

"I'm heading out," Robert called from the bay entrance. "The machine's on, so don't worry about the phone. Nice to have a slow day today so we can shut down early. You good to lock up?"

"Yeah, no problem."

"Sue's making pot roast. You're welcome to join us."

"Thanks, but I'm good." Tyler gestured at the transmission. "I want to finish this up."

Robert studied him for a moment. "You've been working straight through lunch. Everything okay?"

"Fine. Just focused."

"Uh-huh." Robert didn't push, but his expression held a question. "Don't stay too late. And eat something that isn't from a vending machine."

"Yes, sir."

After Robert left, Tyler allowed himself another thirty minutes before admitting he needed a break. His back ached from hunching over the workbench, and his hands were cramping. He needed to call it a day and finish this on Monday. Like Robert said, it was nice to have a slow day once in a while.

He headed to the office, flipping on the light and dropping into the desk chair. His phone sat on the cluttered desk where he'd left it earlier.

Seven missed calls.

Tyler's stomach dropped. He grabbed the phone and scrolled through the notifications. Three calls from Brooke. Two from Gina. One from a number he didn't recognize. One from Nick.

His hands shook as he pulled up the voicemails.

He listened to Brooke's first message: "Hey, it's me. Can you call me when you get this? It's important."

Her voice sounded off. Strained.

Second message: "Tyler, it's me again. I really need to talk to you. Please call me back."

More urgent now. Something was wrong.

Tyler's heart pounded as he listened to Gina's voicemail.

"Tyler, it's Gina. Brooke was attacked on the trail this morning. She's okay, bruised and concussed but okay. She's at my place, and she's asking for you. Please call me back."

The phone slipped from his hand and clattered onto the desk.

Attacked.

Brooke had been attacked.

The note. The threat. This was his fault. Someone had been watching him, had seen him with Brooke, had decided to hurt her because of him.

Tyler grabbed his phone and keys and ran for the truck, his mind racing with fragments of thoughts. Attacked. Concussed. At Gina's place. Brooke asking for him.

The drive to Gina's house took less than ten minutes but felt like hours. Every red light was torture, every slow driver an obstacle. His hands gripped the steering wheel so tightly his knuckles went white.

Images kept flashing through his mind. Brooke on that trail. Someone grabbing her. Someone hurting her. And he hadn't been there. Hadn't protected her. Hadn't even known she was in danger.

Just like before. Just like when the fire took Jen and Garrett.

He'd been hiking that day. Out in the mountains, enjoying the solitude, completely unaware that his entire life was literally burning to the ground. By the time he'd gotten home, the firefighters were already there. The house was little more than charred timbers and ash.

And his family was gone.

Tyler pulled into Gina's driveway and killed the engine, sitting for a moment to collect himself. He couldn't fall apart. Not now. Brooke needed him, and he needed to be strong enough to be there for her.

Even if this was his fault. Even if she'd be safer if he left town and never came back.

He climbed out of the truck and approached the front door. Before he could knock, it opened. Gina stood there, her expression tight with concern.

"She looks pretty rough, but she'll heal," Gina said quietly. "Where were you?"

"Working. My phone was in the office. I didn't— " His voice cracked. "I didn't know."

Gina's expression softened slightly. "She's on the couch."

Tyler stepped inside. The house was warm and comfortable, the kind of place that felt like a home. Nick stood near the kitchen, arms crossed, watching him with an unreadable expression.

And there, on the couch, was Brooke.

The sight of her hit him like a physical blow. A bandage covered part of her head, stark white against her dark hair. Bruises were already forming on her arms. Her face was pale, drawn with pain and exhaustion.

But when she saw him, her eyes brightened.

"You're here," she said, and the relief in her voice nearly undid him.

"I'm here." Tyler crossed the room and knelt beside the couch, taking her hand carefully. "I'm so sorry. I didn't have my phone. I didn't know— "

"It's okay. You're here now."

"What happened?"

Brooke told him, her voice calm despite the tremor underneath.

With every word, Tyler's guilt grew heavier. This wasn't random. Someone had targeted her deliberately. And they'd been silent because they didn't want her to recognize their voice. They knew her. Brooke knew them.

"This is my fault," Tyler said quietly. "The note. It wasn't a prank. Someone was watching me. They saw us together and decided to hurt you. I thought, since it'd been two weeks, we were safe."

"You don't know this was related to the note."

"You don't know it's not." He looked at their joined hands. "Could it have been that game warden? Did you get a good enough— "

"I don't know who it was," she interrupted. "Honestly, I don't even really remember what he looked like. I wasn't thinking clearly the day we found Sheila, and I can't picture him."

"Henry. His name is Henry . . . um, Ayers, I think."

"Sorry. I can't put the name with a face. I don't know everyone in town, you know." She gave a weak laugh.

Tyler sighed. "Maybe I should leave. At least for a little while. If I'm gone, maybe whoever's doing this will stop."

"Don't you dare." Brooke's voice was sharp despite her exhaustion. "This isn't your fault. If you leave, they win. And we lose. And I won't lose, Tyler. I won't quit."

"But— "

"No." She squeezed his hand. "You're not responsible for some psycho attacking me. You're not responsible for what happened to your family. And you're certainly not responsible for Sheila. Bad things happen, and they're not always someone's fault."

Tyler wanted to believe her, and he knew in his head that she was probably right. His heart ached at the thought of walking away, yet the fear that she had been hurt because of him held him back.

"Gina said you're staying here?" he asked.

"Tonight. She doesn't think I should stay alone since I hit my head.

"Good. I'll stay too. On the couch."

Brooke looked at Gina, who lifted her shoulder. "Fine by me."

"Is that okay with you?" Tyler asked Brooke.

"Absolutely."

A knock at the door made everyone look in that direction. Nick moved to answer it, peering through the window first before opening the door.

"It's Boverman," Nick said in a loud whisper.

"The deputy?" Gina asked, looking at Brooke. "Was he going to get another statement?"

Brooke shook her head. "Not that I know of."

"He's out of uniform," Nick said. "Want me to get rid of him?"

"Please," Brooke replied. "I'm not up for his . . . anything."

"No problem, Cuz." Nick winked before opening the door. "Hey, there. Something— "

Adam pushed his way inside. His eyes immediately found Tyler.

"What is he doing here?" Adam's voice was low and dangerous.

"Hey, dude," Nick said, putting his hand on Adam's chest. "You weren't invited inside."

"Get your hands off me unless you want to be arrested for battery on an officer."

Nick removed his hand as he said, "Are you here on official business? Out of uniform?" He looked out the still-open door. "And driving your personal car?"

"As far as you're concerned, I'm always on business."

"Pretty sure that's not how it works."

"Deputy, this isn't a good time," Gina said, moving toward the men.

"I want to know why a murder suspect is in your house with Brooke." Adam pushed past Gina, his attention fixed on Tyler. "Did you do this? Did you attack her?"

Tyler stood slowly, keeping his hands visible. "I was at the shop. Working. Robert can verify that."

"Right. Like he wouldn't lie for you?"

"Deputy Boverman, that's enough," Gina said sharply.

But Adam wasn't listening. He stepped closer to Tyler, his face twisted with anger and something that looked almost like desperation.

"You killed your wife and kid. You killed Sheila. Now you're terrorizing Brooke. Tried to kill her. When are you going to admit what you are?"

The words hit like bullets. Tyler felt something crack open inside him, something he'd kept carefully sealed for years.

"I never touched my family," Tyler said, his voice raw. "I loved them. I would've died for them."

"That's what they all say. Every abuser, every killer—they all claim they loved their victims right up until they're convicted."

"I didn't— "

"The evidence suggests otherwise. The insurance money. The timing. The fact that you left town rather than stay and help find who 'really' did it." Adam's hands clenched into fists. "You're a killer, Gillis. And I'm not going to let you hurt anyone else."

Gina stepped between them. "Get out."

"Not until— "

"Out!" Brooke's voice cut through the tension. She'd sat up on the couch, her face pale but her expression fierce. "Get out of Gina's house. Now."

Adam turned to her. "Brooke, you have to see— "

"I see a deputy harassing someone without evidence. I see you making accusations you can't prove. I see you trying to scare me into believing something that isn't true." Brooke's voice was steady despite the pain she must have been in. "Tyler didn't attack me. He was at work. And even if he wasn't, I know him well enough to know he'd never hurt me."

"You don't know that. You thought you knew Kelsey— "

"Don't," Brooke said sharply. "Don't throw that in my face again. I'm capable of learning from my mistakes without you pointing them out every five minutes."

Adam stared at her for a long moment. Then his expression shifted, became something almost pitying.

"When he hurts you—and he will—don't say I didn't warn you." He turned to Tyler. "I'm watching you. Every move. And when you slip up, I'll be there."

He left, slamming the door behind him.

The silence that followed was deafening. Tyler realized he was shaking, his entire body trembling with the effort of not falling apart.

"Tyler." Brooke's voice was gentle. "Come back and sit beside me."

He crossed back to the couch, sitting carefully beside her. She took his hand again, her grip surprisingly strong.

"I know you didn't do this," she said quietly. "No matter what Adam says. No matter what anyone says."

Tyler couldn't speak past the lump in his throat. He held her hand like it was the only thing keeping him anchored.

That night, after Gina helped Brooke to the guest room and Nick set up blankets on the couch before heading off to his own place, Tyler lay in the darkness and tried to process everything.

Brooke had been hurt. Someone had attacked her, tried to drag her away, tried to do something he couldn't let himself think about too carefully.

And it was probably his fault.

But she'd defended him. Told Adam to leave. Chose to trust him despite everything Adam had said, despite all the reasons she had to doubt.

He closed his eyes and thought about the fire. About Jen's smile. About Garrett's laugh. About the life he'd lost and the questions that had haunted him ever since.

Someone had killed his family. Killed Sheila. Left a threatening note on his truck. Someone had attacked Brooke.

Were they connected? After all these years, had the person who destroyed his life come back to finish what they'd started?

Tyler didn't know. But lying there in the darkness, listening to the quiet sounds of the house settling around him, he made a decision.

He wasn't running this time. Wasn't leaving town to escape the whispers and suspicion. He wasn't letting fear drive him away from the first real connection he'd felt since Jen died.

He was staying. He was fighting. And he was going to protect Brooke, no matter what it cost him.

Chapter 21

Brooke

Brooke woke to the fluttering of unfamiliar curtains and a dull throb behind her eyes. For a moment, she couldn't place where she was. Then her memory came crashing back—the trail, the attack, the pain, Gina's guest room.

She gingerly touched the bandage on her head. Tender. Too tender.

Voices drifted from somewhere else in the house, low murmurs punctuated by the occasional laugh. Brooke sat up slowly, her ribs aching from where she'd been kicked. They'd done X-rays; nothing was broken, but she was bruised and needed to take it easy. She stood, testing her balance. Her head protested, but the world didn't spin. Progress.

The hall bathroom was her first stop. The mirror told a tale that brought tears to her eyes. The bandage covered part of her head. Bruises spread along her jawline, and a small cut marked her cheek. "You, my dear, are a mess," she whispered to her reflection.

After she finished in the bathroom, she returned to her room to change into sweatpants and a top Gina left for her, along with a pair of heavy socks. Deciding she looked as good as possible considering everything, she padded down the hallway to the kitchen.

Tyler stood at the stove, spatula in hand. Gina leaned against the counter with a coffee mug, dressed in scrubs. Nick sat at the table, wearing work clothes.

"Morning," Brooke said from the doorway.

Three heads turned. Tyler's expression shifted immediately—concern mixed with relief.

"Hey." He set down the spatula and crossed to her in two strides. "How are you feeling? Is your head okay? Did you sleep?"

"I'm fine. My head hurts, but I slept okay."

His hand came up like he wanted to check her bandage, then it dropped. "You're just in time, I'm making eggs."

Brooke made her way to the table, shooting a glance at Gina. "Gina's letting you cook?"

"He insisted," Gina replied. "I tried to tell him I'm not much of a breakfast person . . . "

"But I convinced her I make amazing cheesy scrambled eggs."

Brooke sat at the table beside Nick, who studied her with the same worried expression he'd worn last night.

"I came over to check on you," Nick said. "I've got a side job I'm supposed to do today, but I wanted to make sure you were okay first. I can push it off."

"I'm fine. Really."

"She says that a lot," Tyler observed from the stove.

"It's a family trait," Nick said. "Stubbornness runs deep in the Davies bloodline."

"I'm working triage today. I've got a twelve-hour shift starting at nine," Gina said. "I tried to find someone to fill in for me, but . . . " She shrugged. "I'm going to try a few other people, see if I can at least get off early."

"Thanks," Brooke said. "I'll probably get myself together and head home."

"I'd rather you didn't," Gina replied. "Wait until I get back, okay? Or stay another night. That might be best."

Tyler set a plate in front of her—scrambled eggs, toast, and a handful of grapes. Her stomach betrayed her with a low, appreciative rumble.

"Thank you," Brooke said.

He passed plates to Nick and Gina before settling into the chair across from Brooke with his own plate. For a few minutes, they ate in comfortable silence.

"You're right about the eggs," Gina admitted. "They're delicious. More savory than I expected."

"My secret ingredient," Tyler replied, before taking a sip of coffee.

"Secret, huh? I think I'll need the recipe." Gina glanced at her watch. "I need to scoot." She met Brooke's gaze. "I really do want you to stay here today."

"I can stay and keep an eye on her." Nick offered.

"Don't you have that job?" Brooke asked.

Nick shrugged. "I can skip it if you need me."

Brooke looked at Tyler, who met her eyes. "Do you mind staying with me? It's Sunday. You don't work Sundays, right?"

"Right." Tyler's voice was careful, like he was trying not to seem too eager. "I can stay. If that's what you want."

Nick looked between them, his expression shifting from concern to something else. Something accepting. "Okay, then. But, Brooke, call me if you need anything. Anything at all."

"I will. Promise."

Gina and Nick left together a few minutes later, with Gina extracting promises from both Tyler and Brooke that they'd call if anything changed, if Brooke felt worse, or if they needed anything.

Then it was just the two of them in the quiet house.

Tyler cleared the breakfast dishes while Brooke stayed at the table, nursing a second cup of coffee. It was easy, the way he moved around the kitchen while she watched, the quiet between them comfortable instead of awkward.

"You're good at that," Brooke observed as he loaded the dishwasher.

"At what?"

"Being in a kitchen. Making breakfast. The whole domestic thing."

Tyler smiled. "Survival skill. When you're on your own long enough, you either learn to cook or live on takeout."

"I'm terrible at cooking."

"I find that hard to believe."

"It's true. I can make coffee and bake pastries, but actual cooking? Meh. I don't really enjoy it." She took another sip of coffee. "I mean, I cook, of course, so I don't starve, but . . . " She let her voice fade away as she realized she was rambling. *Brilliant, Brooke. Absolutely brilliant.*

She glanced at the counter where her phone sat in a charging cradle. As she slid her chair back, Tyler turned. "Can I get you something?"

"I was going to check my phone. Gina insisted it stay out here on do not disturb . . . you know how she was last night."

"She cares about you. You're fortunate to have a friend like her. Nick too. I know you're cousins, but you seem like you're friends too."

"We are friends," she agreed. "He's only been in town a few months. He had a rough time for a while. Bad breakup, and he was trying to find his footing. But he's good now."

"They were telling me a little about things earlier."

"You mean about how they met? How we all almost died? Those things?"

"Those things." He grabbed her phone. "I know you mentioned it, and I read the articles about it, but wow, Brooke. The whole thing sounds like it was crazy."

He passed her the phone, and when their fingers touched, a jolt shot through her, quickening her pulse. He hesitated for a fraction of a second, his fingers lingering before he pulled his hand back.

Brooke cleared her throat and switched on her phone. Messages started coming in right away. Three texts from Joe, two from Steph, one from Jocelyn, a bunch from the running club and the coffee shop staff, and even a few from customers.

Her dad had left a long, rambling voicemail, offering his place for a few days while she recovered. Phil's text was short and to the point: *Gotta be careful, sis.*

She typed quick responses, assuring them she was fine and thanking them for checking in. She needed to call her dad, but for now, she sent a simple message: *I'm okay. Stayed at Gina's last night. I'll call you later.*

Tyler finished the dishes and joined her at the table, his chair angled so he faced her instead of sitting across, close enough that their knees touched.

"Tell me about your coffee shop," Tyler said. "The real stuff. Not the social media version or what you tell customers."

So she did. She told him about the regulars who lined up before the doors were even unlocked, about Mr. Landers and how he ordered the same thing every single day until one morning he didn't. "Now he orders something different almost every time. Sometimes it's the daily special, but usually it's just whatever sounds good to him that day. It's odd, but I think he's enjoying the adventure."

"Adventures in coffee." Tyler smiled. "I can see that."

She talked about the morning rush—how it had its own rhythm and how she could usually tell what kind of day the town was having just by the way people asked for their coffee.

Tyler listened. Really listened. He wasn't waiting for a pause or steering the conversation somewhere else. He just stayed with her, like he was happy to let her talk and wanted to hear all of it.

"What about you?" Brooke asked. "Tell me about the garage. What's it like working there?"

"Satisfying," Tyler said after a moment. "Something's broken, you figure out why, you fix it. It makes sense in a way most things don't."

"Robert seems like a good boss."

"He is. He and Sue both. They took a chance on me by keeping me on." Tyler's expression shifted. "Robert's known about my history from the beginning. I insisted he know about . . . about what people might say."

"Boverman seems to think they'd cover for you. Lie for you."

"Why would they? Because they need a mechanic?" He shook his head. "That makes little sense. They've got two others."

"But they're only part-timers, right?"

"For now. Andre shows a lot of promise. He's taking some classes at the college. Robert's even paying for those. He's a good kid, and both Robert and Sue know it."

Brooke smiled. She knew Andre as an awkward teen who used to come into the coffee shop with a group of other awkward teens, part of their homeschool community. He started working at the auto shop under Stan Morgan for an on-the-job training program. She hadn't seen Andre in a few years and was glad to hear he was doing well. She shared how she knew him and asked, "How old is Andre now?"

"About twenty, I guess. He doesn't seem too bothered to be working with an accused killer either."

"He probably realizes it's nothing but a rumor."

Tyler shrugged. "Maybe. I haven't asked. It's not the kind of conversation we have in the break room. At least it wasn't. Now the whole Sheila mess makes break room chitchat weird."

Brooke reached for his hand. "But they believe in you. They know you didn't do any of the things Adam is accusing you of."

His fingers laced with hers. "I hope not. I mean, they say they believe me. But sometimes . . . I know I'm expecting a lot of them. Of you."

"You're not expecting that much," she whispered, her eyes meeting his with steady resolve. "I believe you."

"Thanks," he said.

After an awkward few beats, she said, "Mind if we move to the couch? I'm pretty sore, and this chair isn't doing my aching body any good."

"Sorry, of course. I should've thought about that. Do you need some painkillers?"

"I took some when I got up, so I guess I'm set for another couple of hours."

They moved to the living room and settled on the couch, close enough that Brooke could feel the heat radiating off him.

There were a few minutes of uncomfortable silence until Tyler cleared his throat. "Yesterday's run, was it part of your actual Moose Range Run 100 training, or are you still in what you called your building phase?"

She shrugged. "Still base building. I took a few weeks off after doing the fifty-two-mile version of the Moose Range Run back in June. My body and mind needed time to rest and recover. I'll start my actual training plan in January." She paused. "Probably."

"Probably?"

"I don't know for certain," Brooke admitted. "I've been thinking, after everything that's happened . . . maybe I'm not cut out for it."

"What do you mean?"

"I mean, I tried the 100 before, and I had to drop at the turnaround because I timed out. I was a few minutes late for the cutoff, and they wouldn't let me continue."

"That had to sting."

"You have no idea. I mean, I knew the rules going in, of course, but I'm not going to lie, I thought maybe I'd get there and they'd let me slide. So anyway, my name is listed under the DNF section. Did not finish. Right there for everyone to see until the end of time." She forced a smile, though the reality of it still bothered her.

"But you came back this year. You knew you could do it, and you signed up again."

She laughed as she shook her head. "I was a mental case. I'd made an unrealistic training schedule and drove myself too hard. My mind was a mess, and my body was trying to give out, but I still kept pushing. Did Gina tell you why we were caught in the storm up at Bearwater?"

He nodded. "She said it came in early. You all thought you had time to get the run done."

"She's being kind. It's true the storm came in early, but instead of turning around and heading back, like a sane person would've done, I insisted we keep going. I was going to make it to the top of the mountain no matter what. It was only a little over ten miles round trip, and we were close to halfway on the outbound when the snow started. I convinced myself we could make it to the turnaround and back before it got bad."

"But you couldn't."

"No, no way. We were at the steepest part. Joe wasn't used to the kind of climb we needed. The snow and wind were awful. We could've died right there if Gina and Nick hadn't taken over. Somehow, they brought me to my senses."

"They didn't mention any of that," he said, taking her hand. "They've got your back, Brooke."

"Yeah, they do. That day and every day since. Joe too. He wrote the article about what happened up there, and it was very fair. He didn't even completely throw Kelsey under the bus, though she probably deserved it. And his article helped me convince the organizers of the Moose Range Run 100 to allow me to drop to the shorter distance. They don't usually allow a distance change."

"It all worked out pretty well."

She stared at their intertwined fingers. When she finally spoke, her voice was soft. "Except now, I'm rethinking things."

"Rethinking what?"

She could hear the hesitation in his tone. She gave his hand a squeeze. "About the Moose Range Run. Things have been . . . weird lately. And now, with being attacked on the trail yesterday, I'm wondering if I have it in me to do the necessary training."

"Gina said you'll heal, that you'll be fine in a few weeks. If you're not starting your full training until January, you should be completely recovered."

"That's not what I meant. I'm more concerned about the mileage needed. About going out on the trails for a full day on my own. I'm thinking I should just stick to shorter distances. I need to be realistic about my limitations."

Tyler was quiet for a moment. When he spoke, his voice was gentle but firm. "You're the strongest person I know."

Brooke laughed, but it came out bitter. "I'm not strong. I'm terrified half the time."

"Being strong doesn't mean you're never scared. It means you do hard things anyway." He shifted closer. "You got back up after last year. You survived what happened at Bearwater. You fought off your attacker yesterday. That's not someone who gives up."

"But what if I fail again?"

"Then you fail. And you get back up. Again." Tyler's thumb traced circles on the back of her hand. "Look, I'm not a runner like you are. I've never done anything farther than that trail run with the group last week. What was that? About five miles? But I could help you train when you're cleared to run again."

"How?"

"I'll ride my bike on the longer distances. Be your support crew. Make sure you're never alone on the trails. Whatever you need."

The gesture hit her harder than it should have. He wasn't trying to fix her fears or tell her what to do. He was offering to be there. To support what mattered to her, even though he didn't fully understand it.

"Why would you do that?" Brooke asked quietly.

"Because it matters to you. Because I want to be there for you." He paused. "Because I care about you."

Something in Brooke's chest gave way as her heart thumped louder.

"You loved your wife. Your son." She wasn't really asking, just confirming what she already knew.

"I did. Very much."

Brooke leaned her head against his shoulder. "I'm not trying to replace her. I want you to know that."

"I know." Tyler's arm came around her shoulders. "Jen wouldn't want me to spend the rest of my life alone. She'd want me to be happy. To find someone who made me laugh again."

"Do I make you laugh?"

"You make me feel alive. Right now, that's better than laughing."

They sat like that for a while, comfortable in the silence. Brooke's hand rested on Tyler's knee, his fingers playing with the ends of her hair.

"I'm obsessive," Brooke said suddenly. "When I get focused on something, I can't let it go. Training plans, work schedules, whatever. I fixate until it consumes me. It's not healthy."

"Everyone has things they struggle with."

"But mine affects other people. I get so wrapped up in training that I push everyone away. My dad complains he barely sees me. Phil gets tired of my constant talk about mile splits and nutrition. Even the running club gets sick of me, and they know better than anyone else how it is. Steph has run several ultramarathons and has her own level of obsessiveness, and I even drive her crazy."

"They still love you. They all called this morning."

"I know. But I scared them. I scared myself." Brooke lifted her head to look at him. "I've made myself a promise that this time I'm not going all looney bin."

The air between them shifted. Brooke became acutely aware of how close they were, how his hand felt against her skin, how his eyes had gone darker.

She leaned in.

The kiss was different from the ones before. Deeper, more certain. His hand slid into her hair, careful of her bandage. Her fingers found his jaw and traced the line of it.

When they broke apart, she reached for him again. Their faces were inches apart. "I'm falling for you," she said, her voice shaky. "I'm really falling for you, and it scares me."

"Why does it scare you?" He pulled back, his face tightening.

"No." She shook her head. "I'm not saying . . . it's just . . . it's been a while since I had anything resembling a relationship."

"I'm scared too," Tyler admitted. "Terrified, actually. What if being near me puts you in danger? What if yesterday's attack was because of me?"

Brooke took his face in both hands. "Then we're both scared. But I'd rather be scared with you than safe without you."

Tyler pulled her close, his arms wrapping around her like he could shield her from everything outside this moment. "I'm not going anywhere. I'd like us to be together. Get to know each other better."

"I'd like that, too," Brooke agreed.

They stayed on the couch, talking and not talking, the conversation flowing naturally from serious topics to lighter ones. Tyler told her about funny things that happened at the garage. Brooke shared stories about difficult customers and the time someone tried to order a pizza at the coffee shop. They took breaks from talking to share kisses like love-starved teenagers.

Then a knock at the door shattered the peace.

Chapter 22

Tyler

The knock came again, harder this time.

"Probably a delivery guy or something," Tyler muttered as he got to his feet.

"On Sunday?" Brooke asked. He caught his own unease mirrored in the wary look she gave him.

"Missionaries?" he said, trying to use a light tone but failing miserably.

She reached for his hand. "Let me answer."

"Nah." He gave her hand a squeeze. "I've got it. You rest."

He crossed to the door and looked through the window.

Adam stood on the porch with two other deputies Tyler didn't recognize. All three wore their uniforms, badges catching the sunlight. Their expressions were serious, official.

Tyler's stomach tightened. Somehow, he doubted this was a social call.

"Who is it?" Brooke whispered.

"Boverman," he replied.

"That man. I'm going to report him for harassment."

"He's not alone this time."

"Not alone? Edi?" Brooke asked, wincing as she stood.

Tyler moved to the door. Cool air rushed in as he opened it.

"Deputy Boverman."

"Gillis." Adam's expression was flat, professional in a way that annoyed him. "We need to talk to you."

"About what?"

"Can we come in?"

Tyler looked back at Brooke. Her face was pale, and her hands were clasped together. "Why are you here, Adam?" she asked.

"Brooke." He nodded. "You should be resting."

"I was. Until you showed up."

Boverman looked back at Tyler. "I asked if we could come in."

Tyler stepped aside, his heart pounding much too loudly. The three deputies entered, their boots heavy on Gina's hardwood floor.

"What's going on?" Brooke asked.

Adam's eyes flicked to her, then back to Tyler. "There's been another murder."

The words hit hard. Tyler exhaled slowly, his chest tightening.

"What?" Brooke's voice was small, barely more than a whisper.

"A woman was found this morning. There's enough similarity to Sheila's murder that we believe they're connected." Adam paused, his eyes locked on Tyler. "Another woman from Irma High School. Graduated the same year as Sheila. Her name was Monique Stanton."

Tyler's mind raced, scrambling through memories that felt fuzzy and distant.

"Monique?" Brooke repeated. "From the craft store?"

The craft store, the building kitty-corner from the auto shop. He and Brooke had been talking about her the other night. She was a friend of Sheila's from high school.

"Edi said you knew her?" Adam asked.

Tyler lifted his hands, palms up. The gesture felt helpless. "It was a small school. Everyone kind of knew everyone."

One of the other deputies spoke for the first time, his voice firm and official. "Deputy Reeves said Monique was one of the people Sheila mentioned. That you'd all go out together. Listen to music or whatever."

"She might have," Tyler said slowly. "She mentioned several names. Some I recognized, some I didn't."

"But you recognize the name Monique Stanton?"

"I guess. She went to school with us, but we weren't friends. I haven't talked to her in years."

"Is that so?"

"Where is Edi?" Tyler asked, looking over Adam's shoulder toward the patrol vehicles outside. The question came out sharper than he intended.

"She's a witness now. Can't have her arresting our prime suspect. Might be accused of a conflict of interest."

Arrest. Prime suspect. The words hit Tyler like ice water.

"I'm a suspect?" Tyler's voice came out harder than he intended. "How do you figure?"

"We need you to come to the station for questioning," Adam said, ignoring the question entirely.

"Am I under arrest?"

"Not yet. But you are expected to cooperate."

Tyler could feel Brooke watching him, could sense her fear mixing with his own. He turned to face her.

Her eyes were wide, her hands still clasped together. She stood frozen by the couch, like she didn't know whether to move closer or back away.

"I didn't do this," Tyler said. The words sounded hollow and desperate even to his own ears.

Brooke nodded, but something flickered across her face—uncertainty and doubt, a question she wasn't asking out loud but that he could see as clearly as if she'd spoken it.

Was she doubting him? After everything they'd said to each other while snuggling on the couch? After the kissing, the promises, the choice to trust each other?

The thought made his chest ache worse than any accusation Adam could level.

"I have to go with them," Tyler said quietly, forcing his voice to stay even. "I'll call you. Okay?"

"Okay." But she didn't meet his eyes. She looked at the floor, at the deputies, anywhere but at him.

Her refusal to meet his eyes hurt more than Adam's smug look, more than the deputies standing next to him like it was already over, more than being named a prime suspect.

Brooke's doubt cut deeper than anything else could.

Tyler grabbed his jacket from where he'd left it on Gina's chair and followed the deputies out. The mid-September air was cool against his face. He climbed into the back of Adam's patrol vehicle, the back door closing with a hollow thunk that sounded too much like a cell door.

The drive to the station was silent except for the crackle of the police radio and the hum of tires on pavement, giving Tyler time to turn everything over in his head. None of it made sense.

Another murder of someone he knew. A death connected to him. Someone was doing this. Someone was killing these women and making it look like he did. The pattern was too perfect, too deliberate. This wasn't a coincidence.

But who? And why?

The only person who came to mind was the game warden. It had to be him. He's probably the same person who attacked Brooke. But why? Why was he doing it? And why frame Tyler?

The station loomed ahead, all concrete and glass and fluorescent lights that made everything look washed out and harsh. Adam pulled into the lot and parked.

He took Tyler into a side door and down a familiar hallway—the same route he'd walked before, when they'd questioned him about Sheila. At least this time he wasn't taken to booking. That was a plus, he supposed.

Same interview room and same uncomfortable chair. A camera in the corner, its red light blinking steadily.

"Have a seat," Adam said.

Tyler sat. The chair was cold even through his jeans, the metal biting into his back.

Adam settled across from him, a closed folder in front of him, a small notepad to the side. One of the other deputies who'd been at the house stood near the door.

Tyler's hands rested on the table. He focused on keeping them still, on not showing how hard his heart was pounding.

"Seems we've done this before," Adam said, his voice maddeningly calm.

"Seems we have. Seems last time I had a lawyer."

Adam shrugged. "You want your lawyer? Fine." He leaned forward. "Guilty people always ask for their lawyer."

Tyler closed his eyes and let out a sigh. He'd watched enough television to know that it was true.

When Tyler didn't reply, Adam continued, "Where were you on Friday night?"

Maybe it'd be best to answer a few questions, and if things started going bad, then he'd ask for his lawyer. Would the guy even come? Tyler wasn't sure, since he still had no idea who'd sent him in the first place.

"Earth to Tyler. You plan on answering, or should I just lock you up?"

"You should talk to that game warden. Henry Ayers."

Adam smirked. "Talk to Henry about what?"

"He dated Sheila. Maybe he dated Monique too? Maybe he— "

"You trying to tell me how to do my job?"

"Someone needs to."

Adam pierced him with a look. "Where were you on Friday night?"

"I was at home."

"Doing what?"

"Watching television." He almost laughed out loud as he remembered the cop show he was watching. Adam could easily play the hard-nosed, obtuse detective.

"I thought you played darts on Friday nights?"

Tyler crinkled his brow. "Sometimes, yeah. Not this week, though. About Henry— "

"We're talking about you. So, no darts on Friday night. What about Saturday morning? Where were you?"

"Work. I got there about eight."

Adam's eyebrows rose. "Eight? I thought when you worked on Saturdays you started at nine?"

"Customers come in at nine. I get there early to get things set up for the day."

"Can anyone verify that?"

"Robert got there around eight thirty."

"And did you have a customer show up at nine?"

"There were people waiting when Robert unlocked the door."

"You take care of them?"

"Robert handled them. They didn't need repair work but were buying things from the store."

"So, no one saw you?"

"I was working under a hood. But later, we had someone come who needed us to check an indicator light."

"What time was that?"

Tyler shrugged. "Around ten, I guess."

"And you helped them?"

"I helped her, yeah."

Boverman made a note. "So, no alibi for Friday night. No one to confirm what time you actually arrived on Saturday morning." Adam leaned back in his chair, the picture of casual confidence. "No playing darts? Going out with your buddies? Out with Brooke?"

"No." Tyler's jaw tightened. "Brooke went out with a friend on Friday night."

"Which friend?"

"Steph. They'd planned it a few days earlier."

"What'd you think about that? Your girl dumping you on a Friday night for a friend."

"Dumping me? Brooke can see her friends whenever she wants."

"Still, that had to sting. Friday night should be date night, right?"

Adam flipped open the folder. Papers rustled, too loud in the quiet room. "Here's what we know. Both victims—Sheila Jones and Monique Stanton—knew you. Both went to Irma High School at the same time as you. Both died after you returned to Basin County."

He looked up, his eyes hard. "Your wife died under suspicious circumstances before you skipped town in a hurry. The pattern is clear."

"There's no pattern. I didn't kill anyone."

"Then explain how two women you knew from high school end up dead within months of your return."

"I can't. I don't know anything about their deaths."

"And the fire?"

Tyler sighed. *How many times do I have to tell this bonehead deputy the same thing?* "The fire was ruled accidental."

"Officially." Adam's smile was cold, satisfied. "But we both know the truth, don't we? You collected the insurance money and ran. Now this."

Tyler's hands clenched into fists under the table. He supposed it looked bad. He could almost even see Adam's perspective—the lack of an alibi for Friday night, only Robert to verify Saturday morning. And Robert was his boss, his friend, someone whose testimony would be seen as biased.

The connections to both victims were undeniable. His history of tragedy followed him like a shadow he couldn't shake.

But seeing it and accepting it were different things.

Someone was setting him up. Someone who knew his history, knew the victims, and knew exactly how to make him look guilty. Someone smart enough to frame him so perfectly that even the woman he was falling for was starting to doubt his innocence.

But who? And why target him specifically? What had he done to deserve this level of calculated destruction?

"I didn't do this," Tyler said, forcing each word out clearly while he held eye contact. "I don't know who did, but it wasn't me."

"That's what they all say."

The interview lasted another hour. Adam asked the same questions in different ways. Where were you? Who can verify? How well did you know them?

Tyler's answers stayed consistent because they were true. But truth didn't seem to matter when suspicion had already taken root.

Adam closed the folder with a snap. "We don't have enough to hold you. *Yet.* But don't leave town, Tyler. We're watching. I'm watching. And when I find that one piece of evidence that ties you to these murders—and I will find it—you're done."

"You won't find anything," Tyler promised. "I'm not involved. Listen to what I'm telling you and you might find the actual killer."

Adam narrowed his eyes. "I've found him."

Tyler glanced at the other deputy, but he was staring off in the distance, purposely avoiding Tyler's gaze.

Finally, Adam stood. "You're free to go. For now."

When Tyler emerged from the station, the sky had already begun to tint toward evening.

He pulled out his phone and dialed Brooke's number.

It rang once. Twice. Three times.

Voicemail.

Tyler ended the call and tried again, his thumb shaking slightly as he pressed her name.

Voicemail.

He stood in the parking lot, phone in hand, the sick feeling in his gut spreading like poison through his veins.

Was she avoiding him? Had she decided he was guilty after all? Had that moment of doubt he'd seen in her eyes grown into certainty during the hours he'd been gone?

The thought made him want to get in his truck and drive. Keep driving until Basin County was a memory, until he could start over somewhere new where no one knew his name or his history.

But he'd tried that already. For twelve years he'd run, and it hadn't worked.

He wasn't running this time.

Even if Brooke had given up on him. Even if everyone in this town thought he was a killer.

He wasn't running.

Chapter 23

Brooke

Brooke arrived at the coffee shop at five to start prep. Becky came in thirty minutes later.

"Are you okay?" Becky said, gesturing to Brooke's bandage and bruises.

"I'll live."

"You should've taken today off."

"Probably," Brooke agreed. "But I need to be here today. Staying home will drive me crazy. I called in one of our part-timers to help out. She'll be in at eight. Then I can take it easy if need be."

"Good plan," Becky agreed.

By seven, when they unlocked the doors, a line had already formed outside.

Rare for a Monday. Rare for any day.

The first customer through the door was Livi Beckett, who usually came in on Wednesdays on her way back from yoga. She exclaimed about Brooke's injuries as she ordered a sugar-free vanilla latte with oat milk, paid, then lingered at the counter instead of moving to the pickup area.

"Terrible about Monique Stanton," Livi said, her voice pitched just loud enough to carry. "Did you know her?"

"Not well." Brooke kept her tone casual as she rang up the next customer.

"They say she went to school with that mechanic, the one who was at Gina's yesterday when the deputies came. Heard you were there too."

Brooke's hands paused on the register. How did Livi know Tyler had been at Gina's house? The answer came immediately: small town. Someone had seen the patrol cars. Someone always saw everything. She loved living in Irma, but some days . . .

"Tyler Gillis," Livi continued. "Poor man lost his wife and child in that fire years back. I didn't live here then, but my friend Rachael did. Now two women from his past turn up dead right after he comes home. Makes you wonder, doesn't it?"

"Medium coffee, black," Brooke said to the next customer, ignoring Livi entirely.

The morning only got worse from there.

Every customer seemed to have an opinion about Tyler, about the murders, about Brooke's involvement. Some were subtle—meaningful looks, careful pauses in conversation. Others were direct.

"You need to be careful," Mr. Landers said when he picked up his order, a caramel breve extra hot. "A man like that, with his history . . . "

"I appreciate your concern," Brooke said, her jaw tight.

"Just saying. You were friends with that lawyer girl, too, weren't you? The one who got herself mixed up in all that trouble?"

"Have a nice day, Mr. Landers."

Between customers, Brooke stepped into the kitchen and pulled out her phone. Three texts to Tyler last night. Two this morning. No response.

He'd tried to call her last night, but she'd been napping. Who was she kidding? She wasn't napping. But she was in the bedroom and had left her phone in the living room with the ringer silenced. She needed time away from everything. Time to think. When she'd seen the missed call, she'd tried him. Twice. Both went to voicemail.

Gina had texted around seven: *I heard what happened!! Tyler left the station around 6. Not arrested. Just questioned.*

So, he was free. He was out there somewhere, not in a cell, not being held. Just not answering her. She'd texted Gina back, letting her know she was calling a rideshare and going home. She was well enough to be on her own. And it was true. On top of that, she couldn't handle the idea of discussing what happened with Gina or anyone at that moment. She needed to be alone. To process.

If Gina was right, Tyler had left the station fifteen hours earlier, and she still hadn't heard a peep out of him. What did that mean? Brooke typed another message: *Please call me. I need to know you're okay.*

She hit send and shoved the phone back into her pocket.

"Brooke?" Becky appeared beside her. "You've got someone asking for you."

Tyler? "Who is it?"

"Your reporter friend. Joe Monroe. Says he needs to talk to you. Said he's going around to the alley." Becky gave her a look that Brooke couldn't quite interpret.

"Thanks."

Brooke found Joe standing next to her car.

"Hey." Joe nodded when he saw her. "Ouch. That looks like it hurts."

"Some." That was a flat-out lie. Her entire body ached. She should've stayed home, stayed in bed and let herself heal. Let herself cry.

"Thanks for coming out."

"I can't stay long. We're slammed."

"I noticed. Thought about sitting out front, but your place is a zoo. Good to have the business, I guess."

She frowned. "Do you know why it's so busy?"

"Monique," Joe said.

"Yeah. And Tyler and me and . . . " She sighed.

"I've been looking into it . . . the story, I mean, ever since it came over the scanner yesterday morning that there was another body. Then, when I heard it was Monique, I did some digging." He flipped open his notebook.

"You knew Monique?"

"Some. Met her when she was with Sheila once."

"I didn't know you knew Sheila."

He smiled. "Everyone knew Sheila. But listen, there are things you should know."

Brooke's stomach tightened. "What things?"

"Connections. Timeline. Evidence." Joe's expression was serious, his usual easy demeanor replaced by something harder. This was Joe the journalist, not Joe her friend.

"Both victims grew up here, graduated the same year. Both were part of the same social circle back in high school and now. Both knew Tyler."

"Lots of people knew them. It's a small town. You just admitted to knowing them."

"True. But here's what makes it different." Joe pulled out his phone, scrolled, and then turned the screen toward her. "Sheila was last seen leaving the bank where she worked. On a Friday night, around six. Security footage shows Tyler using the ATM at approximately the same time."

"He told me about that. He was getting cash for darts."

"Did he go to darts that night?"

Brooke opened her mouth, then closed it. He'd told her he'd gone to play darts. He did every Friday night except for the most recent. She thought he was going, that's why she'd made plans with Steph, but he didn't.

She'd silenced her phone during the play but noticed he'd sent her a text saying he hoped she was having fun. He was watching a rerun on television, and he'd touch base with her after he finished work on Saturday.

"I checked with the pub," Joe continued. "The Watering Hole, where the dart league plays. Tyler wasn't there that Friday. In fact, no one was playing darts that night. They play on Thursday nights."

The words landed heavily. Tyler had said he went to the pub for darts. That's why he needed cash from the ATM. But if he hadn't gone . . .

"Maybe he played somewhere else," Brooke said, hearing how weak it sounded.

"Maybe." Joe's tone suggested he didn't believe it, but he wrote something in his notebook anyway. "Monique was last seen on Friday at work. Do you know where she worked?"

"Of course. She worked at her aunt's place. They sell yarn and other craft stuff."

"Yeah. The one where they invite people in for sewing circles and such."

"I think she's a knitter, maybe."

"Both knitting and crochet. Monique was the only full-time employee. Do you know where the place is?"

"Sure, it's . . . " Her breath caught. She met Joe's eyes and shook her head. "That doesn't mean anything."

He shrugged. "Perhaps not, but it is interesting that the craft store is so close to the auto shop where Tyler works, wouldn't you agree?"

"What makes them think there's a connection between Monique and Sheila?"

"Preliminary results show Monique died in much the same manner as Sheila. And she was dumped in the woods after she was killed."

Brooke's stomach turned as she remembered that day on the mountain and finding Sheila's body. "Was she buried in a bear cache?"

"Monique was found closer to town. Right at the edge of the national forest."

"Sort of the same as Sheila."

"They were both strangled."

"I didn't know that was how Sheila died. I never thought . . . I guess with finding her the way . . . um, with the bear." She paused and took a breath. "How do you know this? I don't remember reading anything about how Sheila actually died."

He pointed at his chest. "Professional journalist, remember? I have sources."

"But you didn't report on how Sheila died?"

"I was asked not to. Even telling you these things is a breach of ethics. I should've learned my lesson before, but I'm worried about you, Brooke."

She pressed her lips together, her brow tightening as she took in the worry written across his face. She wasn't sure what he meant by learning his lesson before, and she could tell now wasn't the time to ask. "I appreciate you telling me this. But really, Joe, Tyler is innocent."

"He may well be, but you have to admit some things don't fully line up. I'm sure you can understand how the sheriff's department is focused on him."

"The sheriff's department or Adam Boverman? You know he's been harassing Tyler, right? Harassing me, too, in a way."

"It's not just him now. Edi Reeves is now considered a witness since she was at the bank with both Tyler and Sheila."

"Now considered? Why wasn't she a witness when they were accusing Tyler of Sheila's death?"

"She was, but you know the situation with Edi." He raised an eyebrow and gave her a pointed look.

Brooke rolled her eyes. There'd been rumors of nepotism when Edi was first brought onto the sheriff's department. Her uncle was the outgoing sheriff, a man who had held the position for a dozen years but chose not to run for reelection. Instead, he ran for and won a state senate seat.

He still held that office, and there were rumors he planned to run for US senator or representative in the next election. Possibly even governor. His ambition was well known, and many believed Edi advanced by riding on his coattails.

Brooke didn't know much about the inner workings of the sheriff's department, but she had always liked Edi as a person. She was friendly and seemed to go out of her way to help people. She was a little awkward, but Brooke always assumed that was partly because of her size, tall and big-boned.

Since Edi was a couple of years older than Brooke, she had seen how mean school kids could be. She remembered being in elementary school and watching some of the girls pick on Edi. If she remembered correctly, she had been in first or maybe second grade, which would've put Edi in third or fourth. Edi had already been too tall and too heavy, and children could be cruel.

Joe continued, methodical and thorough. "I talked to a few people. Sheila and Monique were close. Best friends, actually, during high school. They were still friendly, but not as close as they had been. Tyler dated both of them, Sheila the summer after he finished high school and Monique early in his senior year."

"I've heard this about Sheila. But who cares?" Brooke said, forcing conviction into her tone. "It was high school. Over fifteen years ago. And so what if he went out with Monique? Everyone went out with everyone. You didn't grow up here, but I did. It's the way it is in a small town."

"Might be, but people have killed for less." Joe closed his notebook. "I'm not saying Tyler did this. I'm saying the evidence points in his direction, and you need to see it clearly."

"Why are you telling me this?"

"Because you're my friend. Because we nearly died when we trusted the wrong person. Kelsey fooled us. Fooled all of us. I'm not going to let that happen again."

"Tyler's not Kelsey," Brooke said.

"How do you know?"

"I just do."

"You need to be smart about this." Joe's voice was gentle but firm. "How many times have we looked back at what didn't click with Kelsey at the time, only to see it clearly now?"

The words stung because they were true. There were signs. Small things Brooke had explained away or ignored. The tension that sometimes crept into Kelsey's voice. The way she'd been so insistent about certain routes. The phone calls she'd walk away from the group to take.

All of it made sense in hindsight.

"What else?" Brooke asked quietly.

Joe hesitated. "The fire that killed Tyler's wife and son. The official ruling was accidental, but there were notes from the investigator. Questions about the timeline, about Tyler's alibi, about the insurance payout."

"Adam Boverman had it in for Tyler, even back then. That's why there are questions."

"Boverman wasn't the person in charge. The Wyoming Division of Criminal Investigation, DCI, was called in. That investigator was the one who had questions. Adam was new to the force, but he agreed with the investigator."

"But those questions were answered. The case was closed."

"The case was closed because there wasn't enough evidence to bring charges. That's different from being cleared." Joe leaned forward. "The DCI investigator revisited the case annually until he retired. He didn't say he thought Tyler was guilty, but he made it clear he wasn't convinced it was a freak accident."

"That . . . that doesn't mean anything. Besides, Adam has it out for Tyler. Everyone knows that."

"Maybe. Or maybe he's been right all along and nobody wanted to believe it."

"What about the investigator? The DCI one. Have you talked to him?"

"He retired two years ago. Sadly, he passed away about six months after."

Everything felt wrong about this. She couldn't believe someone actually thought Tyler was guilty. Adam, sure, but his obsession was unnatural. But to have someone else think Tyler was responsible for the death of his wife and child . . .

"I need to get back to work."

"Brooke— "

"Thank you for telling me. I need to think."

Joe touched her arm, his expression concerned. "Be careful. Please."

Brooke walked back inside the kitchen. The noise hit her immediately—espresso machine hissing, customers talking, Becky calling out orders. It should've been familiar and comforting. Instead, it felt overwhelming.

She pulled out her phone again. Still nothing from Tyler.

The evidence Joe had presented was circumstantial, and all of it could be explained. Tyler being at the bank didn't mean anything; he could've gone for any reason. Missing darts didn't prove anything either—plans change. And the connection to both victims through high school was unavoidable in a small town where everyone knew everyone. Even Monique working practically next door to Tyler didn't have to mean anything.

But taken together, it painted a picture. A pattern.

And Brooke had ignored patterns before. Had explained away concerns, made excuses, and trusted when she shouldn't have.

With Kelsey, that trust had nearly cost her her life. It had put Nick, Gina, and Joe in danger. It had destroyed a friendship and left scars that still hadn't fully healed.

What if she was doing it again? What if Tyler was guilty and she was too blind to see it?

But they'd been seeing each other. Something real was building between them. Her brother said Tyler was innocent when his family died and believed he was innocent now. She believed it too.

But was that belief based on truth, or was it based on wanting so badly to be right this time, to prove her judgment wasn't fundamentally broken?

Brooke didn't know anymore.

She stepped out of the kitchen and into the coffee shop. Customers came and went. Becky handled orders with practiced efficiency. The morning rush continued without pause. She pasted on a smile and moved to the counter.

"I can get the next person here."

Chapter 24

Tyler

The shop felt different on Monday morning.

Tyler noticed it the moment he walked through the bay door at seven thirty. Robert was already there, standing at the workbench with a parts catalog open in front of him. He glanced up when Tyler entered, nodded once, then went back to the catalog.

No greeting. No small talk about the weekend. Just that single nod.

Tyler took his lunch bag to the break room and grabbed his work gloves. Two cars were scheduled for the morning—an oil change and a transmission diagnostic. Simple work, the kind that let his hands stay busy while his mind churned.

He started on the oil change first. It was a Honda Civic, maybe ten years old, with a dent in the rear bumper and a cracked taillight. The owner had left a note about a squeaking noise when braking. Tyler made a mental note to check the pads.

Robert moved to where Tyler was working and stood there watching for a minute without saying anything.

"Everything okay?" Tyler asked, not looking up.

"Fine." Robert's tone was flat. "Got a call from the sheriff's department yesterday afternoon. They wanted to verify your alibi for Saturday morning."

Tyler's hands stilled. "What'd you tell them?"

"The truth. That you were here when I got here, and you were still here when I left for the day. They asked if I was certain about the time, if maybe you could've come in later."

"But I didn't."

"You were here when I arrived, that much is true." Robert shifted his weight. "Thing is, Tyler, this is becoming repetitive. First Sheila, now Monique. People are starting to talk."

"I didn't kill anyone."

"I believe you." But Robert's voice held something Tyler hadn't heard before. Doubt, maybe. Or worry. "Sue's concerned about the business. About what this might do to our reputation."

Tyler straightened, wiping his hands on a shop rag. "You want me to quit."

"I didn't say that."

"You didn't have to."

Robert met his eyes. "I'm saying we need to be careful. This town is small. Word gets around. If people think we're employing someone who— "

"Who what? Killed two women?" Tyler's jaw tightened. "Three, maybe, if you count my wife. And of course, my little boy. But I didn't do it, Robert. None of it."

"I know. But perception matters." Robert rubbed the back of his neck. "Just keep your head down, okay? Do your work, go home, don't give anyone reason to talk."

He walked away before Tyler could respond.

Tyler finished the oil change in silence. His mind kept circling back to Robert's words. *Perception matters. The business. Sue's concerned.*

He'd been so focused on proving his innocence that he hadn't considered what this was doing to Robert and Sue. They'd stood by him when Adam started his harassment, but there was a limit to anyone's loyalty, especially when money was involved.

Sue came in around nine with coffee and a box of scones from somewhere that wasn't Brooke's shop. Tyler noticed but didn't comment.

"Morning," she said, setting the box on the workbench.

"Morning."

She poured coffee into two mugs and handed one to Tyler. They stood there for a moment, neither speaking.

"I'm sorry about Monique," Sue said finally. "I knew her. Not well, but I'd see her at the craft store sometimes. She worked there."

"I heard."

"Right across the street from here." Sue's tone was careful. Measured. "Must have seen her around, I'd think."

Tyler took a sip of coffee. It was too hot and burned his tongue. "Maybe. I didn't really know her."

"But you went to school together."

"I graduated eighteen years ago."

"I heard you dated."

He paused with the mug halfway toward his lips. "Dated? Monique and me? We never dated."

"In high school? When I was picking up treats, the woman in line said— "

"I never dated Monique."

Sue nodded slowly. The expression on her face made it clear that she believed the woman in line over Tyler. "Robert told you about the sheriff calling?"

"Yeah."

"We're not trying to make this harder on you, Tyler. We just need to protect ourselves."

"I understand."

"Do you?" Sue's expression was worried. "Because I'm not sure you do. This town is talking. About you, about the murders, about Brooke."

"What about her?" Tyler asked quietly.

"People saw the patrol cars at Gina's house on Sunday. They know you were there. They know Brooke was there." Sue set down her mug. "And I heard about her being attacked on Saturday. I'm glad it wasn't too serious."

"It was serious enough."

She dipped her chin. "I drove by her coffee shop on the way to work. The place is packed. Everyone wants to see her, wanting to know what's going on between you two."

Tyler's chest tightened. He'd been avoiding his phone, avoiding Brooke's texts. He was trying to give her space, to give himself space while he sorted out whether he should keep seeing her. He hadn't considered that staying away might not be enough, that just being associated with him was causing problems.

"I should go," Tyler said. He wanted to stay and fight, to prove his innocence and be with Brooke. But now that just seemed stupid. It would hurt people he cared about. It would hurt Brooke.

"Go where?"

"Leave town. Go somewhere else where I'm not bringing trouble to people who don't deserve it."

"That's not what I'm saying." Sue touched his arm. "I'm saying be smart. Figure out who's doing this and clear your name. But until then, maybe keep some distance from people who could get hurt by association."

The phone rang, and she gave him a smile. "We'll figure this out."

"Sure," he muttered.

She reached for the phone on the shop wall, an old-fashioned kind that rang with an obnoxious bell and had a cord. He could hear her but not make out the words. After a moment, she called, "Tyler, it's for you."

His first thought was Brooke. He'd ignored her texts and calls, and now she was trying his work line. As he neared Sue, he mouthed, "Who is it?"

She shrugged. "Not sure. A guy."

Adam Boverman. It had to be him.

He reluctantly took the receiver. "This is Tyler. Can I help you?"

"Tyler Gillis?"

"Yes?" Not Adam. Tyler didn't recognize the voice, but from the way the man stumbled over his name, it sounded like the guy must have had Bloody Marys for breakfast. Or, more likely, Old Milwaukee.

"Sheila wasn' . . . enough for ya? Had ta . . . go an' . . . have Monique too?"

"Who is this?"

"Ya know who dish is."

"Sorry, pal. I don't."

"Rusty. Rusty Jones. Sheila's husband."

Slur and all, that came through clear as a bell. "I'm, uh, sorry for your loss— "

"Shave it. I'm gonna make sure you pay."

The line went silent. Tyler shook his head as he hung up the phone.

"Who was that?" Sue said, startling him.

"Uh . . . Sheila's husband."

Sue's mouth formed an *O* as she shook her head. "Wow. Sorry. I had no idea."

"It's fine. I know you didn't."

Tyler returned to work, trying to pretend like the call hadn't bothered him, but it had. This entire thing bothered him.

Rusty calling me at work, threatening me like that . . . why? Unless Rusty is the killer and is the one framing me.

Tyler's hands stopped all motion as he considered the possibility. Robert said Rusty drove an old Trans Am and had been to the shop before. Tyler remembered the car, but not the man who drove it. Typical, really.

It hadn't been that long since they worked on it. July, maybe, right after Irma Days? Maybe three weeks before Sheila's death? *Does that mean something?*

He slipped into the steady rhythm of diagnosing and repairing, hands occupied and thoughts kept at bay.

Sort of. Brooke kept popping into his mind. Her hair. Her smile. The way her lips felt against his. How she made him feel alive after so many years of merely existing.

Her texts from yesterday were still unread on his phone. He'd seen the notifications—six messages and two missed calls. Each one was a reminder that he was hurting her by staying silent. But what was the alternative? Drag her deeper into his mess?

Brooke's reputation was at risk. People were watching her and questioning her judgment because she'd been seeing him.

He knew she'd been put through the wringer before with Kelsey. And, exactly like then, Brooke had done nothing wrong. Nothing except choosing to trust the wrong person.

Better to stay away and protect her by not being part of her life.

The decision should've felt right. Selfless. The mature thing to do.

Instead, it felt like failure. Like he was running again, the way he'd run when he couldn't face another day in Irma surrounded by the memories of Jen and Garrett. He couldn't take it then, and wasn't sure he could take it now.

Four o'clock came. Andre and Robert were working on something. He told them he was heading out. Andre lifted his head and said, "See you later," but Robert only grunted. Tyler cleaned his workspace, put away his tools, and grabbed his lunch bag from the break room.

He drove home on autopilot. Turn left out of the parking lot, straight for three blocks, right on Cedar, second house on the left. He had a small rental with peeling paint and a lawn that needed mowing. He intended to mow yesterday, but taking care of Brooke while she was injured was more important.

Inside, the house was quiet. Too quiet. Tyler dropped his lunch bag on the counter and stood in the kitchen, not sure what to do next.

Usually, he'd lift weights. The garage had a bench and a decent set of free weights he'd bought secondhand when he first moved back. Forty-five minutes of lifting usually cleared his head, burned off whatever stress the day had piled on.

But today, the idea of being trapped in the garage, alone with his thoughts, felt unbearable.

Brooke always said running helped clear her mind. She talked about it sometimes after Wednesday night runs— how the rhythm of her feet hitting the ground, the steady breathing, and the movement itself made everything else fade away. Tyler ran in high school, but it was never like that for him. It was just sports, a way to stay active and enjoy time with his friends.

Even running with her a few times since they met hadn't brought on the passion she had. He preferred lifting, the immediate feedback of weight against muscle and the clear proof of progress.

But running sounded good today. Maybe he'd feel closer to her when he couldn't actually be close to her.

He changed into athletic shorts and a T-shirt, laced up his shoes, grabbed his keys, and headed out.

The lake was ten minutes away, a popular spot with a paved path that looped around the water. Three miles total, mostly flat. Brooke had mentioned it once as a good place for easy runs.

He pulled into the parking lot as the sun started dropping toward the horizon. A few other cars were scattered across the spaces—evening walkers, probably, or other runners taking advantage of the cooler temperature.

Tyler killed the engine and reached for the door handle.

That's when he saw her.

Brooke stood beside her SUV three spaces down, her back to him. She wore leggings and a tank top with her hair pulled back in a ponytail. Even from here, he could see the bandage on her head. It was a smaller size than yesterday, but it was still there.

Tyler's heart kicked hard against his ribs.

Chapter 25

Brooke

Brooke stood in the parking lot, staring out at the lake and the paved trail beyond. It had always been one of her favorite places, somewhere she could come in any weather and run. Today, though, it felt wrong. Like she should turn around and leave.

She wasn't physically up to it, but that wasn't the point. She needed to be here. She needed the fresh air, the quiet, and being outside gave her the space to think.

She needed to breathe.

Plus, she worried that if she didn't go today, she'd be too scared to ever go again. She'd chosen the lake because it was well used and wide open. There was no place for anyone to hide.

Even if she couldn't run, she could walk. Sort of. She certainly wasn't going to be doing any speed walking, but what could she expect?

She checked her messages, hoping Tyler had replied to her text while she was driving but she didn't hear the notification. Nothing.

Maybe she should put the phone away and let the rhythm of movement ease her aching heart. She rubbed her forehead, her fingers drifting toward the bandage. Her head still hurt—her entire body, really—but it was nothing compared to how much she missed Tyler.

More than anything, she needed to hear from him, to talk to him and find out how he was holding up. As hard as the last twenty-four hours had been for her, they were nothing compared to what he was facing.

The thought of calling him lingered. He should have been off work. Maybe he would answer this time. There was probably a valid reason for not responding before. She stood there, thumb hovering over his name in her contacts.

A car door closed, and Brooke looked behind her.

Tyler stood three spaces down beside his truck, one hand still on the door handle.

They stared at each other across the parking lot.

Her heart kicked into a faster rhythm. All the things she'd wanted to say to him, all the texts he hadn't answered, all the doubt Joe had planted earlier—it all tangled together in her throat.

Tyler took a step toward her, then stopped.

"Hey," he said.

"Hey." Her voice sounded like it belonged to someone else.

"I didn't know you'd be here."

"I didn't plan to be." Brooke tucked her phone into her pocket. "Are you going for a walk?"

"Thought I'd try running." He gestured at his athletic shorts and T-shirt. "You always say it clears your head."

"Does it?"

"Don't know yet. Never tried it that way before."

Brooke noticed the tension in his shoulders and the dark circles under his eyes, the way he held himself like he was bracing for another hit. "I could run with you," she heard herself say. "If you want."

He gestured to her head. "Are you supposed to be running?"

She gave a small, shrugging smile. "Probably not. The doctor said to take it easy for a few days. I should probably walk."

"You probably should."

"I don't want to keep you from getting the workout you were hoping for."

Tyler hesitated. "It's probably good to walk, too, right?"

"I'm sure it is. There're all sorts of studies about walking and mental health."

He studied her face like he was trying to read something there. "Okay."

They started toward the path together, not quite walking side by side but close enough to talk.

Their walking pace was faster than a stroll but not a power walk. It was a good pace for the way Brooke's body felt. Their steps fell into a steady rhythm on the pavement. Other people were on the path—an elderly couple power walking, a woman with a stroller, two teenagers on bikes.

Normal people doing normal things.

Brooke tried to focus on her breathing. In through the nose, out through the mouth.

But her mind kept circling back to Joe's words and how he'd been putting things together. The evidence and connections he found painted a picture she wasn't comfortable admitting to.

She wanted to ask Tyler about it, to have him explain everything away so she could stop doubting him.

But what if he couldn't?

They rounded the first bend. The path curved along the water's edge, trees on one side and the lake glittering in the evening sun on the other. The days were getting shorter. Soon, fall would arrive, and then the middle of October, when she needed to register for the Moose Range Run 100.

What might her life be like by then? She'd be physically recovered from her injuries before then, but would she still be wondering about Tyler? Would there still be accusations and innuendo?

"You didn't answer my texts," she said quietly.

Tyler paused before replying, "I know."

"Why?"

"Because I thought staying away was the smart thing to do. Sue told me your coffee shop was packed today, that everyone wants to know about us, that people are gossiping and questioning and judging you for being with me."

"I can handle gossip."

"You shouldn't have to." Tyler's jaw was tight. "You've been through enough—with Kelsey and everything that happened at Bearwater, and now with the attack. You don't need my mess added to your life."

Brooke walked beside him in silence. The path stretched ahead, curving back toward the parking lot. "I heard things too," she said finally. "About you and Monique. That you dated in high school."

"I didn't."

"That's not what people are saying."

"People are wrong." Tyler stopped walking and turned to face her. "I never dated Monique. I barely knew her. But somehow that rumor is all over town now."

"You heard it too?"

"Yeah, Sue told me. Said a woman in line at the donut shop told her. I don't know where it started or why people are saying it, but it's not true."

Brooke studied his face. His frustration was evident, but he also looked tired and worn down. But he didn't look like someone who was lying.

"Joe Monroe said you dated both of them. Sheila and Monique."

"Joe's wrong. Or his sources are. I dated Sheila for a couple months when we were kids. That's it."

They started walking again. The conversation had broken something open between them, the careful distance they'd been maintaining dissolved.

"What else did Joe say?" Tyler asked.

Brooke walked him through it all. The evidence, the timeline, the doubts about the fire, and the other investigator who wouldn't let the case rest. Tyler listened quietly, his expression growing darker as she spoke.

"Someone's framing me," he said when she finished. "Someone who knows my history, knows these women, and knows exactly how to make me look guilty."

"Who would do that?"

"I don't know. But I'm going to find out." He looked at her. "I didn't kill anyone, Brooke. Not Sheila, not Monique, not my wife and son. I need you to believe that."

"I want to believe it."

"But you're not sure. We're back to that again, huh?"

Brooke didn't answer. The truth was complicated and messy, and she didn't know how to put it into words.

They walked in silence for a while.

"We're not back to that," she finally said. "I know you weren't responsible for what happened to your wife. And I believe you about Sheila and Monique too."

"Do I hear a *but* in your voice?" he asked.

"Not exactly, it's just . . . Joe said there was a question about whether you actually played darts the night Sheila died. Plus, you didn't go to The Watering Hole on Friday for darts. I thought you would. That's why I went to the play with Steph."

"I don't know where your friend is getting his information, but I *was* playing darts the night Sheila died. Not at the Watering Hole. I haven't played there in months, not since they changed from Friday night darts to Thursday night darts. Bronco Willie's has darts on Friday night."

He reached for her arm, and they both came to a stop, eyes locking. "And I didn't go this past Friday night because the guys I usually play with are gone hunting. It's archery season, and they're up at their elk camp."

She held his gaze as she nodded. "That makes sense." She almost reached for him, wanting that connection, but the moment passed and they started walking again, soon reaching the parking lot.

They stopped near Brooke's SUV. The sun had dropped lower, painting the sky in shades of orange and pink. It was a beautiful evening, but the wrong circumstances.

Brooke reached for Tyler's hand.

His fingers closed around hers automatically before he seemed to realize what she'd done. "People will talk."

"They're already talking."

"It'll get worse."

"Probably." But she didn't let go.

Tyler looked down at their joined hands, then back at her face. Something passed between them—understanding, maybe, or recognition of how complicated this had become.

Brooke liked him. Maybe more than liked him. Maybe loved him, though it was too soon to be certain of that. The connection she felt when they were together was real, the way he made her feel safe despite everything happening around them.

She wanted to believe him. Everything he said made sense. She wanted to choose trust over doubt, to prove that her judgment hadn't been broken by Kelsey.

But what if she was wrong again?

Tyler's thumb brushed across the back of her hand. "I should go."

"Yeah. Me too."

Neither of them moved.

The parking lot was emptying out as evening settled in. The lake reflected the sunset, all gold and pink and darkening blue. Somewhere, a dog barked. Normal sounds. Normal evening.

Nothing about this felt normal, and at the same time, it was completely normal. It felt comfortable.

"Brooke," Tyler started, then stopped. "I don't know what to say."

"Me neither."

He let go of her hand. The loss of contact felt more than physical, like something important slipping away.

"Be careful," Tyler said. "Whoever's doing this, they're still out there."

"You too."

He walked to his truck, and Brooke watched him go, her hand still warm from where he'd held it.

She got into her SUV and sat there as Tyler's truck pulled out of the parking lot.

Then she put her head on the steering wheel and tried to figure out what she was supposed to do next.

Chapter 26

Tyler

Thirty miles separated Elkridge from Irma—far enough, Tyler hoped, that they wouldn't run into anyone who knew them.

He glanced across the truck cab at Brooke. She'd dressed up for dinner—dark jeans and a blue sweater that made her eyes stand out. Her hair was down instead of pulled back in the ponytail she usually wore for work or running.

"You look nice," Tyler said.

"Thanks." A faint blush crept across her cheeks as she smiled at him. "You clean up pretty good yourself."

Tyler felt heat rise in his face. He'd worn khakis and a button-down shirt, wanting to make an effort for their first real date in public, even if they'd driven to another town to do it.

The past few weeks, since their walk around the lake, they had been careful and quiet. They saw each other at his place or hers, but never out where people might notice.

He had thought about going to the Wednesday night runs with the group, but Brooke was still only walking. The temptation to walk with her, to hold her hand and be the couple they were in his mind and heart, would be too strong.

She said she was ready to start running again. Once she did, joining the club might make more sense. He would still see her, but he'd keep his distance.

He was protecting her reputation. At least, that's what Tyler told himself. But maybe he was protecting himself too—from the judgment, from the whispers, from Adam Boverman's constant surveillance.

He never knew when Boverman would show up. More than once, Tyler left for work in the morning to find him parked on the street, either in his patrol car or his personal vehicle. Or he'd be parked near the auto shop when Tyler got off.

A few days ago, when Tyler went to Brooke's place, Adam was in front of the neighbor's place. Tyler kept on driving, calling Brooke after he got down the street to a place he could park.

Brooke said she'd had enough. Tyler didn't know exactly what she'd done, but he hadn't seen Adam since. Not even in his regular course of duty. It was almost as if the man had simply disappeared. It'd only been a couple of days, but it was a nice feeling and spurred their date tonight.

Without Boverman lurking around, they felt more confident in seeing each other. Not confident enough to go out to dinner in Irma, but still. Tyler had to admit, even the drive down felt special. Romantic, even. They took his truck, their hands finding each other's whenever they could.

The restaurant was on Elkridge's Main Street, a steakhouse that had been there since the seventies. It was already dark when they arrived, and the restaurant was lit up with white lights along the eaves and woven through the trees. The outdoor patio was closed, but it still looked inviting.

Tyler wondered why he'd never eaten here before. Thirty miles wasn't much of a drive as far as Wyoming distances were concerned, and Elkridge was still part of Basin County. He'd always heard the food was good. If the reviews were accurate, maybe this could be a special place for him and Brooke. Maybe it could become "their place."

Tyler parked and went around to open Brooke's door.

"Such a gentleman," she said, smiling.

"My mama raised me right."

Inside, the restaurant was busy, probably what would be expected on a Saturday night. The hostess led them to a table for two near the back. It was the perfect private spot.

They ordered—salmon for him and steak for her. She ordered a glass of red wine, while Tyler stuck with soda. The waitress brought bread and water and left them alone.

"This is nice," Brooke said. "Being out somewhere together. Like normal people."

"We are normal people."

"You know what I mean."

Tyler did know.

The meal was good, but the conversation was better. Brooke told him about a difficult customer at the coffee shop who'd demanded a refund because her latte wasn't hot enough. Tyler shared a story about a car that had come in making a noise Robert swore was possessed.

For almost an hour, Tyler managed to let the murders slip to the back of his mind. The accusations, Adam's constant scrutiny, all of it faded beneath the warm glow of the restaurant lights and the way Brooke's laughter curled around him like something he didn't deserve but wanted anyway. It felt right. It was exactly what he'd hoped the night would be.

The server brought the check, and Tyler grabbed it instantly. Brooke looked like she wanted to protest until he shook his head. "I told you, my mama raised me right." He slipped in enough cash for the bill and a generous tip.

He took a sip of water, not wanting the time to end. "So, you think you're well enough to run tomorrow?"

"It's been two weeks. Two weeks today. The headaches are gone, and the bruising is mostly gone. The cut is still tender when I catch it with my brush, but I'm good. Even Gina agrees I can do it as long as I take it easy. And you know how Gina is. Old mother hen." She smiled.

He knew it was true. Gina, Steph, and another friend named Jocelyn were always there for Brooke.

Even so, Tyler knew Brooke hadn't told them they were seeing each other again. Her cousin Nick didn't know either, since he'd no doubt tell Gina. That's what couples do.

And Brooke certainly hadn't told Joe Monroe. He'd done several reports on Monique's death and the connection between her and Sheila. He never used Tyler's name in the reports, but there were plenty of suggestions as to who the primary suspect was. Enough hints were dropped that anyone who'd been paying attention could put things together.

A shadow fell across their table.

Tyler looked up. A man stood there, around forty, with thinning hair plastered to his forehead and a belly shaped by too many nights spent leaning against a bar. His face was ruddy, his eyes sharp and unfriendly.

"Tyler Gillis," the man said.

Tyler stiffened. "Can I help you?"

"Thought it was you."

Brooke leaned forward in her seat. "Hello," she smiled, her voice friendly. "Something we can help you with?"

He ignored her and stared at Tyler. "You don't recognize me?"

Tyler stared at the man for a moment. He was vaguely familiar, but Tyler couldn't place him or put a name on him. Someone from the shop, maybe? Or from before when he lived in Basin County. A classmate, maybe? "Sorry, no . . . "

"I'm Rusty. Rusty Jones." The name came out sharp and accusatory. "Sheila's ex-husband."

The restaurant noise faded. Brooke gasped, and several diners nearby looked their way.

"I'm sorry for your loss," Tyler said carefully.

"Are you?" Rusty's voice rose. "Because from where I'm standing, you don't look sorry at all. You look like you're out on a date, having a good time, like you didn't kill my ex-wife."

"I didn't kill anyone."

"That's not what I heard." Rusty leaned closer. His breath smelled like alcohol. "You were there. At the bank. Same time she left work. Same night she died."

"Lots of people use the bank."

"Not lots of people dated her. Not lots of people had reason to want her dead."

Tyler's hands clenched under the table. "I didn't want Sheila dead. I barely knew her anymore."

"Liar." Rusty grabbed the edge of the table. "You killed my Sheila, and you killed Monique. And you're going to pay for it."

"Rusty." Brooke's voice was calm but firm. "You're upset. We understand that. But Tyler didn't hurt anyone."

"Who are you? The girlfriend everyone's talking about?" Rusty's laugh was ugly. "Better watch out, sweetheart. You might be next."

Tyler stood. "That's enough."

"Or what?" Rusty straightened to his full height, still shorter than Tyler. He had weight on him, though, most of it around his middle. "You going to kill me too?"

"I'm going to ask you to leave us alone."

"I don't think so." Rusty shoved the table, slamming it into Tyler's thighs and knocking him back a step.

The restaurant had gone quiet. Everyone was watching now.

Tyler steadied himself. "Walk away."

"Too late."

Rusty swung, wild and fast. Tyler got an arm up in time, but Rusty's other hand drove in low and hard, cracking into his ribs. Pain tore through his side.

Tyler lost his footing and went down hard. Rusty was on him immediately, his fist slamming into Tyler's jaw. Stars burst across Tyler's vision.

Brooke shouted something, sharp and urgent. Chairs scraped across the floor. Rusty had him pinned, one knee driving into his chest, hands clamped around his throat.

Tyler clawed at Rusty's wrists, trying to pry them loose, but the angle worked against him and Rusty had all the leverage. Pressure pounded behind his eyes. His vision tunneled. Then the weight vanished. He sucked in a ragged breath and rolled onto his side, coughing.

Through watering eyes, he saw Brooke standing over Rusty, the broken wooden chair still in her hands. Rusty lay on the ground, clutching his shoulder, his face twisted with pain and surprise, splinters scattered around him.

"Stay down," Brooke said, her voice shaking, holding the jagged chair above him.

Rusty looked at her, then at Tyler, then at the restaurant staff rushing toward them.

"She hit me," Rusty said, like he couldn't believe it.

Two servers reached them. A man who looked like a manager was already on his phone, probably calling the police.

"We're leaving," Brooke said. She dropped the broken chair and reached for Tyler's hand. "Now."

Tyler let her pull him to his feet. His ribs screamed, and his jaw throbbed where Rusty had connected. But he could stand.

They moved toward the exit, but the manager stepped in front of them.

"You need to wait for the police," he said.

"That man attacked my boyfriend," Brooke said. "We defended ourselves."

"You broke a chair. You're going to pay for it."

"Fine. Send me a bill." She fished a business card out of her pocket and thrust it at the man before pushing past him, Tyler following. They made it to the truck before anyone came after them.

Tyler's hands shook as he pulled his keys from his pocket. Brooke took them from him.

"I'll drive."

"You sure?"

"Absolutely."

She pulled out of the parking lot as sirens sounded in the distance, getting closer.

"They're going to find us," Tyler said. His voice was rough from Rusty choking him.

"Let them. He attacked you first. Everyone in that restaurant saw it."

Tyler touched his jaw, wincing. It was already swelling. "You hit him with a chair."

"I did."

"You could've been hurt."

"You *are* hurt." Brooke's hands were white-knuckled on the steering wheel. "He had you down and was choking you. I wasn't going to just stand there."

Tyler looked at her, taking in the shake in her hands and the fierce set of her jaw as adrenaline faded.

She'd fought for him. Literally picked up a chair and hit someone to protect him, despite all the doubt, despite what people would say, despite the risk to her own reputation and safety.

She'd chosen him.

"Brooke," Tyler started, but didn't know how to finish.

"Don't." She glanced at him, then back at the road. "This wasn't your fault."

"Still. I hate that it happened."

"I hate it, too, but it did. I'm just glad you're okay."

She reached across the console and took his hand. Her fingers were still trembling.

Tyler squeezed back. He held on like she was the only solid thing in a world that kept trying to knock him down.

They drove the rest of the way in silence, the kind of silence that didn't need filling, the kind that came from understanding.

When they reached Irma, Brooke drove to Tyler's house instead of hers. She helped him inside, found ice for his jaw, and checked his ribs.

"You should see a doctor," she said.

"I'm fine."

"You're stubborn."

"So are you."

She smiled at that, a real smile despite everything.

Tyler caught her hand as she pressed the icepack to his face. "Thank you. For back there. For saving me."

Her eyes filled with tears. She looked like she was going to say something, but instead, she leaned in and kissed him, careful of his injured jaw, her lips soft against his.

When she pulled away, she said, "If you're sure you're okay, I'm going to head home."

He caught the look she gave him and couldn't quite make it out. He wanted to suggest she stay, but the words wouldn't come. It felt like he'd be asking for too much. Besides, he was hurting and knew he'd be terrible company.

"I'm good. See you tomorrow?"

"Sure." She smiled.

Chapter 27

Brooke

Sunday morning arrived with Brooke doomscrolling social media. She'd been awake for hours.

Sleep had been sporadic, the kind that made her wonder if she had ever truly slept. Certainly not deep sleep. Eventually, she gave up on it. Every time she closed her eyes, she saw Rusty's hands around Tyler's throat, watched Tyler's face turn red, then purple, and heard the crack of the chair hitting Rusty's shoulder.

She helped Tyler get home last night, then called an Uber to take her back to her place. She had been tempted to stay, to make sure he really was okay, but that would never do.

Even sleeping on the couch brought too much risk of someone noticing she had spent the night. Not that she wasn't an adult who could do what she wanted, but with the way things were . . . she sighed and dropped the phone onto her nightstand.

She went to the kitchen and set the kettle on the stove. The sound of it heating gave her something to concentrate on. She measured the coffee beans and focused on the grind, keeping her mind anchored to the noise instead of Tyler.

When the beans were ready, she filled the french press with hot water to warm it. She emptied it as the kettle began to whistle and poured a slow stream of boiling water over the grounds. The sharp scent rose and spread through the room. She stirred the mixture, counted to thirty, and finished pouring the water. As the coffee steeped, she fixed her eyes on the swirl, finally letting some of the thoughts that had kept her awake most of the night settle in.

Rusty Jones was out of line, likely fueled by too much beer and grief and anger over his ex-wife's death. But still, out of line or not, Brooke kind of understood. Tyler had already been tried and convicted by the press and the Basin County grapevine.

She realized now they were dumb to think going to Elkridge would be safe. The old saying that Wyoming was a small town with long streets held true.

She pushed the plunger slowly, counting to ten to avoid rushing. Patience was the key to a perfect french press.

With her coffee perfectly dressed with heavy cream and a splash of vanilla sugar, she made her way to the couch.

What kind of life could they even have together?

Last night gave her a glimpse of how it might be. They couldn't even go to dinner in another town without violence finding them. Rusty had recognized Tyler, made a scene, and attacked him in a restaurant full of people.

And Brooke had broken a chair over the man.

The thing was, she'd do it again. Brooke knew she would. She was convinced Rusty could kill Tyler. The booze and anger prevented him from using good judgment. Or maybe Rusty was simply a bad person. Either way, Tyler's life was in danger, and Brooke did what she had to do.

Still . . . she hated being put in that position. She'd never been in a fight before. Never had to defend someone by using furniture as a weapon. She ran a coffee shop. She trained for ultramarathons. She lived a quiet, normal life.

Or she had, before Tyler.

Brooke pulled her knees to her chest. The bruises from her attack two weeks ago were mostly faded now. She still had yellow-green marks on her arms where she'd fought back, and the cut on her head had healed to a thin line under her hair.

She'd survived that. Survived being attacked on the trail by someone in a ski mask. Survived wondering if she was going to die alone in the woods.

And now she was with someone the entire town—the entire county, maybe even the whole state—thought was a murderer.

Lots of people were convinced Tyler was guilty. She heard it every day at the coffee shop. Customers who used to be friendly now gave her looks, whispered when they thought she couldn't hear, or questioned her judgment.

Just like with Kelsey.

Except this was worse because she'd chosen Tyler. She'd decided to be with him despite the warnings, despite the evidence, despite everyone telling her she was making a mistake.

What if they were right?

No. Brooke shook her head. Tyler wasn't guilty. She knew that and believed it completely.

But belief didn't change reality. It didn't change the fact that being with him meant constant scrutiny, constant judgment, constant fear that violence would find them again.

The coffee shop had always been a place where people felt comfortable. Now it felt tense. Some regulars stopped coming. Others still came, but their actions were different than before this mess started.

The shop was still busy, busier than before, but the energy had changed. Patrons lingered with watchful eyes, phones at the ready, as if waiting to see what would happen next and record it to share with the world.

Even though she and Tyler avoided going out in public in Irma, people still drew the connection between them. After last night, she was certain there'd be plenty of talk.

She knew things at the auto shop were no different. Customers still brought in their vehicles, but some asked Tyler not to handle the work himself. He didn't say anything, but she could see the concern in him and knew he was worried about his job, worried Robert and Sue would get tired of the constant circus and scrutiny.

Brooke knew the trouble wouldn't stop until someone uncovered who had really killed Sheila and Monique. She also knew Adam Boverman was fixated on Tyler's guilt, and she suspected he wasn't even searching for the real killer.

Edi Reeves was still off the case and now considered a witness, which was a shame because Brooke knew Edi believed Tyler was innocent. A few days earlier, she had stopped by the coffee shop and dropped hints that Brooke had noticed. Woven through the hints was a clear message that, regardless of his guilt, Brooke would be wise to avoid Tyler.

So much for Edi being a friend. She might have thought Tyler was innocent, but she wasn't willing to stand beside him. A fair-weather friend, that's what she was.

At least Adam had stopped staking out her house, and Tyler's house and work. Brooke knew that was thanks to her friend Steph.

When Brooke had finally had enough, she'd called Steph and asked if there was anything she could do to help with the continued harassment. Steph made a phone call to the sheriff, and things had been better.

Steph used to be engaged to the sheriff's son, and as far as he was concerned, she was family. Family pulled a lot of weight in Basin County.

Steph told Brooke the sheriff had been very careful in what he said, but she got the impression the harassment was all Adam and his own private vendetta. Steph was unsure of the sheriff's opinion on Tyler, but he was intent on solving the case and had the Wyoming Division of Criminal Investigation reviewing it. The DCI should be responding soon about the next steps.

"Next steps" sounded both promising and scary. Brooke was confident about Tyler's innocence . . . most of the time. It was the dark of night when her mind swirled and she had doubts. Or times like now, when for no reason at all, things seemed completely wrong.

She couldn't deny she cared for Tyler. There was something that had caught her attention that first day on the mountain after finding Sheila's body in the bear caches. It was magnetic and real, yet also very dangerous. She didn't worry about her physical safety, not the way people said she should, but she still worried.

Brooke stood and went to the window. Sunday morning in Irma—a few cars on the street, someone walking a dog. Normal life happened all around her while she felt like she was drowning.

She should stay away from him. For her business. For her sanity.

The thought made her chest ache.

But it was the right thing to do. The smart thing. The mature thing.

They needed to take a break. She needed space to think, to breathe, to figure out what she wanted without Tyler's presence clouding her judgment.

Brooke picked up her phone and stared at Tyler's name in her contacts.

She should go to his place and talk to him face to face. That's what adults did. That's what people who cared about each other did.

But she knew what would happen if she saw him. His eyes would meet hers and reveal the truth: his innocence, his hurt, his hope that they could make this work. She'd change her mind and convince herself they could get through this together.

She couldn't afford to change her mind. Not about this. Not when the stakes were this high.

Brooke opened a text message.

Her fingers shook as she typed.

I can't do this anymore. Last night was too much. I need to take a break. I'm sorry.

The words looked harsh on the screen. Cold. Not at all what she felt inside.

But if she tried to explain, she'd talk herself out of it. She'd find reasons to stay, to fight, to keep trying. And she couldn't do that. She couldn't risk it.

She hit send before she could delete it.

Brooke stared at the screen, waiting. Her heart pounded so loud she could hear it in her ears.

Finally, a message came through.

I understand. I don't want to hurt you anymore. Take care of yourself.

That was it. No argument. No pleading. No asking her to reconsider.

Just acceptance.

Brooke read the message three times. Four times. She waited for more, or for some sign she had misread it.

He understood. He was letting her go without a fight.

She should feel relieved. This was what she wanted—space, distance, a chance to rebuild her life without the constant weight of Tyler's situation dragging her down.

Brooke set the phone down and returned to the couch, sinking into it as she stared at the blank wall, tears stinging her nose.

They were done. She had ended it. It was the smart choice, the safe choice. So why'd it feel like the biggest mistake of her life?

The coffee on the side table had gone cold. Sunday stretched ahead of her, empty and quiet. She should do something—go for a run, go to church, clean the house, call Gina or Steph or Jocelyn—but she couldn't make herself move.

She had chosen safety over love, her business and her reputation over the man who had made her feel alive.

Brooke pulled the blanket tighter around herself and closed her eyes. She tried to tell herself it was the right choice. She tried to convince herself. But her heart refused to listen.

Chapter 28

Tyler

Tyler stared at his phone.

The message sat on the screen. *I understand. I don't want to hurt you anymore. Take care of yourself.*

His thumb hovered over the keyboard. He wanted to type more, wanted to tell her he loved her, that they could make this work, that he didn't want to lose her. He wanted her to write back and say it was all a terrible mistake, that she'd had a moment of weakness but was over it now. That she wanted to be with him. But a new message didn't arrive.

He set the phone face down on the kitchen table.

Deep down, he'd known this was coming. He didn't blame her for ending things. Being with someone like him couldn't be easy for her, not with people talking and whispering, or Adam showing up out of the blue and arresting him or taking him in for questioning, or Rusty attacking him and Brooke stepping in, putting herself in danger.

She did the right thing. The best thing, really. If he were any kind of man, he would've done it himself. Instead, he'd been wrapped up in Brooke, in how she made him feel, in who she was. All he wanted was to be with her.

Tyler touched his jaw. The swelling had gone down some overnight, but it still hurt. His ribs ached when he breathed too deeply. There was bruising around his neck. Nothing major but noticeable in the right light. It was a small price to pay for being stupid enough to think they could have a normal date and be a normal couple.

The house was quiet. The day stretched ahead of him with nothing to fill it.

He went to the kitchen window. The lawn still needed mowing. That was something he could do. The paint on the trim was peeling too. He'd told the landlord he'd handle it in exchange for a break on the rent. Maybe today was the day. Outside, the air had that early-October chill that Wyoming always brought, cold enough to bite but not yet settled in. Winter might hold off long enough for him to do the job.

He should've taken care of the trim weeks ago, but since he'd met Brooke, spending time with her took priority over almost everything else.

Now he had all the time in the world.

Tyler filled a glass with water and drank it at the sink. The cold soothed his sore throat.

He was convinced Brooke had saved his life last night. If she hadn't hit Rusty when she did, things could've gone differently. Rusty was drunk and angry and not thinking straight. He might have actually killed Tyler right there in that restaurant.

And Brooke had stopped him.

Then she'd driven Tyler home, made sure he was okay, and called herself an Uber rather than stay.

Because staying would've been too much. Too close. Too dangerous.

Tyler understood. Ordering the Uber had been a conscious decision. She could've stayed, they could've . . .

No. This was for the best. Now she could live her life without his mess holding her back. She could run her coffee shop without customers whispering about the murderer she was dating. Train for her ultramarathon without worrying about him. Live the life she deserved.

Tyler set the glass down and walked into the living room. He sank onto the couch and stared at the blank television screen.

He was alone again, back where he started when he returned to Irma nine months ago.

At least Brooke was safe.

Tyler's phone buzzed. He grabbed it too fast, hoping it was Brooke changing her mind.

It was Robert. *Everything okay? Heard about the restaurant.*

Tyler typed back. *Fine. Just a misunderstanding.*

It wasn't exactly the truth, but he didn't want to tell his boss that some guy tried to kill him. Besides, it was obvious he'd already heard. And if Robert heard, so had the cops. Boverman would have a new excuse to harass him.

Sue wants to know if you need anything.

I'm good. Thanks.

By tomorrow, everyone would know about the fight. About Brooke defending him.

More gossip. More judgment. More reasons for people to believe he was guilty.

Tyler went to the window. A car drove past. Normal Sunday morning traffic. People going to church or brunch or whatever normal people did on Sundays.

He hadn't felt normal in years and hadn't gone to church since Jen and Garrett died. Sometimes, he missed it. Mostly, he just felt guilty about not going.

His phone buzzed again. This time it was a number he didn't recognize.

This is Edi. Heard about last night. You okay?

Tyler hesitated before responding. *How'd you get my number?*

I'm a cop. I have ways. Seriously though, are you all right?

Bruised but fine.

Good. Stay safe, Tyler.

He stared at the message. Edi believed him. Robert and Sue believed him. Even Brooke believed him, though she'd chosen to walk away.

But believing him didn't change reality. Didn't find the real killer. Didn't clear his name.

Didn't keep Brooke safe. Tyler's mind kept circling back to that.

What if staying away from her doesn't actually keep her safe? The thought made his chest tight.

Someone was killing women from his past, even if he hadn't been close to them. Someone had left a threatening note on his truck. Someone had attacked Brooke on a trail.

And now Brooke had defended him publicly. She'd hit Rusty with a chair in front of a restaurant full of witnesses. Had made it clear she was on Tyler's side.

What if that made her an even bigger target?

What if the real killer saw her as a threat? As someone who needed to be silenced?

Tyler grabbed his phone and pulled up Brooke's contact. His thumb hovered over the call button.

But what would he say? That he was worried about her? That staying away might not be enough? That whoever was doing this might come after her anyway?

She'd think he was being paranoid. Or manipulative. That he was trying to find an excuse to keep her in his life.

Maybe he was.

Brooke was smart and careful. She wouldn't take unnecessary risks. She'd be fine.

Except she'd already been attacked once. Already been dragged off a trail by someone strong enough to overpower her despite her fighting back.

If that person came after her again, would she be able to defend herself?

Tyler's hands clenched into fists. He couldn't protect her if he stayed away, couldn't be there if something happened, couldn't do anything except sit in his house and hope she was safe.

Hope wasn't enough.

Staying away from Brooke was supposed to keep her safe. But if the killer saw her as a threat, distance wouldn't matter.

The only way to truly protect her was to find out who was doing this, clear his name, and remove the target from both their backs.

He should've been doing this all along. In some ways he had, but the truth was, he was making little headway in finding out who the killer was. He thought maybe Rusty had killed Sheila, but after last night, he wasn't sure. Rusty was drunk, no doubt about that, but he was also hurting. Tyler knew grief well enough to recognize it in someone else.

Who did that leave? The game warden—Henry. He'd shown up the day they found Sheila. Tyler assumed it was because he was working in the area. He'd gone to Sheila's funeral, and that's when Sue learned he'd dated Sheila.

Then he stopped at the shop and said he was there to order a case of oil, but it had sounded like an excuse, especially when Robert told him he could get the same stuff at the superstore down the road without waiting for it to come in.

But the way he had just happened to arrive at the same time Tyler did, walking into the building with him, and the subtle threat he made when he left . . . looking back on it, it seemed a little too coincidental.

Tyler sank into the sofa, turning over the situation with Henry in his mind. Maybe it was a coincidence that he had been the one to show up when dispatch called. Just like it was a coincidence that Tyler was there that day.

They weren't supposed to be hiking that trail. They had planned on another route, one in a different section of the wilderness area, but Robert had said he heard the loop trail was a good one to take.

Tyler leaned forward. "Well, that's interesting," he murmured.

The change in plans had come from Robert. Everything was set for the other trail until he and Sue arrived that morning to pick him up. Sue had no idea the plan had shifted and had been looking forward to the original hike, which promised both a challenging climb and a rewarding view at the top. Robert, however, said he wasn't up for it. His back had been bothering him, and he preferred something easier.

Robert did sometimes complain of a stiff back now and then. But he'd said nothing about it on the hike, and he seemed perfectly fine when they came across Brooke and then Sheila's remains. In fact, he hadn't mentioned it since then.

He reached for his phone. His finger hovered over Robert's name.

What are you doing? he asked himself as he put it back on the table. *Gonna call your boss and accuse him of murder? Accuse him of changing our hiking plans so we could magically stumble across the body of someone he killed? Brilliant career move.*

Besides, it was a stretch. Why would Robert kill Sheila? He could think of one obvious reason, but Robert didn't seem the type to cheat on Sue. And then Monique? Why kill her? Unless Monique knew Robert was seeing Sheila.

Or maybe it was the other way around. Maybe Robert was seeing Monique. Sheila knew about the relationship and . . . and what?

Sheila was blackmailing Robert. Hmm. Tyler could see that. Sheila told Robert she'd tell Sue about him and Monique, and he killed her. Maybe he killed Monique because she knew Robert killed Sheila. It was still a stretch but could fit.

Robert could've left the note on his truck, too, simply by slipping out the door while they were working. What about Brooke? Would Robert have attacked her?

He hated to think it could be Robert, but with him and Henry both as possibilities, at least he had somewhere to start instead of sitting around waiting for another body to turn up.

Because he couldn't live with himself if that body was Brooke's.

Chapter 29

Brooke

Brooke stared at her phone for the hundredth time that Sunday afternoon. The text thread with Tyler sat open, their final messages glaring back at her.

She'd made the smart choice. The safe choice. The choice that protected her business and her reputation, and, most importantly, her heart.

So why'd it feel like the worst mistake of her life?

Brooke set the phone down and pulled her knees to her chest. The house was too quiet. Too empty. She'd spent the morning sulking, the afternoon pacing, and now the evening was stretching ahead with nothing to fill it.

If she was smart, she'd go for a run. The doctor had cleared her for easy runs. No speed work yet, just a slow jog to clear her head. But even that felt like too much.

All she really wanted was to wallow in self-pity. No, that wasn't it. What she wanted was to call Tyler and tell him she'd made a mistake. Better yet, go to his house and beg him to take her back.

But she knew she couldn't do that. The whole situation gnawed at her. The evidence, the timeline, it all pointed to Tyler, and yet none of it felt right. It was too . . . perfect.

Brooke grabbed her phone and pulled up Joe's number before she could talk herself out of it.

He answered on the second ring. "Hey, you okay? I heard about last night."

She shook her head, brushing past the part about last night. Of course he had heard. Everyone probably had. She was surprised her phone hadn't been buzzing nonstop. "I need your help."

"With what?"

"I need to know everything about Tyler. Really know it. Not what Adam says, not what the evidence suggests. The actual truth."

"Brooke— "

"You're an investigative journalist. You seem to have contacts on top of contacts. And you just know things. If anyone can figure this out, it's you."

"I've been looking into it," Joe said carefully. "You know that. But I'm not sure getting more involved is a good idea."

"You think I'm not already involved?"

"You are, but this could be different."

"Why?"

"Because you might not like what we discover." His voice was gentle but firm. "Can you handle it if Tyler really is guilty? If the evidence is right and your instincts are wrong?"

The question hit hard. Brooke thought about Kelsey. About how wrong she'd been, how her judgment had nearly gotten them all killed. About the pit in her stomach that said maybe this was the same thing happening again.

"I need to know," she said quietly. "Even if it destroys me. I can't live with this uncertainty. Besides, I'd rather find out the truth myself than read about it in the paper later."

Joe was quiet for a long moment. "All right. Come over. We'll go through everything."

★★★★★

Joe's townhouse was small but organized—up to a point, anyway. It held entirely too much stuff for Brooke's liking, but she understood it reflected who he was. Newspaper clippings and printed articles covered one wall. In the corner, a multi-paneled desktop setup glowed on a narrow table, looking like the command center of a one-man newsroom. His laptop sat open on the coffee table, multiple tabs crowding the screen.

"Want something to drink?" he asked. "Coke? I also have iced tea."

"Coke is great," she said.

He brought them each a can of soda and motioned to the couch. "I have some things already queued on the laptop for us."

"You've been busy," Brooke said, settling onto the couch.

"I've been working on this off and on since you found Sheila's remains." Joe grabbed a notebook from the desk. "The thing about murder investigations is that they're built on timelines. Who was where and when. What they were doing. Who can verify it."

"And Tyler's timeline doesn't look good."

"It leaves questions." Joe flipped open the notebook. "Let's go through it. Not assuming anything. Just looking at facts."

He started with Sheila. First detailing how she moved to Irma as a young girl, her dad taking a job with an oil company based in Basin County, overseeing operations in northwest Wyoming.

She attended Irma schools from kindergarten through her high school graduation. Around the time Sheila entered middle school, her dad lost his job. There was some talk of wrongdoing on his part, possibly embezzlement of company funds, but nothing further came of it past rumors.

"The Irma grapevine," Brooke said. "It's always been strong."

"Yep. I reached out to a few people I know who are around the same age as Sheila's dad. Got a lot more info than the little bit the newspaper ran with. Her dad had a rough patch. Couldn't find work for about eighteen months. Sheila's mom waitressed and took odd jobs. I'm sure it was a difficult time for the family."

Joe shared a few more things about Sheila's adolescent years, including how her dad eventually found a job and things seemed to return to normal for the family.

"After graduating from Irma High School, she went to Casper for college. Sometime during those first months, she met her first husband, Shane Jenkins. They were married in mid-December, and she didn't return to college after winter break." Joe flipped the page.

"Like her dad, Shane worked for an oil company, but instead of being upper management, he was a rig worker. Two weeks on, two weeks off. The marriage lasted less than two years. Sheila returned to Irma after the split. She held a variety of jobs and eventually met Rusty Jones. I believe you know Mr. Jones." Joe paused to meet Brooke's gaze.

She rolled her eyes. "Yeah. Don't remind me."

"Rusty has a history of his own. Last night wasn't the first time he's been in a barroom brawl."

"We were at a steakhouse. Not exactly the place for brawling."

"Still . . . He's been arrested for similar activities before and spent more than one night in the drunk tank. During his marriage to Sheila, the cops responded to noise disturbances several times."

"Was he hitting her?"

Joe shook his head. "There were never any arrests for domestic violence and no evidence of it happening. A few police reports suggested Sheila may have been the instigator."

"Sounds like it was a toxic marriage."

"Indeed. As the marriage neared its end, she started working at the bank. There was some scuttlebutt about her having an affair with her manager, and that's what led to her divorce from Rusty. Chances are, she had her sights on Mr. Manager as husband number three, but he took his wife and left town before that happened."

Brooke leaned back in her chair. "I remember hearing about that. I had just opened the coffee shop around that time." She paused as memories of various conversations came back to her. "Wasn't one of the reasons the bank manager left because Rusty threatened him?"

"Bingo," Joe said. "He threatened not only the manager but the man's wife too. He was essentially stalking both of them. Even showing up at a restaurant where they were having dinner."

She shook her head. "Wow. That sounds very familiar."

"Doesn't it?"

"She dated a lot," Brooke said, trying not to sound too accusatory. Since her death, there had been plenty of rumors about how many people she went out with. "There's a game warden— "

"Henry Ayers. He was seeing her earlier in the year. They went to an event at the Elks Lodge for Valentine's Day and saw each other off and on for a few weeks after."

"So why isn't Adam bothering him like he is Tyler?"

Joe shrugged. "Hard telling. But Henry is definitely someone to consider. Back to Sheila. The weekend of her death, she was last seen leaving the bank on Friday evening around six. Security footage showed Tyler at the ATM around the same time. The ATM was at the front of the building, and they could just catch a glimpse of Tyler's truck in the camera. He'd parked along the curb."

"Did Sheila go out the door by the ATM? I thought staff used the back door and parked in the lot?"

"That's right. She went out the side door nearest the employee lot, not the door near the ATM."

"Do you have footage of her leaving?"

"No, I couldn't get it."

"How'd you get this?"

"Better for you not to know."

She understood Joe had contacts, and maybe not all of them were ones that should be public. "Do you have any other video footage? Showing either Sheila or Tyler?"

"There're a few things. You know that traffic light on Grand Avenue and Seventh? The one with the camera? There's footage of both of them going through there. About seven minutes apart. Tyler first, then Sheila."

"Which proves he didn't nab her at the bank."

"Right. He says he played darts that night. I checked at the Watering Hole, but they didn't have league that night."

Brooke nodded. "They don't have darts on Friday nights there now. They play at the Watering Hole on Thursdays. He plays at Bronco Willie's on Fridays."

He smiled. "I was going to mention I found that out since we talked last. I asked around. Who knew darts were so popular that they play at different bars on different nights?"

"Anything to pass the time around here."

"I guess. Anyway, Sheila wasn't at either of those bars that night. We don't know where she was. After the stoplight camera, there's nothing. No one admits to seeing her. Not until . . . " He tilted his head.

"Not until I found her Sunday morning in a pair of bear caches." Brooke swallowed hard as the memories of finding Sheila's body washed over her. "But she wasn't killed on the mountain. Just left there, right?"

"Yes, the theory is she was killed somewhere else and dumped. The bear saw an opportunity and took it."

Brooke made a face and shook her head. "Poor Sheila."

They moved on to Monique. Joe described an early childhood in a small town in Alabama before moving to Irma in the middle of sixth grade to be closer to family.

"Monique and Sheila were instant friends. They, along with a handful of other girls, formed a tight clique. They were part of what many people called the popular crowd, though they seemed to relish their popularity more than most." He took a long drink of his soda. "Tyler was part of the popular group, too, you know."

"I know my brother Phil and Tyler were good friends, and Phil had plenty of other friends."

"Which means they were immune to the antics of Sheila, Monique, and their group."

"Phil knew about it. He said they were the classic mean girls."

"Yep. They went out of their way to target students they thought were beneath them. I have statements from many former classmates, both men and women, who said the girls did everything they could to make their lives miserable." Joe shook his head.

"It didn't stop after high school either. As adults, both Monique and Sheila were known gossips. Sheila had been spoken to repeatedly by her bank supervisors. Monique worked for her aunt at the craft store, where she was originally in charge of the knitting and crochet circles. Too many of the conversations were being spread around, so her aunt stopped letting her participate in the circles."

"Did that stop the gossip?"

"According to the aunt, it did."

"And her death?"

"Monique's timeline is less clear. Her aunt left around three o'clock that day, but Monique stayed to close up. The building's alarm was set at five, exactly when it should've been."

"And then?"

"Nothing until her remains were found Sunday morning. In a different section of mountains than Sheila. She was also strangled."

"The same day Adam showed up at Gina's place and took Tyler in for questioning."

"Right. But let's not forget you were attacked on Saturday morning while out for your run."

Her hand went to the still-tender cut along her scalp. "I haven't forgotten."

He made a note in his notebook. "We know Tyler was at work that day."

Brooke nodded. "Robert verified that."

"But he doesn't have an alibi for Friday night. You went to Jocelyn's play with Steph. You thought he was going to play darts."

"I didn't know his friends that he usually played with were gone elk hunting."

"So, he doesn't have an alibi for Friday night. He works practically next door to where Monique works. There're rumors they dated in high school— "

"Tyler says that's a lie."

"And I'm leaning toward agreeing with him. While several people have said they heard Tyler and Monique dated, no one confirms it. Your brother even laughed about it, saying no way."

"You talked to Phil?"

"I've spoken to just about everyone who may have info on their history. But Tyler's lack of an alibi doesn't help him any."

"You think he killed her Friday night, dumped her, and went into work Saturday morning like it was just a normal day?"

"I think it's possible." Joe's expression was troubled. "I don't want it to be true, Brooke. But the timeline fits."

Brooke stood and walked to the window. Outside, the street was quiet. Normal. Like the world wasn't falling apart around her.

"What about motive?" she asked without turning around. "Why would Tyler kill them?"

"The theory stems fully from their dating in high school."

"But you just said you can't prove he dated Monique. And really, it was years ago." Brooke turned to face him. "If Tyler wasn't here, if he never came back, who would be the main suspect?"

"You're assuming they'd still be murdered."

"Because I don't believe Tyler is guilty."

"Who else had motive, access, and opportunity? Who else is smart enough to make Tyler look guilty? And why frame him?"

"Who else connects to both victims?"

"That's the question." Joe pulled his laptop closer and started typing. "Both women lived here for most of their lives. Both were part of the same friend group. Both worked in town."

"What about their personal lives? Relationships? Conflicts?"

"Sheila was twice divorced. Shane Jenkins doesn't live in the state, and as far as I can tell, they haven't had contact since the divorce was finalized. Rusty Jones has a temper, clearly, but he also has an alibi. He was visiting relatives out of town the weekend Sheila died. He knew Monique, since Sheila and her had been friends during their rocky marriage, but he has an alibi for that night too. He was working an overnight shift at the factory."

Brooke thought about Rusty's hands around Tyler's throat, about the rage in his eyes. She could see him doing it, but his alibis sounded solid. "What about Monique?"

"Never married. No kids. Lived alone. She'd worked at her aunt's store off and on since she was in high school. She and Sheila maintained their friendship, often going to bars and different events. We know Sheila mentioned a few people from the old gang going out when she was talking to Tyler at the bank."

"Yeah. Edi mentioned that too."

Joe scrolled through his notes. "Both women were strangled. Same method. Location of the crime is unknown. Same type of dump site—remote, no witnesses, bodies found later."

"Which suggests the same killer."

"Right. And that killer knew the area well enough to hide bodies where they wouldn't immediately be found, knew both victims well enough to get close to them, and had the physical strength to overpower them."

Brooke sighed. "Tyler fits all of that."

"Probably dozens of people do, but not all of them have history with both of them, even if it is ancient history."

"Then we need to find those dozens of people."

Joe studied her for a long moment. "You really think he's innocent."

"I think someone's lying. And I think we need to find out who."

Chapter 30

Tyler

Tyler was halfway through an oil change on Monday afternoon when Robert appeared in the bay doorway. He'd been tempted to ask Robert about the change in hiking plans, but couldn't come up with a reason that wouldn't sound out of left field and like he was accusing Robert.

"You've got a visitor," Robert said. "Joe Monroe."

Tyler straightened, wiping his hands on a shop rag. "The journalist?"

"That's the one. He's in the office."

"Did you tell him I'm working?"

Robert shrugged. "I told him you were due for a break. I've read some of the pieces he's put out about this. I think he's fair. And I know he's a friend of Brooke's."

Tyler let out a breath. If Robert had played any part in Sheila's death, he wouldn't want an investigative reporter hanging around, would he? Tyler didn't think so . . . unless somehow Robert was using Joe as part of the frame job.

Whether Robert was involved or not, Tyler knew he had to be careful. Journalists brought questions, speculation, and stories that twisted facts to sell papers. He had learned that when Jen died. Joe, though, was different.

As Robert had said, he was Brooke's friend. He was part of the running club, someone she trusted. That should count for something. At least he hoped.

"Okay. Guess I'll talk to him." Tyler nodded, wondering if that was a good thing or a bad thing.

He hadn't told Robert that Brooke had broken up with him. Even though he hadn't advertised that they'd been secretly seeing each other for weeks, he supposed Robert was smart enough to figure it out, considering what happened in Elkridge. Surprisingly, there'd been no contact from Adam Boverman about it. Not yet, anyway.

He found Joe standing in the break room, looking uncomfortable.

"Hey," Tyler said. "What can I do for you?"

"I need to talk to you. About the case." Joe met his eyes. "Brooke and I have been investigating."

The words hit Tyler square in the chest. Brooke. "Oh, yeah? When was this?"

"Yesterday. She called me. How's the jaw?" He motioned to where Rusty had clobbered him.

"Fine." At the moment, it didn't hurt. Nothing on him hurt now that he knew Brooke was still investigating, still trying to prove his innocence even after their breakup. "Did she ask you to come here?" Tyler heard the hope in his own voice and hated how obvious it was.

"Not exactly. But we've been going through everything together—timelines, alibis, evidence." Joe pulled out his notebook. "And I need to ask you some questions."

Tyler gestured at the chair. "All right."

They sat, and Joe flipped through pages of notes. "I know you were playing darts at Bronco Willie's the night Sheila died. But darts ends around, what, ten o'clock?"

"Usually. Earlier sometimes. Later other times. Just depends on how much beer is flowing."

"And that night?"

"Probably about ten.

"You left as soon as you were done?"

Tyler nodded slowly. "Yeah. I was tired and wanted to get home. Plus, I had plans for the next morning. You know about that."

"One of your buddies said you took off pretty quick." Joe looked up from his notebook. "So, you have an alibi until ten, maybe ten fifteen. Then nothing until you met Robert and Sue at eight the next morning."

"I went home. Went to bed."

"Alone."

"Yes, alone."

"They can't pinpoint the exact time of Sheila's death," Joe continued. "The coroner's estimate puts it somewhere between late Friday night and early Saturday morning. That gap in your alibi—that's why Adam thinks it's you."

Tyler's jaw tightened. "I didn't kill her."

Joe shrugged. "From an investigator's perspective, you don't have an alibi for the window when she likely died." Joe turned a page. "And Monique—you have no alibi at all for Friday night. Your dart buddies were at elk camp. Brooke went out with Steph."

"I was home. Alone. Again."

"Right. So, no alibi for either murder during the critical windows. Plus, Adam is still convinced you killed your wife and son. Everyone knows you dated Sheila in high school. And there's a rumor going around that you dated Monique too."

"That's not true," Tyler said sharply. "I never dated Monique. We barely knew each other in school."

"I believe you. Brooke's brother said the same thing. Laughed about it, actually. Said there was no way."

"Phil knows. We were friends back in high school. I would've told him if I was seeing someone."

"But someone's spreading this rumor." Joe leaned forward. "That's what doesn't add up. Who benefits from you looking guilty? Who's actively working to make the case against you stronger?"

Tyler thought about the note left on his truck, about the attack on Brooke, about the way evidence kept appearing that pointed directly at him.

"Someone's framing me. I've thought that all along. Brooke and I have talked about it. It has to be someone who knows me well enough to make it look convincing."

"Yeah, that's what Brooke said too. But who?"

Hearing her name again made Tyler's chest ache. "How is she?"

"Scared. Confused. Trying to figure out if she can trust her own judgment." Joe's expression softened slightly. "But she hasn't given up on you. She called me yesterday and said she needed to know the truth. We spent hours going through everything."

"She did that for me?"

"She did that for herself. She needs to know if you're innocent or if she's making the same mistake she made with Kelsey." Joe paused. "The mistake several of us made with Kelsey. I know Brooke blames herself, thinks that trusting Kelsey means she's a bad judge of character, but Kelsey fooled all of us. Even me, and I don't trust anyone."

Tyler snorted. "Probably what makes you good at your job."

"I'd like to think so. But anyway, about Brooke, she's fighting for you even when she thinks staying away is safer."

Tyler stood and walked to the small window overlooking the parking lot of the hardware store next door. A customer was loading something into their trunk. He glanced at the craft store across the street, where Monique used to work.

"I've been thinking about who might want to frame me and why. Honestly, I have no idea." He turned back to face Joe. "There's this game warden— "

"Yep. Henry Ayers. He's on my list. Who else should be on it? That's the question. Let's work through it. Who knew both victims?"

Tyler thought about mentioning Robert, but it still didn't feel right. Yesterday he almost had himself convinced Robert was having an affair with either Sheila or Monique, but he still hated to believe that, hated to make any accusations that might come out and cause trouble for Robert or Sue.

"Half the town." He shrugged. "They've both lived here practically forever and worked locally. Everyone knew them."

"But who knew them well? Who had access to them? Who could get close enough to kill them without raising suspicion?"

"Again, half the town. You've lived here for a while now, right? You know how this place is."

"I've only been here since February, but yeah, I'm beginning to realize how it is. You went to school with them. Both Brooke and Phil said they had a bit of a reputation. Very cliquish."

"Cliquish? I don't know about that. They weren't very nice to people sometimes. I'll admit, I never thought much about it. It was high school. Who cares?"

"Brooke said there were a few others in their group. Do you remember any of them?"

"I don't know. Maybe." Tyler thought back, trying to recall faces and names. "There was another girl—Stacy something. A few others, maybe. I think they were cheerleaders. Not Monique. She wasn't. But Sheila and the others were. I knew them, but we didn't hang out much outside of school. And I don't know much about what happened while I was gone."

"What about conflicts? Did Sheila or Monique have enemies?"

"It was high school," Tyler said bluntly. "Everyone had conflicts. Raging hormones and all that. They made life difficult for people they decided weren't worth their time, targeted kids who didn't fit in."

Joe made a note. "So potentially a lot of people who might hold grudges."

"Yeah. But enough to kill them all these years later? That doesn't even make sense."

"People have killed for less." Joe tapped his pen against the notebook. "What about more recently? Any conflicts you know about?"

Tyler thought about the conversation at the bank. Sheila mentioned getting together with old friends. She'd been friendly, normal, like they were just people who used to know each other.

"Sheila wanted to organize a reunion of sorts," Tyler said. "She mentioned it to Edi and me. Said we should all get together, listen to music, have drinks."

"Did that happen?"

"No. She died before anything was planned."

Joe wrote something down. "Who else was she planning to invite?"

"Monique, probably. I think she mentioned her. A few others, but I didn't recognize any of the names. She wanted to get the old gang back together."

"Was Edi part of the old gang?"

"No, not really. She graduated the same year, but they weren't friends."

"But Sheila invited her to the reunion?"

"Maybe they're friends now? Have I mentioned we all left high school behind a long time ago?"

"You've mentioned you left high school behind. But I've heard there are several people in this town who were a big deal in high school and think they are the same big deal years later, when they aren't."

"Huh?"

"Someone told me Sheila pretty much peaked in high school. Her life had been a train wreck since then, but she hadn't seen it. She still thought she was the popular girl."

Tyler thought about when he talked to Sheila at the bank. He could see that, he supposed. But it still made little sense.

They talked for another twenty minutes, going through connections and possibilities. Nothing concrete emerged, but patterns started forming. Both were victims from the same high school crowd. Both were killed after Tyler returned to town. Both were connected to him through rumor or fact in ways that made him look guilty.

"Someone knows you," Joe said finally. "Knows your history, your routines, your connections. They're using that knowledge to set you up."

"But why?"

"That's what we need to figure out." Joe closed his notebook. "Brooke and I are going to keep digging and look for connections we're missing. I'll interview people who knew Sheila and Monique. Maybe the three of us should work together?"

"You think she would? Want to work with me, I mean."

"I can ask her. You have any plans tonight?"

Tyler didn't even try to hide his smile. "Nope."

"Let me reach out to Brooke and see what she thinks. You guys can come to my place. I'll grill some burgers. We'll go over everything together and see what comes up. Maybe I'll see if her brother wants to join us. He seems to have his finger on the pulse of the community."

Tyler chuckled. "You make it sound like Phil's nosy."

"He does hear all the buzz at the print shop."

"It'd probably be good to bring him in on this," Tyler agreed. "One thing I do know, we need to be careful. Whoever's doing this has already killed twice. And I'm positive Brooke was attacked because of this. I don't want her getting hurt again."

"We'll be careful." Joe stood. "But we need more evidence. More proof. Right now, we have questions but not answers."

Tyler walked him to the main entrance. "Thank you. For helping. For believing me."

"Thank you for talking to me. For what it's worth, I think Brooke made a mistake breaking up with you. She's scared, and I get that. But you two are better together than apart."

After Joe left, Tyler stood by the door, staring at nothing.

Brooke was still fighting for him. Still investigating. Still trying to prove his innocence, even though she'd ended things.

He'd agreed to the breakup because he thought it'd keep her safe, thought distance would protect her from whoever was targeting him.

But Joe was right. They were stronger together.

Right now, he had work to finish. But tonight, thanks to Joe, he was going to see Brooke.

Chapter 31

Brooke

Brooke pushed through the back door of the coffee shop and headed toward her car in the alley when her phone chimed.

She tried to balance the coffee in one hand while digging her phone out of her daypack. It didn't go as planned, and she missed the call.

"Well, fine," she muttered, setting the cup on the hood of her SUV.

The missed call was from Joe. She tamped down her disappointment. It wasn't that she didn't want to hear from him—she hoped he'd learned more since yesterday. Still, part of her had been hoping it was Tyler. Every time her phone rang or a message came through, she wanted it to be him.

She couldn't stop thinking about him. About the text she sent yesterday morning. About his reply, that had been so understanding, so quick to agree that staying apart was best.

The breakup was supposed to protect them both, keep her reputation intact, and keep her safe from whoever was targeting people connected to Tyler.

Instead, she felt empty. Broken. Like she was making the biggest mistake of her life.

She called Joe back.

"Hey," he said when he answered.

"Hey, yourself. What's up?"

"Do you have plans this evening?"

She leaned against her car. "Not really. I need to get a run in. I should've done it yesterday, but you know how my day went. Why? Did you find something?"

"I went to see Tyler today. We talked for a while but didn't finish. He's meeting me at my place after work around six thirty. Thought you might want to join us."

Brooke's heart kicked into a higher gear. "I don't know if that's a good idea."

"Why not? You're the one who asked me to investigate. You wanted to know the truth."

"I do. But— "

"But what? You scared to see him?"

Yes. That was exactly it. She was terrified to see Tyler, terrified that being near him would make her want to take back everything she'd said and make her forget all the very good reasons they needed to stay apart. She was terrified that seeing him would open the hole in her heart even further.

"Brooke," Joe said gently. "You broke up with him yesterday. But you spent part of the day moping and the rest of it investigating his case. You haven't given up on him. So why are you hiding?"

"I'm not hiding."

"Aren't you?"

She kicked her car's tire with her heel. "What if I can't trust my judgment? What if I'm wrong about him? It's like Kelsey all over again. You know that."

"It's not like Kelsey. We discussed this yesterday, remember? Besides, what if you're right? What if he's innocent and you walk away from something real because you were too scared to take the risk?"

The words hit hard. Brooke closed her eyes, thinking about Saturday night at the steakhouse. The way Tyler had looked at her across the table. The way he'd stood up to Rusty. The way she'd grabbed that chair without hesitation because Tyler's life was in danger.

She'd fought for him then, literally hit someone to protect him. And she'd do it again in a heartbeat.

She'd fight for him without thinking. But staying meant something else entirely.

"Come to my place," Joe said. "Half past six. I'm going to ask Phil to join us too."

"Phil? Why are you inviting my brother?"

"For the historical perspective partly, and partly because, like you, he owns a business in town. A business where people talk."

"You mean gossip?"

"That too. But really, if you decide you can't handle seeing Tyler, you can leave. But at least give yourself the chance."

After they hung up, Brooke leaned against her car, rhythmically kicking the tire for several minutes. The noise her heel made as it connected with the tire was both comforting and irritating.

She thought about Tyler's hands, always stained with grease no matter how much he scrubbed them. The way he'd looked at her that first day on the mountain, calm and steady when she was panicking. How he listened, actually listened, when they talked. The way he'd kissed her, like she was something precious.

She thought about the note on his truck. The attack on the trail. The murders of two women who'd gone to high school with him all those years ago. About the death of his wife and child and how she knew he still loved them and missed them.

She thought about Adam Boverman's certainty. The evidence. The timeline. All the reasons staying away made sense.

She thought about Joe's words. *You're the one who asked me to investigate. You wanted to know the truth.*

The truth. That's what this came down to. Not what people thought. Not what the evidence suggested. But what she knew in her bones to be true.

Tyler was innocent.

And she loved him.

The realization hit her with sudden clarity. She loved him. Not despite the danger or the suspicion or the gossip. Not because she was trying to prove something to herself or the town.

She loved him because of who he was. A man who'd lost everything and kept going. A man who'd come back to face his past instead of running from it. A man who looked at her like she was worth fighting for.

A man who'd agreed to let her go because he thought it'd keep her safe.

She hit the key fob and unlocked her car. She didn't care what the town thought. She needed to be with him and tell him she'd made a mistake, that they were stronger together than apart.

Brooke started up her car and began to pull forward. That's when she saw it. The coffee cup sat on the hood where she'd left it. "Brilliant, Brooke," she muttered, putting the car back into park and retrieving the now-cold coffee. She made a face as she took a sip.

"Life's too short," she said, taking the cup to the dumpster. "Too short for cold coffee and pretending I don't want him."

Brooke stepped out of the shower. Her run was exactly what she needed, an easy half hour. Her body handled it well. She knew she had a lot of training ahead of her if she was going to complete the Moose Range Run 100.

If was the big question.

Registration opened in a week and a half. She'd need to be ready the minute it opened to guarantee herself a spot and not be waitlisted. If she got in, she'd have a little over eight months until race day. She was still in what she considered the base building phase. Her hard training wouldn't start until late January. And, unlike last year, she needed to make sure to build some flexibility into her plan.

She'd definitely learned a hard lesson about how crazy training could make her, and she wasn't going to let that happen this time. She was even thinking about taking Tyler up on his offer to train with her. He admitted he may not be able to run the distances she did, but he could bike alongside her. The idea of it sent a warm feeling through her.

"Don't get ahead of yourself," she told her reflection in the fogged-up mirror. "See how it goes tonight. Maybe he won't even want you anymore. You're too wishy-washy. Besides, maybe you don't even want to do that stupid race. There's no reason you have to put yourself through that torture."

She gave herself a nod, knowing that even though it'd be smart to forget about running a hundred miles up and down the steep mountainsides, giving up that dream felt almost as hard as giving up Tyler.

Brooke rushed to get ready, putting her hair up instead of styling it while taking a few minutes for her makeup. A skirt, blouse, and sandals would do. At the mirror by the front door, she gave her makeup a final check. "Here goes nothing."

The drive to Joe's townhouse took less than ten minutes. Brooke parked on the street and sat for a moment, gathering her courage.

What if Tyler didn't want her back? He really might think she's too wishy-washy—or had already moved on? What if seeing her again just made things harder for him?

Stop it, she told herself firmly. *I don't get to make decisions for him. If he wants space, he can tell me himself.*

She looked up and down the street. Not seeing Tyler's truck anywhere. "Hmm. Maybe I'm not the one who has cold feet. Might as well see this through."

She climbed out of the SUV and headed for Joe's door. She didn't see Phil's car anywhere either.

Joe answered on the first knock. "Knew you'd come."

"Yeah, well . . . " Brooke stepped inside. "Tyler's not here?"

"Not yet. He should be here any time." Joe gestured toward the couch. "Phil's on his way too. He had a late job come in, but said he's wrapping it up and will be here in fifteen minutes or so. Want something to drink?"

"No, thank you. I'm good."

She sat, then stood, then sat again. Her hands wouldn't stay still. She smoothed her hair, checked her phone, and smoothed her hair again.

"You're nervous," Joe observed.

"I broke up with him yesterday. Via text. Now I'm showing up to tell him I was wrong. Of course I'm nervous."

"He'll be glad to see you."

"You don't know that."

"I do, actually. We talked about you today. He asked how you were doing and if you were okay." Joe's expression was knowing. "That man is in love with you, Brooke. Even if he hasn't said it yet."

The words filled her with warmth and sent a smile across her face. "What if— "

A knock at the door cut her off.

Brooke's heart jumped into her throat. Joe moved to answer it, and there was Tyler, standing in the doorway with exhaustion written across his face.

Then he saw her.

Everything about him changed. His expression shifted from tired to happy to something else. Something that made Brooke's knees weak.

"Brooke," he said, and just her name in his voice was enough to make her certain she'd made the right choice coming here.

"Hi."

Tyler stepped inside, his eyes never leaving hers. Joe said something about getting drinks and giving them a minute, but Brooke barely heard him. Her entire world was Tyler.

The black eye Rusty had given him looked painful. And he looked like he hadn't slept well, like maybe he'd been up all night thinking about her the same way she'd been thinking about him.

"I wasn't sure you'd be here," Tyler said.

"Joe called. Asked if I wanted to come."

"Are you glad you did?"

Brooke took a step closer. "Yes."

"I'm glad you're here. I wanted to call earlier and tell you that the breakup was a mistake, that we're better together."

"I wanted to tell you the same thing."

They stood there, three feet apart, the space between them charged with everything unsaid. Brooke wanted to close the distance, wanted to touch him, kiss him, make sure he was real and here and hers.

But she needed to say it first. Needed him to know.

"I love you," Brooke said, the words tumbling out before she could second-guess them. "I don't care what the town thinks. I don't care about the danger or the gossip or any of it. I love you, and I want to be with you."

"Brooke— "

"Let me finish." She took another step closer. "I was scared. I *am* scared. But not of you. I'm scared of losing you. I'm scared of getting this wrong. Scared I'm going to mess things up. And I might. I'm a mess sometimes, and I do stupid things. But staying away from you isn't the answer. Fighting for us is."

"I love you too," Tyler said, his voice rough with emotion. "Mess and all."

The distance between them disappeared. Brooke wasn't sure who moved first, but suddenly she was in his arms, and he was holding her like she was the only solid thing in a world gone sideways.

"I'm sorry," she whispered against his chest. "For the text. For pulling away."

"Don't be sorry. You were trying to protect yourself." Tyler pulled back enough to look at her. "But Joe's right. We're stronger together."

When they broke apart, Joe was standing in the kitchen doorway with a satisfied smile.

"Glad that's settled," he said. "Now, can we get to work? We need to sort out who is framing Tyler and prove it before they kill again."

Chapter 32

Tyler

Tyler couldn't take his eyes off Brooke. She sat close to him on Joe's couch, her hand in his. Every time their eyes met, his chest tightened with something he couldn't name.

She loved him. She had said it out loud, in front of Joe, without hesitation.

And he loved her back, more fiercely than he had realized he could.

"All right," Joe said, appearing from the kitchen with three bottles of water. "I've got burgers ready to grill. We can eat first, if you want, or go over everything first. Your call."

Tyler glanced at Brooke. "What do you think?"

"It's nice out," she said. "Maybe we could sit on the patio? You could grill while we talk?"

"Works for me." Joe headed back to the kitchen. "Tyler, can you help me carry things out?"

They moved food and drinks to Joe's small patio. The evening air was cooling down. Joe fired up the grill while Tyler set plates and condiments on the table.

"Phil should be here any minute." Joe gestured toward the slider. It was open with the screen in place. "We'll hear when he gets here."

"I would've thought he'd be here by now," Brooke said, checking her watch.

"Maybe something came up?" Tyler suggested.

"He would've called," Joe said. "He's probably— "

A knock at the door interrupted him. Joe looked at Tyler. "And there we go. Mind grabbing the door?"

Tyler walked back through the house and opened the door. Phil stood there, but his usual easy smile was gone, replaced by a tight, concerned expression.

"What's wrong?" Tyler asked.

Phil held up a piece of paper. "Pulled up behind your truck. When I was walking by, I saw this stuck under the windshield wiper."

Tyler's stomach dropped. He took the paper, his hands already shaking.

Generic printer paper. Same as before. But the message was different.

Two threats neutralized. All your fault! You made this necessary!!

"You found this on my windshield?" Tyler managed.

"Yep. I parked, walked by, and there it was."

Tyler rushed past Phil out into the street. His truck sat at the curb, exactly where he'd left it twenty minutes ago. He scanned the street in both directions. There were a few parked cars and an elderly woman walking a dog down the block. Nothing suspicious. No one watching.

"Did you see anyone?" Tyler called back to Phil.

"No, sorry."

Tyler stared at the paper in his hand. *Two threats neutralized.* Sheila and Monique. *All your fault! You made this necessary!!*

The murderer blamed him, but he still didn't know why.

His chest went tight. Brooke. If the killer thought she was another threat . . .

He jogged back inside. Brooke and Joe were already in the living room, Phil explaining what he'd found.

"Let me see it," Joe said.

Tyler handed over the note.

Joe studied it, his journalist brain already working. "Does it say the same thing as the last note?"

"Same kind of vibe," Tyler said. "Different words."

"What's 'threats neutralized' mean?" Brooke asked, reading over Joe's shoulder. "I mean, obviously they're talking about Sheila and Monique. But that's a weird way to phrase it."

"Yeah." Joe frowned. "It's odd. And familiar somehow."

"We should call it in," Tyler said. "Tell Boverman— "

"No." Brooke's voice was sharp. "Adam has his own agenda. We can't trust him with this."

Tyler sighed. She was right, but Adam was still law enforcement. "He probably should know, though."

"I think Brooke's right," Phil said. "Boverman's been after you since the fire. He's not going to investigate this objectively."

"Then we call Edi. I gave her the first note."

"I thought Edi was persona non grata," Phil said. "Ordered off the case."

"She was, but this is different."

"Is it?"

Joe was still staring at the note. "Let's eat first and talk through everything. Then we can decide about calling someone." He motioned toward the patio. "Come on. I need to flip the burgers."

Joe took care of the burgers while Tyler, Brooke, and Phil settled in at the small table. Joe had brought out a folder of printouts—articles, timelines, and notes from his investigation.

"Start with the basics," Joe said, transferring burgers to a plate. "Both victims lived here for years. Sheila moved to Casper for a short time for college and an ill-fated marriage, but came back. Monique never left. She started working at her aunt's craft store in high school. She had a few other jobs, too, when the store was too slow to give her full-time hours."

"They were good friends," Phil added. "I remember them from high school, though they were a couple of years behind us. They were popular with the boys."

"With the boys," Brooke repeated, shaking her head.

"What? They were. They went out of their way to be friendly. It's not much of a surprise, and it didn't end with high school. When Sheila returned to Irma from Casper, she was on the prowl. Went to the bars. Drank too much. Went home with whoever. She had a reputation."

Tyler knew Phil was right. He'd heard plenty since Sheila's death. Monique, too, though it seemed she'd slowed down on dating and drinking in recent years.

"And both women were considered troublemakers of sorts," Joe added.

"Mean girls," Brooke said. "In high school, at least. Phil said they went out of their way to torment those who were less popular or underclassmen."

"Does that matter?" Tyler asked. "I mean, it was high school."

"Boverman's entire theory of why you killed Sheila hinges on you two dating in high school," Brooke said, serving herself some salad. "If Adam can say that matters, I can say that being mean girls matters."

"Don't forget there's a rumor floating around that Tyler dated Monique." Phil laughed.

"Don't remind me." Tyler shook his head. "Wish I knew who was saying that. Monique and I barely ever even spoke."

"There's something else we need to consider," Phil added. "They were both dumped in the woods."

"Beartooth Mountains," Brooke said softly.

"Right. Found in remote locations, dumped after death." Joe brought the burgers to the table and sat down. "The killer knows the area. Knows how to hide bodies. Has physical strength."

Tyler reached for a burger. His appetite was gone, but he knew he needed to eat. "That describes half the county."

"But not half the county has a connection to both victims." Joe pulled out a timeline. "Look at this. Sheila died sometime Friday night or early Saturday. Tyler has an alibi until about ten o'clock—darts with witnesses. But after that, nothing until meeting Robert and Sue at eight the next morning."

"I was home," Tyler said. "Alone."

"I believe you, but from an investigator's perspective, that's a gap." Joe turned to another page. "Monique died between Friday night and Saturday morning, just like Sheila. Only this time, Tyler has no alibi at all. He was home alone the entire evening."

"My dart buddies were at elk camp," Tyler explained to Phil. "Brooke went out with Steph."

Brooke squeezed Tyler's hand. "We've been over this. The alibis are weak, but it doesn't mean anything."

"No," Joe agreed. "But it makes him look guilty. Which is exactly what someone wants."

"Both of them were killed on a Friday night or a Saturday morning?" Phil said. "And found on Sunday? That sounds like a pattern."

"It is," Joe agreed. "But we don't know what that pattern means."

"Whoever did it was off during that time?" Phil suggested.

"Off?" Brooke said. "Off work?"

"Right," he agreed with a nod.

"Not a stretch," Joe said. "Weekends off are common."

Tyler knew Joe was right, but it was interesting that both women were killed in the same timeframe. And he didn't have an alibi for either time.

They ate while going through the file—articles about the murders, timelines Joe had constructed, lists of people connected to both victims.

Joe was reaching for his burger when he stopped midmotion. "That's it!"

"What's it?" Tyler asked.

"Can I see the note again? The one Phil just found on your windshield."

Tyler pulled it out of the folder and handed it to Joe.

Joe nodded as he read it. "The wording. 'Threats neutralized.' That's not how regular people talk. That's law enforcement. Military." Joe picked up the note again. "Civilians don't say 'neutralized.' They say killed. Murdered. Something direct."

Ice slid down Tyler's spine. "You think this is from a cop?"

"Or someone with military training. But given the context— " Joe looked around the table.

"Adam," Tyler said immediately. "He's been obsessed with proving I'm guilty since the fire."

"But Adam's been vocal," Brooke pointed out. "He arrested you in front of half the town. He shows up everywhere you go. Why would he send anonymous notes?"

"To scare me. To make me leave town."

"Because he's a psycho." Phil leaned back in his chair. "An obsessed psycho. He's been after you since Jen died, Tyler. You know it. I know it. Everyone does."

"Boverman writing the note makes sense," Joe said, tapping the word neutralized with his finger. "Not only is he with the sheriff's department, but he was in the Army before that."

"He was in the Army?" Brooke asked, her eyes wide. "And this is like an Army phrase?"

Joe shrugged. "Some military would use the phrase. Adam was an MP, so it fits."

"Military Police. I guess that makes sense." Brooke shook her head. "You think he'd kill two women just to frame Tyler for it because . . . because what? He thinks Tyler killed Jen and Garrett? That seems a little extreme."

"I told you, he's a psycho," Phil muttered.

"Is he, though?" Tyler asked. "I agree he's obsessed with me. And I could maybe see him planting evidence and framing me. But add in the murder of two women as part of that frame job, and it seems like Brooke said. Extreme."

"He's been stalking you," Phil said. "Arrested you for Sheila's murder. Took you in for Monique's murder. Insists that you and she used to date. I'd put money on him being the one who made that up and spread it around town. I wouldn't even be surprised if somehow he'd made sure Sheila's ex-husband—what's his name?"

"Rusty," Tyler and Brooke replied in unison.

"Yeah. Him. Wouldn't surprise me a bit if Adam is behind that incident too. Like he sicced him on you. Followed you two to Elkridge and then called Rusty and told him where you were."

"That's a stretch." Brooke shook her head. "I mean, really. Why do that? Besides, if we are saying Tyler is being framed, then that means Adam is a killer. He doesn't seem like a killer."

The way she said it had Tyler looking at her. Does she know Adam better than he thought?

Brooke crinkled her forehead. "Would a game warden use words like that? Neutralized."

Tyler nodded, while Joe said, "Maybe so."

"Game warden?" Phil asked.

Joe briefed Phil on Henry. "So, we know Henry dated Sheila, but I haven't found any direct connection between him and Monique other than the fact that the women were friends. They didn't date or double date or anything. He could've killed both of them, but . . . " Joe shrugged. "I'm still looking into it."

"But it could be him, right?" Brooke asked. "The wording might fit?"

"Neutralized might be used when talking about wildlife," Phil said.

Tyler leaned back in his seat as he turned over the words on the note—not only the words, but the fact it was left on his truck. His truck parked in front of Joe's condo.

Is Adam following me again? That could make sense. The game warden, though, doesn't make much sense. How would he know where to find me? I don't even know him and have only spoken to him the one time at the shop.

He sat up in his chair. Robert knew he was coming over to Joe's. After Joe left the shop, Robert asked how it'd gone. Tyler had told him they were going to figure out who was framing him and that they were meeting up after work.

A sick feeling came over Tyler.

"What's wrong?" Brooke asked, touching his arm.

He shook his head. "What if it's Robert?"

"Robert?" She crinkled her brow. "Your boss?"

He nodded.

"Dude?" Phil shook his head. "You can't go accusing your boss of being a murderer and framing you for it. Not if you want to keep your job. Or have any job in Irma."

Tyler raised his hands. "I know . . . it sounds crazy. But did I ever tell you why we were on the loop trail that day? Robert suggested that hike. We were going somewhere else, one of the peaks, but he said his back hurt and he wanted to take the loop since it's mostly flat."

He glanced at Brooke, who gave a nod and said, "It's an easy one."

"Right. And I didn't think anything of it until yesterday, when I was remembering why we went there."

Phil shook his head. "Seems a stretch to accuse your boss of murder because he had a backache and wanted to take an easier hike."

Tyler shrugged. "It does, but— "

"But what if he was seeing Sheila and killed her and was some kind of sicko who thought it'd be fun for his wife to find a body?" Phil made a face.

"She didn't find the body," Brooke said softly. "I did. But I wouldn't have found it if I'd stayed on the trail. None of us would have."

"I think it's worth exploring," Joe said, though his voice lacked conviction. He made a note on his paper. "So, we have Henry, Adam, and Robert."

Phil laughed and shook his head. "I still can't believe you're accusing your boss."

"I'm not accusing him," Tyler said, though he knew that wasn't exactly true. "I'm just saying, someone killed them and is framing me. Robert knew I was coming here tonight. He makes more sense than the game warden. Unless he'd been following me around like Adam does."

"But Adam stopped following you," Brooke said. "You haven't seen him lately, right?"

"True." Tyler nodded. "I haven't *seen* him."

"Doesn't mean he hasn't been around," Phil said. "My money is on him. He's had it in for you all these years."

Joe turned to Tyler. "Tell me again about the first note. What exactly did it say?"

"I'll do one better," Tyler said, pulling out his phone. "I took a picture of it before Edi arrived. She has the original."

It took him a couple of minutes to find the picture, his mind more on the way Brooke had been sure Adam couldn't be a killer than on finding the photo. *Stop it, Tyler,* he told himself. *She loves you. She told you she loves you. Don't go borrowing trouble.*

"Here it is." He handed his phone to Joe.

Brooke leaned toward it. "I didn't know you photographed it. You never showed me."

"Didn't seem right to show you," he admitted. "But I wanted a record. Just in case."

She smiled at him and reached out to take his hand. "Smart."

Joe read it out loud. "'*You should've stayed away. You have blood on your hands. Who's next?*' The words are different, but the paper looks pretty much the same. It's a printout. Typed in what looks like Arial font, printed, then cut to size with scissors. Odd, but that's what was done with both of them."

"The other one seems more normal, though, don't you think?" Brooke asked. "I mean the wording."

Phil scoffed. "Nothing normal about either note."

Joe nodded. "Both are odd. The wording is a little strange in both of them. Seems to me they were written by the same person. Too many similarities not to be. Or . . . " Joe paused as he looked to Tyler. "Who all knew about the first note?"

"Sue and Robert, before we called in Edi. She bagged it and took it with her."

"Not Adam?"

"No. Adam . . . no. I called Edi. She came, said it was probably a prank but took my complaint. Chances are good, though, she showed it to him. Boverman and the rest of the sheriff's department. You heard about the note, right?"

"Not until Gina told me about it, and that was after Brooke was attacked— " Joe glanced at the timeline he'd written out " —two weeks later."

Brooke she gave a shudder and closed her eyes. She'd recovered from the physical wounds, but Tyler knew she was still scared to go running where someone could hide.

She opened her eyes and found him watching her. She gave him a faint smile.

"We should probably call Edi about this note too," Brooke said.

"Should we?" Joe asked, leaning forward. "What if it's not Adam leaving the notes? What if it's Edi?"

Chapter 33

Brooke

Brooke stared at the note lying on Joe's patio table. *Two threats neutralized.* The clinical language made her skin crawl.

"We need to talk about keeping you safe," Tyler said, his hand tightening on hers.

"I'm fine."

"You've already been attacked once," Phil said bluntly. "Someone grabbed you on a trail and tried to drag you into the woods. You didn't get a look at their face, right?"

"You know I didn't."

"But do you think it was Adam?"

Brooke stared at the note as she thought back to that awful day. "It could've been Adam. The height is right."

"What about the game warden? Could it be him?"

She shrugged. "I don't know. I only saw him from a distance." She closed her eyes and thought back to that day. "He was standing next to Edi . . . no, I don't think so. He was shorter than her by several inches. Edi is about the same height as Adam. Same build too. The game warden is shorter."

"Could it have been Edi?" Joe asked, his voice soft.

"I never would've thought it was a woman, but Edi . . . she's tall."

"And big," Phil added.

"Phil." Brooke pursed her lips. "Be nice."

"Hey, I'm telling the truth. Edi's always been a big girl. Back in elementary school, kids teased her something awful. You remember, Tyler? They'd chant, 'Edi, Edi two-by-four can't fit through the schoolhouse door.'"

Tyler shook his head. "I don't remember doing that."

"Not you. Not me either, but some of them did. Like . . . " He glanced out toward the yard, as if trying to remember. "Sheila. I'm pretty sure she was one of them."

"Sheila used to make fun of Edi?" Joe sat up straight. "What about Monique?"

Phil shook his head. "She didn't live here when we were young. Not until . . . "

"Middle school," Joe said, shuffling through his notes. "I'm pretty sure she moved to Irma sometime around then."

"Yes," Brooke said. "You told me before about this. Sixth grade. Then Monique and Sheila were best friends."

"Thick as thieves." Phil nodded. "They were always together. Had a few others in their posse, too, but if Sheila was around, you could count on seeing Monique too."

"And Edi?" Joe asked, making a note on his timeline.

"Nothing really changed for her. She was always on the outside looking in. I don't think it bothered her much. She wasn't part of the popular crowd, but she didn't need to be."

Joe's pen stopped moving. "Why is that?"

"You know about Edi's family?"

"Can't say I do. She hasn't been the focus of my research. Something I intend to remedy with this new information."

Phil detailed how Edi's family had long ties with the community and plenty of money. "Her mom's a Goldworth."

"As in former US Senator Davidson Goldworth?"

"That's her grandpa. I take it you've heard of him."

Joe snickered. "Everyone's heard of Davidson Goldworth."

Brooke knew he was right. Goldworth had been a major political figure, and his failed reelection had been all anyone talked about for weeks. Even Brooke, away at college by then, had heard plenty.

She rarely thought about the connection between Edi and Senator Goldworth, although she knew Edi had grown up wealthy. You'd never guess it now. Edi worked steadily as a deputy, drove an ordinary-looking car during her off-hours, and had told Brooke more than once, usually while stopping in for coffee, about her modest condo and her two cats.

"Back to Brooke," Phil said, pointing at her. "She's been attacked once already."

"I already told you, I'm fine," she said, giving her brother a look.

"Fine is not the word I would use. You could've been killed."

"I fought them off."

"Because hikers showed up," Tyler said quietly. "What if they hadn't? What if next time there's no one around?"

The fear in his voice stopped her protest. She looked at his face and saw the genuine terror there. This wasn't about controlling her. It was about not losing her.

"Okay," she said. "I'm already being extra careful. I never go anywhere alone."

"Not enough." Phil shook his head.

"What do you suggest?"

"You should move home. Dad's there most of the time. You'd never be alone."

Brooke made a face. "Don't remind me."

"What's wrong with Dad?"

"Nothing's wrong with Dad. But I'm thirty-two years old. I'm not moving back into my childhood bedroom because I'm scared."

"Hey, I live at home. It's not that bad. Besides, it's not about being scared. It's about being smart."

"I can be smart and stay in my own house."

Tyler cleared his throat. "What if I stayed with you? At your place. Just until this is sorted out."

The offer hung in the air. Brooke felt heat creep up her neck. Tyler quickly added, "I can stay in your extra room."

"So, you two are really together?" Phil asked, looking between them.

Joe grinned. "Oh, you missed it earlier. Right after Tyler got here. Very romantic."

"Joe," Brooke warned.

"What? It was. The whole 'I love you; I love you too' thing. Very sweet."

Phil's eyebrows shot up. "You said that? Out loud? In front of people?"

"In front of Joe," Brooke said, lifting her chin. "I did. We did. We love each other."

"It's about time," Phil said, his face splitting into a genuine smile. "You two can be good together. If you both wouldn't be such boneheads." He bugged his eyes out at her.

"Thanks, bro," she said, rolling her eyes.

Even with his silliness, Brooke felt something warm in her chest. Phil's approval mattered more than she realized. He'd been Tyler's friend first, had believed in his innocence when others didn't. Having his support for their relationship felt like a blessing.

And he was right about her being a bonehead. She'd been so indecisive about Tyler. Sometimes, she was sure they could make it work, and other times she was full of doubt. Not because she thought he was a killer, more because she was still a mess from what happened with Kelsey. That whole thing still stung and left her questioning her own judgement.

That ended now.

She supposed she should talk to her dad about Tyler too. She'd mostly kept a lid on the relationship since it was so complicated, but the truth was, she could no longer deny her feelings and didn't care who knew.

"So that settles one problem," Joe said. "Tyler stays with Brooke for now. What else?"

"We take the evidence to the sheriff," Tyler said. "Show him the notes, explain our concerns."

"About one of his deputies possibly being a killer?" Phil shook his head. "That's not going to go over well."

"It has to be done," Joe said. "We can't sit on this. Two women are dead. There's been another threat. The sheriff needs to know."

Brooke thought about the sheriff. She knew him casually—he came into the coffee shop sometimes and always ordered the same thing. Black coffee and whatever pastry looked good. He was fair, from what she'd heard. But asking him to investigate one of his own people?

"Steph could help," Brooke said suddenly.

"Steph?" Joe asked.

"Yeah. She was engaged to the sheriff's son. That ended . . . oh, I guess about a year and a half ago. Steph was treated like family. And she's still friendly with most of them. Even her former fiancé and his new wife. She could get us a meeting, make sure he takes it seriously instead of dismissing it as paranoia."

"That's not a bad idea," Joe said, already pulling out his phone. "Mind if I call her now?"

"Go ahead."

Joe stepped back inside the house, his voice fading as he moved toward the living room.

Phil stood and started clearing plates. "I'll clean up. You two talk."

Once they were alone on the patio, Tyler turned to face Brooke fully. The sun had dropped below the Beartooth Mountains, casting long shadows across the small space. He looked tired but determined.

"I meant what I said," Tyler told her. "About staying with you. Whatever happens, we face it together."

"Even if it's dangerous?"

"Especially then." His hand came up to cup her face. "I love you, Brooke. I'm not going to let doubt keep us apart. Not anymore."

She leaned into his touch. "I love you, and I'm not going anywhere. I'm finished letting fear make my decisions."

"We're really doing this?"

"We're really doing this." She smiled. "Fair warning, though—I'm terrible at sharing my space. I like things a certain way. And I'm not great at compromise. And you already know how I can sometimes fixate on things."

"I'll take my chances."

They kissed, soft and sweet, a promise of more to come.

When they pulled apart, Brooke rested her forehead against his. "This is going to be complicated."

"Everything worth having is."

Phil appeared in the doorway. "Joe's still on the phone with Steph. Sounds like she's on board to help."

They went back inside. Joe was pacing near the couch, phone to his ear, nodding along to whatever Steph was saying.

"Yeah, I think that could work," Joe said. "Okay. Call me back when you know. Thanks, Steph." He hung up and turned to the group. "She's going to reach out to the sheriff tonight, see if she can set up a meeting for tomorrow morning."

"What'd you tell her?" Brooke asked.

"Just that we have evidence related to the murders that needs to get to him directly. I didn't go into details about suspecting a deputy."

"Smart," Phil said.

Tyler checked his watch. "I should head to my place and pack a bag. It's getting late."

"I'll follow Brooke home and wait there until you arrive," Phil offered.

"You don't have to do that," Brooke said.

"Yes, I do. You're my little sister. Someone's threatening you. I'm not leaving you alone."

The protectiveness in his voice made her throat tight. "Thanks, Phil."

They gathered their things and headed for the door. Joe walked them out to the street where their vehicles were parked.

"Be careful," Joe said. "All of you. If we're right about this, the killer may find out we're getting close."

"We will," Tyler promised.

Brooke climbed into her SUV, looking in the rearview mirror as Tyler walked to his truck. Phil was already in his car, engine running, waiting to follow her.

The drive home felt longer than usual. Every shadow seemed suspicious. Every car behind her could be a threat. By the time she pulled into her driveway, her hands were shaking.

Phil parked on the street and followed her to the door. "Let me check inside first."

"Phil— "

"Humor me."

She unlocked the door and let him go in ahead of her while she waited in the entry. He moved through the house methodically, checking the upstairs bedrooms first. When he returned to the living room, his expression was satisfied.

"So . . . little sister," Phil said, with a smirk. "You and Tyler. Two official love birds."

"Stop." She walked past him and into the kitchen. He followed.

"And he's really staying in the spare room?"

She turned around, hand on her hip. "I'm a grown woman, Phil. I can have him stay with me if I want. Besides, do you really think we can't control ourselves?"

"I think you and Tyler could make a great life together. But I know how you get. All obsessed with things. Like your running. This investigation. I don't want to see you spiral again. Maybe . . . maybe you should take things slow."

Brooke braced herself against the counter. She knew he was right about the way she could get. But she also knew her feelings for Tyler were real. She would never replace Jen and Garrett in his heart, yet she understood there was a place for her, too, one that was entirely her own.

"I've got this," Brooke said, and for the first time in a long while, she meant it.

Chapter 34

Tyler

Tyler guided the brake caliper back into position and reached for the mounting bolts. The Silverado's front pads were shot. He threaded the bolts by hand first, then reached for the torque wrench.

The repetitive work gave his hands something to do while his mind wandered back to this morning.

Waking up in the same house as Brooke had been perfect. Better than he could've imagined.

He'd heard her moving in the kitchen before his alarm even went off, the coffee maker gurgling, her footsteps on the hardwood. Normal household sounds, but somehow they filled him with a kind of happiness he hadn't felt in years. Sounds he could imagine waking up to every day. Sounds he wanted to enjoy forever.

It felt right in a way that both comforted and terrified him.

He'd found her at the counter, already dressed for work, sipping from a glass. She smiled when she saw him, that genuine smile that made something in his chest soften and tighten at the same time.

"I made coffee." She gestured toward the pot and a travel mug next to it. "I usually just drink at the shop, but I wasn't sure if you'd have time to come in."

"What are you having?"

"Electrolytes. I try to get these in before I start on the coffee, especially on days after a run. It works better for me."

They'd driven to the coffee shop together, Tyler following her in his truck just to make sure she got there safely. He'd watched her unlock the back door, sipping from the mug she'd given him, waiting until she disappeared inside before heading to work himself.

She promised to wait until he showed up this afternoon. She assured him she had work to do and could wait for him to follow her home. With any luck, they'd have answers by then.

Tyler tightened the last bolt and lowered the Silverado off the jack.

He kept trying not to think about how he would've preferred waking up in the same room as Brooke. The same bed. Would've preferred reaching for her in the early morning light, pulling her close, feeling her warmth against him.

He understood they needed to not rush that part of the relationship. Not only for Brooke, who'd been burned before by trusting the wrong person, but for him too.

It wasn't that he'd lived as a monk since Jen died. There'd been women over the years. A bartender in Montana who'd understood he wasn't staying. A teacher in Idaho who'd ended things when she realized he'd never be fully present. A nurse in Indiana who'd told him that he was still grieving and maybe always would be.

He'd never lied to any of them. Never pretended he had more to offer than temporary comfort. And none of them had pushed for more than he could give.

There hadn't been feelings involved. Not real ones. Just two people finding comfort with each other for a while before moving on with their separate lives.

But this was different.

What he was building with Brooke was real. Deep. The kind of connection he'd thought died in the fire along with everything else.

He knew it, felt it in the way his heart rate kicked up when she walked into a room. The way her laugh made him want to find reasons to hear it again. The way her hand fit inside his like it belonged there.

Tyler planned to keep it that way. To protect what they were building. To not mess this up by rushing or pushing or letting his own needs override what was best for both of them.

And until she was safe—until the real killer was caught—he needed to be at the top of his game. He couldn't risk a moment of letting his guard down. Couldn't allow Brooke to be hurt because he was distracted or careless or not paying attention to the threat.

Besides, deep in his bones, he knew they needed to wait. Maybe even wait like he and Jen had, until their wedding night.

Tyler moved to the next vehicle on his list, a Honda with a check engine light. He hooked up the diagnostic scanner and waited for it to read the codes.

He was determined to enjoy the time they had. However long it lasted. However it ended up. He tried to not get his hopes up that this could be a forever thing. Because that was what he wanted more than almost anything.

After work, they were going on a run together. He promised to make dinner. He brought a few things over from his place last night with this in mind—a couple of elk steaks, compliments of his dart-playing buddies, along with pasta and a salad. Easy to make and delicious.

The scanner beeped. Tyler noted the codes and disconnected the tool.

He checked his watch—11:53. Almost lunchtime.

He'd heard nothing from Joe about the meeting with the sheriff.

No call. No text. Nothing.

Joe and Steph were supposed to meet with the sheriff at ten. Maybe he'd believe them. Start an investigation and keep his possibly guilty deputies under surveillance.

Or something.

Tyler sighed. He didn't know exactly what the procedure would be for something like this. He could only hope the sheriff would examine the evidence with an open mind.

Somehow, Tyler knew not hearing from Joe didn't bode well.

Steph had been confident she could help and could convince the sheriff to listen. Maybe something went wrong with the appointment? Maybe the sheriff got called out to an emergency?

Or worse, the sheriff had listened and dismissed their concerns outright.

He could call Joe and ask what was happening. But Joe would've reached out if there was news. The fact that he hadn't meant there wasn't any. At least not good news.

Tyler shoved the phone back in his pocket and returned to the Honda.

The waiting was the worst part. Not knowing. Not being able to act. Just working and thinking and checking his watch every few minutes like that would somehow make time move faster.

Two women were dead. Someone had left threatening notes on his truck. Brooke had been attacked on a trail, nearly dragged into the woods by someone strong enough to overpower her.

And they were sitting here, waiting for permission to investigate. Waiting for someone in authority to take them seriously.

It made him want to put his fist through something.

But that wouldn't help. It wouldn't protect Brooke, wouldn't prove his innocence, and wouldn't catch the real killer.

So Tyler did what he'd always done. He worked. He focused on the task in front of him. Kept his hands busy and his mind as quiet as he could manage.

And he waited.

Chapter 35

Brooke

Brooke sat on her couch, phone in hand, checking it for the hundredth time. 5:15. Nothing new from Joe. He'd sent a text to both her and Tyler around one o'clock. It was short and cryptic: *Late start. Things happening now. Head straight to Brooke's after work and wait.*

Tyler paced near the window, occasionally pulling the curtain aside to look at the street.

"Maybe we should just call him," Brooke said.

"He'll reach out when he knows something."

"It's been hours since we've heard anything."

Tyler turned from the window. "I know."

The waiting was getting to her. Joe had told them to stay at the house, but they'd changed into their running clothes anyway, hoping to squeeze in a few miles before sunset.

Now the light was fading fast. The sky had already taken on that deepening blue that warned night was close, and her nerves still hadn't settled since the attack. She was far too skittish to run in the dark, even with Tyler beside her. And Joe's last message had been clear: stay inside until they knew more.

"I think I'm going to go on the treadmill," Brooke said. "Better than sitting here waiting. You could use the walking pad if you want. I have them both set up in the office."

"Sure. That might be good. Not exactly the same as going for a run together, but close." He smiled as he dropped the curtain.

Brooke's phone buzzed. Joe's name flashed on the screen.

"It's him," she said, answering immediately. "Joe? What's happening?"

Tyler crossed to the couch, sitting beside her. She hit the speaker button so they could both hear.

"Sorry it took so long," Joe said. His voice sounded strained. "It's been a long day. The sheriff didn't believe us at first. Took forever going through the evidence, asking questions, trying to poke holes in our theory. Then he had a meeting he couldn't miss, and we had to wait, and . . . " Joe sighed. "Anyway."

"But he believes you now?" Brooke asked.

"I'm not sure *believes* is the right word. Let's say he sees enough to have concerns. Enough concerns to bring both Adam and Edi in for questioning. He agreed that both have been acting suspiciously and there needs to be a proper investigation."

Tyler's hand found Brooke's. "When?"

"Immediately. Only . . . "

"Only what?" Tyler asked.

"It seems Edi might have gotten wind of what was going on. She heard something or figured it out somehow. By the time they went to find her, she was gone."

Brooke's chest tightened. "Gone where?"

"No one knows. Her car's missing. Phone's off. She just disappeared." Joe paused. "But that pretty much confirms it was her, right? Innocent people don't run. I'd love to see what the sheriff thinks now, see if he believes us, but he's unavailable."

"Where's Adam?" Tyler asked, taking Brooke's hand.

"He's here. They questioned him, and while no one told me directly, he's no longer a suspect. Especially not with Edi missing. Everyone's looking for her. City police, highway patrol . . . everyone. Adam's going out soon to help them. I wanted to call you right away, though. Just in case."

"In case what?"

"So you'd know. While they don't know where she is, they found things. Things in her desk. Her locker. Even in her patrol car."

"Things?" Brooke leaned toward the phone. "Things that suggest she's guilty?"

"Nobody's saying that. Not to Steph and me, anyway. But yeah. That's the impression I'm getting. Really, though. Stay inside. She's desperate. And desperate people do unpredictable things."

They talked for a few more minutes, Joe promising to call if he heard anything else. When Brooke hung up, the house felt too quiet.

"It's almost over," she said, trying to convince herself as much as Tyler.

"Yeah. Almost."

Neither of them moved from the couch. The relief Brooke had expected to feel hadn't come. Instead, there was just tension, a sense of waiting for something else to happen.

Tyler stood suddenly, his head tilted. "Did you hear that?"

"Hear what?"

"Outside. I thought I heard— " He moved to the window again, peering through the curtain. "There. Movement. By your SUV."

Brooke joined him at the window. The early evening light made it hard to see clearly, shadows lengthening across her driveway. Then she saw it too. A figure moved near her vehicle, crouched low.

"Go upstairs," Tyler said, his voice urgent but controlled. "Lock yourself in your bedroom. Call 9-1-1."

"Tyler— "

"Now, Brooke. Please."

The fear in his voice galvanized her. She grabbed her phone and ran for the stairs.

Brooke reached the bedroom and closed the door, turning the lock. Her hands shook as she dialed.

"9-1-1, what's your emergency?"

"Someone's breaking into my house. I'm at 412 Elm Street. My boyfriend is downstairs. The intruder . . . we think it's— " Her voice caught. "Please hurry."

The operator's questions blurred together. A crashing sound came from downstairs. Heavy footsteps shook the floor. Tyler's voice cut through, above all else.

"Edi. What are you doing here?"

Edi's voice was too quiet for Brooke to make out the words, but she caught the tone. It was off, almost singsong.

Brooke opened the bedroom door and crept into the hallway. She leaned against the hallway table and nearly knocked over a lamp, but managed to catch it. She stepped toward the top of the stairs and peered down. The front door hung open at an odd angle.

"You need to leave," Tyler said. "The sheriff knows. This is over."

"It's not over." Edi's voice rose, sharp and desperate. "It's never been over. Not since you came back. Not when you were gone either. It's always been you."

"Edi, please. Just leave. We can talk about this at the station."

"Talk?" Edi let out a harsh laugh. "I've been talking to you for months. Years, even. You never heard me. Never saw me. Just like in high school. Just like always."

"I don't understand— "

"I loved you!" she screamed. "I've always loved you. And you never even looked at me. Not the way you should. I mean . . . why not? You were always so nice to me. I thought . . . I thought, maybe . . . remember how we used to always talk? When I worked at the county office, and you'd need to get your titles changed over for your latest project car?"

"I do, Edi. You were great. Always very helpful."

Brooke pressed her hand over her mouth, phone still to her ear. The operator was saying something about units being dispatched and staying on the line, but Brooke couldn't respond. If she said anything, they'd hear her.

"I was so certain." Edi's voice took on a new quality, something almost nostalgic. "That day when you brought in that old Jeep, you said how you'd got it for a song and it was going to be beautiful when you were done. I understood you, Tyler. I understood what you were saying, even though you didn't say it. I knew your wife would understand too."

"My wife? The old Jeep? You mean . . . Edi, what did you do?"

"It was an accident. I went to tell her the truth. That you loved me. That you were going to leave her. But she laughed at me. *Laughed.*" Edi's voice broke. "We fought. She fell. Hit her head. I panicked. Set the fire to cover it. I didn't know Garrett was there. You said you were taking him hiking. You told me just the day before you were taking him hiking.”

“He was sick.” Tyler’s voice was raw. “He was home sick, and you killed him? Killed both of them.”

“I didn’t mean to! I loved you! Everything I did was for you!”

“They thought I did it. Did you . . . you framed me?”

“Only a little bit. I had to. Don’t you see? If they arrested you, you’d need me. You’d need my connections. My family’s money. But they didn’t have enough evidence. I didn’t do things right, and you left instead. You left, and I had to put my life back together without you.”

“I’m sorry, Edi. There was never— ”

“I took care of you after Sheila too. Remember? The lawyer who showed up? I sent him.”

“You sent the attorney?”

“I tried to take care of you. Even with Brooke.”

Brooke heard the way Edi said her name. Full of hate.

“When she wouldn’t stay away from you, I tried to warn her. Tried to scare her on that trail. But she fought back. She always fights back.”

There was a sharp noise, followed by the scrape of furniture moving across the floor.

“No, no, no,” Edi sang, the words almost playful. “You stay right there. Keep your distance.” She gave a soft, almost pleased laugh. “You think I didn’t notice those muscles you came back to Irma with?”

Her tone sharpened. “They’re not going to do you any good. Not when I have the gun.”

“Everything’s fine, Edi.” Tyler’s tone was placating. Brooke could almost imagine him raising his hands, trying to calm her.

“Fine? You really think so, Tyler? You think it’s fine?”

"It can be, Edi. We can— "

Edi laughed, a kind of laugh that sent a sick feeling through Brooke.

"It's not fine, Tyler. It won't ever be fine again. When that reporter walked in today, along with the prissy woman who teaches at the college, I knew."

Brooke leaned against the wall. They should've planned better. Steph should've arranged for the sheriff to meet her and Joe at a different location. It was too late for that now. It was now up to Tyler to keep Edi calm and talking until help showed up.

"Where's your little girlfriend? That's what she is, right? Your girlfriend?"

"She's safe. She went out the back door when you came in the front."

Glass shattered as Edi let out a string of profanity. "No, no, no. That is not how this is supposed to happen. She must be here. I planned it so it ends here."

A wave of understanding rushed over Brooke. Edi didn't plan on any of them walking away. Not Tyler. Not Brooke. Not Edi.

Tyler must have understood too. "Edi, let's talk about this. We're just having a conversation, right? Two old friends."

"Old friends? Sure. You know, I was over you. I really was. Then you came back. And I thought finally. *Finally*, we could be together. But you wanted Sheila. I saw you at the bank. The way you looked at her."

"I didn't want Sheila. We were just talking."

"She wanted that reunion. Wanted to bring everyone together. I was never part of that group, Tyler. They tortured me. Made my life miserable. So I took care of her. For you. For us."

Another glass broke.

"And Monique," Edi said. "During the interview, when Adam and I questioned her about Sheila's death, she made a joke. About how fat I was in high school. How I should thank her and Sheila for motivating me to lose weight. She laughed. Just like Sheila used to laugh. Just like they all laughed."

"Ma'am? Ma'am, are you still there?" the operator asked.

Brooke knew she couldn't answer. Edi thought she'd made it out the back door. If Edi found her, she'd be as good as dead. They all would be.

"You know what, Tyler?" Edi's voice drifted up the stairs. "I don't believe you. She wouldn't leave you. Not her precious Tyler. She's still here somewhere."

"She's gone," Tyler said, but there was strain in his voice now. Fear.

"Then you won't mind if I check."

Footsteps. Edi was moving toward the stairs.

"Edi, don't— "

The gunshot cracked through the house like thunder.

Tyler's cry of pain followed immediately after.

Brooke scanned the hallway for something to use as a weapon. Her eyes landed on the heavy ceramic lamp. She set her phone down and yanked the lamp free, the cord tearing from the wall socket.

She moved to the top of the stairs. Through the spindles, she could see Tyler on the floor near the couch, clutching his calf. Blood seeped between his fingers.

Edi stood over him, gun still raised. "Where is she, Tyler?"

Brooke couldn't let Edi shoot him again. Couldn't hide while Tyler bled out on her living room floor.

She started down the stairs, the lamp clenched in both hands like a club. Edi heard her and turned. Their eyes locked.

"There you are," Edi said, swinging the gun toward Brooke, smiling. A wide smile that was the creepiest thing Brooke had ever seen. Edi leveled the pistol, taking a bead on her.

Tyler lunged and hit Edi in the thigh as she pulled the trigger. The wall behind Brooke exploded in a spray of drywall.

Her ears rang, but Brooke kept moving, sprinting down the stairs. Tyler and Edi struggled. Edi screamed obscenities while Tyler grunted with effort.

And worst of all, Edi still had the gun.

With a fierce swing, Brooke brought the lamp down. It connected with Edi's shoulder with a crack.

Edi stumbled sideways. The gun fell from her hand and skittered across the floor toward the kitchen. But before Brooke could process that small victory, Edi recovered and charged.

The impact knocked the air from Brooke's lungs. They crashed into the bookshelf together. Books rained down around them. Then Edi's hands were around her throat, squeezing.

Brooke clawed at Edi's wrists, trying to pry her fingers loose. But Edi was the stronger of the two, and the pressure kept building. Brooke's vision started to go dark around the edges. Her lungs screamed for air.

Then the pressure lifted, and Brooke took in a ragged, desperate breath. Tyler yanked Edi backward. She hit the coffee table, and the whole thing collapsed under her with a crash.

Brooke doubled over, gasping. Each breath hurt like swallowing broken glass, but she'd never been so grateful for air. When she looked up, Tyler stood between her and Edi. His sweats were dark with blood around his calf, but he kept his weight balanced, ready.

Edi scrambled to her feet. Blood streamed from her nose. "If I can't have you, no one can. We'll all be together. All of us. Forever."

She dove for the gun.

Tyler shoved her as Edi's fingers closed on it. Edi grabbed his leg—the wounded one—and Tyler's face went white as he went down hard. Then they were rolling across the floor, a tangle of limbs and violence.

Brooke's hands were shaking, but she forced herself to move. The lamp had shattered when she'd hit Edi with it. She looked around wildly and spotted the heavy brass candleholder on the mantel.

Brooke brought the candleholder down as hard as she could on Edi's back.

Edi screamed, and Brooke hit her again, this time across the arm with a resounding crack.

"You broke my arm, you— "

Brooke swung the candleholder, catching Edi in the stomach. She made an *oomph* sound.

As Brooke drew back, ready to strike again, Tyler said, "Don't move, Edi. Brooke, take a step back, honey. I've got the gun."

Sirens wailed outside, growing louder and closer as Brooke took several steps back, away from the injured woman.

Edi whimpered, and the sobs followed. "Just shoot me," she whispered through her tears. "Shoot me and get it over with."

"Not happening, Edi," Tyler said. "You're going to get the help you need."

"Help?" She shook her head. "I don't need help. I need you, Tyler. You've always been the one. We can still be together."

"Police!" The call came from the front door.

"We're here!" Brooke called.

Adam stepped in first, gun trained ahead, the others fanning out behind him.

"This is the sheriff's department and Irma Police! Nobody move!"

"It's over," Tyler said as the gun clattered to the floor. His hands shot up.

Brooke dropped the candlestick and mirrored him.

Adam spoke into the radio on his collar. "Scene secure. Send two buses."

"Let's get you to the couch," Adam said to Tyler. "She shot you?"

"Yeah." Tyler nodded. "Not bad, I don't think."

Tyler sank onto the couch as the deputies checked Edi for injuries. One of them confirmed her arm was broken, so they didn't cuff her, but they still helped her to her feet. "We'll take her outside," the city officer said.

The wail of approaching sirens made it clear that at least one ambulance was on its way.

"I'm sorry," Adam said to Tyler. "I was so sure it was you. So certain. I missed everything."

Tyler nodded and looked like he was going to say something, but the EMTs came into the house, and everything became a new kind of chaos.

One of them led Brooke to a chair and started questioning her about her injuries. "I'm not hurt," she insisted. Her voice was odd. Shaky. Her hands were shaking too.

Within a few minutes, they had Tyler on the gurney, and the EMT was walking alongside Brooke as they all headed toward the ambulance.

"It's best to get you checked out," the EMT said. "We'll make sure you don't go into shock."

Inside the back of the ambulance, Brooke sat on the bench with a blanket pulled tight around her. One of the EMTs was taking care of Tyler while he lay on the gurney.

She leaned forward and kissed his cheek. "It's really over," she whispered.

He reached for her hand. "Yeah. It's really over."

She threaded her fingers through his and held on.

Chapter 36

Tyler

Tyler shifted his weight on the crutches and tried to find a comfortable position against Brooke's kitchen counter. His leg was healing well. The bullet had gone clean through the meaty part of his calf without hitting bones or major vessels. But standing for long periods still made it ache.

The clock on the microwave read 5:47 a.m. Thirteen minutes until the Moose Range Run 100 registration opened.

Brooke's living room was crowded. Gina and Nick had claimed the couch, each cradling a mug of coffee, while Steph and Joe sat together on the stools at the breakfast bar, talking softly. The rest of the running club filled the remaining space, settling into chairs that had been dragged in or standing wherever they could squeeze in.

The atmosphere felt like a party, celebrating not just Brooke's decision to register for the race but everything they had come through together. Surviving. Moving forward.

And they were doing it all before daylight on a Thursday. It was one of the strangest things Tyler had ever witnessed, and also one of the most wonderful. These were Brooke's people. Even Phil showed up, grumbling about weird runners and their early morning hours, but he was there.

Brooke moved through the crowd with scones and pastries. Tyler watched her, marveling at how she'd bounced back. Not long ago, she'd nearly been strangled to death in her own living room. Now she was hosting a registration party as if it were the most natural thing in the world.

She caught him staring and smiled; that genuine kindness still made his chest tight. He smiled back.

"Five more minutes," Steph announced, checking her watch. "You ready, Brooke?" She pointed to the laptop already open and waiting.

"I think so." Brooke set down the tray and wiped her hands on a towel. "Maybe. I don't know."

"You're ready," Gina said firmly. "Registration is the first step. You've got a solid training plan—one that's not too crazy—to carry you through."

"Not too crazy is the key," Nick said, giving Brooke a wink.

Tyler knew about how obsessed Brooke had become when she'd tried to run the Moose Range Run before. And he knew she wasn't sure about doing it this time. She waffled on whether or not to register.

After everything with Edi, after the attack and the confrontation and nearly dying, she'd told Tyler she wasn't sure she could commit to the training. Wasn't sure she had it in her. And if she did commit, she wasn't sure she could keep her sanity.

Tyler had promised to help however he could. Bike alongside her on long runs once his leg healed. Drive support on training days. Whatever she needed. They'd spent many hours on the computer building a training schedule that felt reasonable.

Gina and Steph had both looked it over and agreed it made sense. Steph said it was enough to give her the miles she needed to complete the distance, and Gina thought it seemed sensible for maintaining her mental health. Plus, it provided some flexibility in case of weather or other issues.

She'd been open with all her friends about what she was facing. About the doubts she had and the toll the training—and the race itself—might take on her. The running club had rallied around her, offering encouragement and practical help.

The support had made the difference. Brooke had gone from "I can't" to "Maybe I can" to "I'm doing this" over the course of a week.

Tyler was proud of her. More than that, he was grateful to be part of her journey. Part of her life.

The coffee shop had seen a surge in business after everything came out. People apologized and showed up to support Brooke. She handled it all with grace and focused on the people who'd stood by her from the start.

Tyler had been in regular contact with Robert and Sue. They'd apologized for ever doubting him, though Tyler waved off the apology. They'd supported him when it mattered. He felt a little bad for ever thinking Robert might have been behind the murders and figured some day he might even tell him about his suspicions. Then again, maybe not. Phil had been right about it never being a good idea to accuse your boss of murder if you wanted to keep your job.

They were holding his position for him. The doctor said another two or three weeks, and he'd be cleared for light duty. Robert assured him he'd find something for him to do, even if it was sitting on a stool and organizing tools. Tyler was looking forward to it. The routine. The normalcy.

Edi was in a mental health hospital after being declared currently incompetent to stand trial. Tyler didn't know if there would eventually be a trial once she stabilized, or if she'd spend the rest of her life in treatment.

He was okay with either outcome. What Edi had done was unforgivable, but she clearly wasn't in her right mind and hadn't been for a long time.

Tyler wanted justice. He wanted Edi to face consequences for what she'd done. But not until she was capable of understanding those consequences. Not while she was still trapped in whatever delusion had driven her to violence.

There were still several unanswered questions as to what all Edi did and why. He still had no idea why she'd left the notes on his pickup truck.

He'd asked Adam about it, but Adam said something about not commenting on an open investigation, then followed up with how Edi didn't seem to know what all she did and didn't do, and had even suggested she hadn't acted alone. Tyler didn't think anyone believed that, but Joe said there was an investigation happening for an accomplice.

Tyler also assumed Edi was behind the rumors about him dating Monique but had no proof. The things he knew were bad enough.

He carried the weight of Jen and Garrett's deaths differently now, knowing it hadn't been an accident, knowing someone had deliberately taken them from him. That grief would never fully heal. Brooke seemed to understand, even recognizing that the revelation of Edi's betrayal reopened the original pain. She'd offered him space, and he loved her all the more for it.

"Two minutes," Steph called out.

The room went quiet. Everyone shifted closer to where Brooke stood with her laptop open on the kitchen counter.

Tyler moved beside her, balancing on his crutches. She glanced up at him, nervous energy radiating off her.

"You've got this," he said quietly.

"What if I don't get in? What if it fills up before— "

"Then you get your name on the waitlist. You said yourself that not everyone who signs up can run. If you don't make the waitlist, you try again next year. But you're getting in. I can feel it."

Joe appeared on Brooke's other side, his own phone out and ready. "I've got the backup registration page loaded. Just in case your computer freezes or something."

Tyler studied Joe for a moment. He'd been around a lot lately. He said he was working on a book about the case—interviewing people and gathering details. He'd asked Tyler for several sit-down conversations, and Tyler had agreed to most of them.

Joe was nice enough and was a good friend to Brooke and the rest of the running crew.

But there was something else there. Something Joe wasn't saying. Tyler had caught him a few times staring off into space with an expression that didn't quite fit the moment. Had noticed the way he sometimes deflected personal questions. Tyler also knew Steph had mentioned something similar to Brooke about how she'd like to get to know Joe better, but he didn't make it easy.

Everyone had secrets. Tyler knew that better than most. Maybe Joe's were harmless. Maybe they weren't.

Either way, Tyler would keep an eye on him. Not because he didn't trust Joe with Brooke—she could take care of herself—but because after everything they'd been through, Tyler had learned to pay attention to his instincts.

"Thirty seconds," Steph announced.

Brooke's hand found Tyler's. He gave it a soft squeeze before letting go. She had work to do.

"Ten. Nine. Eight."

The room counted down together.

"Three. Two. One. Go!"

Brooke's fingers flew across the keyboard. Tyler watched the screen as she navigated through the registration process. Name. Address. Emergency contact—she listed Tyler without hesitation. Payment information. Waiver signed electronically.

"Submit," she whispered, clicking the final button.

The page loaded, and a confirmation message appeared.

Congratulations! Your registration for the Moose Range Run 100-Mile Trail Run has been received.

The room erupted in cheers. Gina hooted. Steph clapped. Phil started chanting Brooke's name.

Brooke stared at the screen like she couldn't quite believe it. Then she turned to Tyler, her face breaking into the widest smile he'd ever seen.

She kissed him. A real kiss, full of joy and relief and promise.

When they pulled apart, she was laughing. "I did it. I actually did it."

"You did it," Tyler agreed.

Around them, her friends celebrated. Coffee and treats were forgotten as they congratulated Brooke, talked about training plans, and made promises to support her through the next months of preparation.

Brooke lifted her hands and called for quiet, her smile wide and her eyes filled with tears. "Thank you all so much. I can't even tell you how much it means to me to have you here." She paused and met her brother's gaze. "Especially those of you who are not early risers."

Phil lifted his coffee cup. "You deserve it, sis. All of this and more. I'm proud of you."

She nodded. "I'm glad you're here." Brooke glanced around the room. "Glad all of you are here. I mean it when I say I wouldn't be doing this without your support. And I also wanted to thank those of you who have already offered to help me train and volunteered to be part of my crew or to pace me during the Moose Range Run."

Brooke gave Tyler's hand a squeeze. She'd specifically asked him if he'd be willing to run with her on the last long leg. Instinctively, he knew it was an honor and something he had to do.

"That all said," Brooke continued, "I'm not the only one with a big race happening in the next few months. Steph is doing the Frozen Divide 100 in March and is already training for it, though we all know her real training will begin after the snow starts since it's a self-sufficient winter race."

"So no pacers for me," Steph said. "But I'd welcome anyone who wishes to be at the start or finish."

"I'll be there," Jocelyn promised. "No way would I miss you setting a new personal best."

Steph shrugged. "That's the plan anyway. Hopefully, everything comes together and the course is kind to me this year."

Tyler had heard stories about the winter races Steph had done, and how the weather could turn brutal and ruin everything, even when she had trained and prepared as much as possible.

"You'll be fine," Jocelyn assured her. "And I've already reserved a house near the race." She glanced around the room. "Let me know if you want to be there to cheer

Steph on. It's the middle of March, so check your calendars."

"And check your calendars for the first weekend of July," Steph said. "That's when Jocelyn is running her first marathon. She'll need us there to cheer her on."

The conversation continued as the group made plans to attend Steph's race in March, Jocelyn's race in July, and the Moose Range Run in June for Brooke.

Tyler stayed where he was, Brooke's hand in his, watching her glow with excitement and marveling at this group and how they were more family than friends.

This was their future. Not perfect. Not without challenges. But together. Building something real out of the wreckage of their pasts.

He'd lost everything once and thought he'd never have this again—a partner, a community, a reason to look forward instead of back.

But here he was. In Brooke's kitchen. Surrounded by people who cared. Planning for a race eight months away, like the future was something he could count on.

Brooke caught his eye again. "Thank you," she mouthed.

He didn't need to ask what for. He knew. For believing in her. For staying. For being there through the worst and promising to be there for what came next.

Tyler pulled her close, careful of his crutches, and held her while the celebration continued around them.

Epilogue

8 Months Later

Brooke's legs had stopped feeling like legs somewhere around mile eighty. Now they were just these things attached to her body that moved when she told them to, more or less. Each step sent protests through muscles she didn't know she had.

"You're doing great," Tyler said. He'd seen her off yesterday morning at nine and met her at Antler Creek Outbound around noon. He'd wanted to be at the Rendezvous aid station, the turnaround point, at midnight, but Gina insisted he rest so he could pace her today.

Tyler had been waiting when she arrived at Antler Creek Inbound, mile 82.5, a little before two in the afternoon, twenty-nine hours into her run. Seeing him, cheering and calling her name, gave her a new drive that even overrode the exhausting pulling at every cell in her body.

"I'm dying."

"You're not dying. You're finishing."

Having him run next to her for the rest of the way had been amazing. Every time she thought she couldn't take one more step, he'd say something or do something that kept her going.

"Look there," he said. She could hear the smile in his voice.

Brooke looked up to see a young girl waving an Otter Pop. Almost There aid station, the last one before the finish. She was starting to think she just might make it.

"You're almost finished," the little girl said as she handed them each their frozen treat.

Tears stung Brooke's eyes. She was doing it. She was really doing it. Only two miles remained. She'd been running for thirty-three hours. Through daylight and darkness and daylight again. Through pain and doubt and moments where she'd wanted to quit so badly she could taste it.

But she hadn't quit.

"We're getting close," Tyler said as they raced down the sidewalk toward the finish line at Freedom Park.

"You keep saying that." They picked up speed. She didn't think she had anything left, but they were definitely moving faster.

"Because it's the truth. You are doing this, Brooke."

She nodded and kept moving, her shoes pounding on the sidewalk in rhythm with Tyler's.

"Turn here," Tyler said, guiding her left into the park. She was grateful for the cue; she was so tired she could barely tell where she was supposed to go, even with all the signs and cheering. At this point, she was moving almost entirely on instinct.

"There." Tyler pointed ahead, where a small crowd had gathered. "See them?"

Brooke squinted. Her vision had gone fuzzy around the edges hours ago, but she could make out familiar shapes.

Gina jumped up and down. Nick was beside her, his arm around her waist. Joe had his camera. Steph was clapping. There were others from the running club, too, who'd crewed for her through the night, sleeping in shifts so someone was always there when she needed them.

When she arrived at an aid station exhausted, hungry, and disoriented, they were there to take care of her.

"They've been waiting," Tyler said.

"For hours probably."

"They'd wait days if they had to. You've got this. The finish is just ahead. Can you see it?"

Brooke wanted to cry. Or laugh. Maybe both. She'd dreamed about this moment for years. Obsessed over it. Failed at it. Almost gave up on it entirely.

And now she was here.

"I can see it," she whispered.

"That's right, babe."

"I'm going to make it."

"You're going to make it."

The crowd was louder now. Gina's voice cut through the noise, shouting Brooke's name. Nick whistled. Joe moved closer to the finish line with his camera raised.

Something caught the sunlight on Gina's left hand. A ring. She filed that observation away for later, her brain too fried to process anything beyond putting one foot in front of the other.

"Hundred yards," Tyler said. He was still right beside her, matching her shuffling pace even though she knew he could run circles around her right now. "You ready?"

"For what?"

"To finish strong."

Brooke almost laughed. Strong wasn't happening. She had nothing left.

But then she thought about everything that had brought her here. The training through winter cold and spring mud. The long runs that tested her limits. The mental work of not obsessing, of trusting her body, of letting Tyler and her friends help carry the load.

Everything with Edi. The attack. Nearly dying. Fighting back.

Surviving.

She'd survived. And now she was finishing.

"Go ahead," Tyler said quietly. "Cross that line. I'll be right behind you."

Brooke found something that wasn't quite a kick but was more than her shuffle. Her legs protested, but they moved. Faster. The finish line grew closer.

Twenty yards. Ten.

The crowd was screaming now. Her name. Her number. Pure noise that wrapped around her and pulled her forward.

Five yards.

Brooke's arms lifted automatically, breaking the plane of the finish line with everything she had left.

The announcer's voice boomed across the speakers. "Brooke Davies from Irma, Wyoming! One hundred miles! Congratulations!"

Her legs gave out. She stumbled, but Tyler was there, catching her, holding her up, pulling her close.

They swayed together. Brooke buried her face in his chest.

"I did it," she whispered.

"You did it."

Then he was spinning her around—slowly, carefully, mindful of her exhausted body. She laughed, the sound breaking into something between joy and tears.

He kissed her. Her friends were there now, surrounding them, but Brooke only felt Tyler. His arms. His warmth.

His steady presence that had carried her through training and racing and everything before that.

"I'm so proud of you," he said against her mouth. "I knew you'd do it."

"We did it," she corrected. "Both of us."

He pulled back enough to look at her. "Yeah. We did."

Someone draped a blanket over her shoulders. A finisher's buckle appeared in her hands. Gina was crying. Nick was grinning. Joe's camera clicked. Steph wrapped Brooke in a careful hug and suggested it was time for a burger and a beer.

"Yes, please." She laughed.

Through it all, Tyler stayed beside her. His hand found hers and held on.

One hundred miles. Almost thirty-three hours. Every step a choice to keep going.

Brooke looked up at Tyler and saw her future reflected in his eyes. Not perfect. Not without challenges. But together.

They'd made it. Both of them. Through loss and fear and doubt and violence and everything that tried to break them.

They'd made it. Together.

Steph Pierce thought the hardest part was the race. She's about to find out she was wrong.

Her story continues in
Continental Crisis: Deadly Miles Book 3.

Thank you for spending your time with the people of the
Basin County Running Club!

If you have five minutes, you'd make this writer very
happy if you could write a short review on Amazon,
Goodreads, BookBub or your favorite book review site.

I appreciate you!

Ready for more?
Join my reader's club and receive an exclusive
Beartooth Betrayal Bonus Scene.

Grab your story at MillieVaughn.com/BB-Bonus

Also by Millie Vaughn

Absaroka Ambush

Gina Connolly doesn't need anyone. She's built her life on control with a steady job, careful boundaries, and zero emotional risks. Depending on someone only leads to heartbreak.

Nick Davies is the last complication she wants.

He came to their small Wyoming town with no clear future and no intention of staying. The chemistry between them is instant. Inconvenient. Dangerous.

Continental Crisis

Steph Pierce has worked her whole life for one goal. Every mile she trains brings her closer to the race she has dreamed of, and nothing will stop her.

Jack Swisher thought a fresh start would be simple. A former Olympic biathlete with everything to prove, he arrives in Basin County ready to claim the race Steph has been planning and immediately makes an enemy of her.

Find these titles at MillieVaughn.com

Check out Millie's cozy post-apocalyptic fiction books, written as Millie Copper, at MillieCopper.com.

Author Note

Hello, Dear Reader,

Thanks so much for reading *Beartooth Betrayal: Deadly Miles Book 2*. I hope you enjoyed spending time with Brooke, Tyler, and the rest of the Basin County Running Club.

The fictional race that Brooke trained for and ran, the Moose Range Run, is based on a real-life event called the Bighorn Trail Run. In 2025, my husband ran the 52-mile distance of the Bighorn, completing the distance in fourteen hours and twenty-five minutes. Joe's finish was amazing and wonderful, and less than an hour later he was already talking about the Bighorn 100. He'll run that in June of 2026.

My husband is a bit like Brooke in his training. He gets obsessive and frets if he misses a run, so keeping him balanced falls to me. On race day, I will be his crew chief, meeting him at aid stations to keep him hydrated and fueled. The Bighorn has fantastic aid stations, staffed by the same volunteers each year. Joe is already eyeing the one that serves bacon and hoping his stomach agrees.

Ultramarathons are brutal on the body. Runners often struggle with digestion, and some even hallucinate. Not surprising given that a hundred miles can take thirty hours or more with little rest. Joe is hoping for a twenty-minute break at the turnaround, depending on his pace.

Seeing it laid out like this, it feels like an unusual pastime, and even more unusual that someone would choose to put themselves through it. LOL. And yet, he does.

Exploring the mindset of an ultrarunner adds a new dimension to my *Deadly Miles* books. Anyone who willingly pushes their body to those extremes is far from typical. They move through life with a different mindset. You'll get a better glimpse of this mindset in Book 3, *Continental Crisis*. It's going to be a wild ride!

Thanks for reading,
Millie Vaughn

Acknowledgments

Thanks to:

Ameryn Tucker, my editor, beta reader, and daughter wrapped in one. I had a story I wanted to tell, and Ameryn encouraged me and helped me bring it to life.

Dauntless Cover Design for the amazing cover.

And extra special thanks to my husband, a real-life ultra-runner, who acts as my technical advisor.

Three more daughters and a teen son, who willingly listen to me drone on and on about story lines and ideas while encouraging me to "keep going."

My amazing Street Team! Thanks so much spending your time reading the *Deadly Miles* installments.

And to you, my readers, for spending your time with the people of the Basin County Running Club. I hope you'll stay tuned for more love and adventure. If you have five minutes, you'd make this writer very happy if you could leave a review. I appreciate you!

About the Author

Millie Vaughn writes clean romance, mystery, and suspense. She delights in placing her characters in impossible situations where they must discover the strength, faith, and courage to find their way out.

When she's not plotting twists and tender moments, she calls Wyoming home. Though she travels whenever she can, she dreams of one day living in a van by the river or out of a backpack somewhere in Europe, but she can't leave her little homestead for that long.

Millie Vaughn is the not-so-secret pen name of bestselling Cozy Apocalyptic Fiction author, Millie Copper.

Find Millie at MillieVaughn.com
Instagram: Instagram.com/MillieVaughn_Author
Facebook: Facebook.com/MillieVaughnAuthor